INTO THE DARKNESS

Katie Reus

Cover art: Jaycee of Sweet 'N Spicy Designs
JRT editing
Author website: www.katiereus.com

Into the Darkness/Katie Reus. -- 1st ed.
ISBN-10: 1942447469
ISBN-13: 9781942447467

eISBN: 9781942447450

For Kari Walker. Thank you for all that you do.

Praise for the novels of Katie Reus

"Sexy military romantic suspense!" —USA Today

"...a wild hot ride for readers. The story grabs you and doesn't let go."
—*New York Times* bestselling author, Cynthia Eden

"Has all the right ingredients: a hot couple, evil villains, and a killer action-filled plot. . . . [The] Moon Shifter series is what I call Grade-A entertainment!" —Joyfully Reviewed

"I could not put this book down. . . . Let me be clear that I am not saying that this was a good book *for* a paranormal genre; it was an excellent romance read, *period*." —All About Romance

"Reus strikes just the right balance of steamy sexual tension and nail-biting action....This romantic thriller reliably hits every note that fans of the genre will expect." —*Publishers Weekly*

"Prepare yourself for the start of a great new series! . . . I'm excited about reading more about this great group of characters."
—Fresh Fiction

"Wow! This powerful, passionate hero sizzles with sheer deliciousness. I loved every sexy twist of this fun & exhilarating tale. Katie Reus delivers!" —Carolyn Crane, RITA award winning author

Continued...

"...a captivating, heated, romantic suspense that will pull you in from the beginning and won't let you go until the very last page."
—Amy, So Many Reads

"A sexy, well-crafted paranormal romance that succeeds with smart characters and creative world building."—Kirkus Reviews

"*Mating Instinct*'s romance is taut and passionate . . . Katie Reus's newest installment in her Moon Shifter series will leave readers breathless!" —Stephanie Tyler, *New York Times* bestselling author

"Both romantic and suspenseful, a fast-paced sexy book full of high stakes action." —Heroes and Heartbreakers

"Katie Reus pulls the reader into a story line of second chances, betrayal, and the truth about forgotten lives and hidden pasts."
—The Reading Café

"Nonstop action, a solid plot, good pacing, and riveting suspense."
—RT Book Reviews

"Sexy suspense at its finest." —Laura Wright, *New York Times* bestselling author of *Branded*

CHAPTER ONE

Rhea smoothed a hand down her dress—a freaking *dress.* It had been probably about fifty years since she'd worn one. Maybe longer. Ugh. What the hell was she doing anyway? Frowning at her silly self, she pushed open the door to the training room. She'd left a couple blades down here and—

"Holy hotness!" Spiro's dark eyes widened as he caught sight of her—until Solon slammed a fist into his face, sending him flying back across one of the training mats.

"That's weak, dude. Can't get distracted by a pretty female." Solon shook his head as Spiro quickly jumped to his feet. But not before shooting her a quick wink.

Feeling some of her tension ease, but not much, she headed around the length of the mats since she was wearing heels. Well, kitten heels. She wasn't doing more than two inches. It didn't matter that she had shifter agility and balance, high heels were stupid. And whoever had invented them hated feet. And women.

As she reached one of the tables, she smiled and picked up her two new titanium blades. Sharpened to perfection. For the most part she preferred to fight in her wolf form, but she loved having blades with her. Weapons were offensive to her animal side but as a woman and a warrior, she appreciated the beauty of such superb craftsmanship. True art. And these were—

"You're always giving me grief about my new weapons yet here you are looking like you want to start making out with these beauties." Solon strode up, a towel thrown around his neck.

She glanced past him to see Spiro heading out. "You guys done?"

Solon shrugged, running a hand over his dark skull trim. "Yeah, he got tired of getting his ass kicked."

"Liar," Spiro shouted as he left the room.

He leaned against the table, eyebrows raised. "So? What's up with the dress?"

"What do you mean?" She avoided his gaze as she slid the blades into their custom-made sheaths.

"Come on. This about all those texts you've been getting from someone you think I don't know about?"

Rhea narrowed her gaze. She'd been calling and talking with a certain Alpha dragon shifter for the last eight months but hadn't told Solon about it. She and Solon might be best friends but some things she wanted to keep private. Besides, her texts were just friendly and she didn't have to tell Solon everything. God, why did she feel so defensive? "What do you think you know?"

Grinning, he kissed her forehead. "I know that he's a goner once he sees you in this dress."

She cleared her throat. She wasn't going to respond to that statement because it would be confirming she'd dressed up for a male. The thought was ridiculous even to her, but . . . she couldn't help herself. Because Conall Petronilla would be here soon and Rhea felt stupidly excited to see him. Their friendship had taken her off guard, but she found herself looking forward to hearing from him every day. "So, what are you up to tonight?"

He grinned, showing off perfect white teeth. "Heading up to Bo and Nyx's club."

She snickered. "I'm sure the night will end well for you then." The male had absolutely no problem finding female companionship. Rhea was from a different generation though and would never be as relaxed about sex as him. Not to mention she'd once been hurt badly by a male. After losing her almost-mate, then living through hell, casual sleeping around held no appeal.

She held her covered blades at her side. "I'll walk you out. Victoria said she wanted to talk to me about something to do with the wedding." Rhea couldn't imagine what her packmate could want to talk about though. She wasn't in Bo and Nyx's wedding, though she was happy for the half-demon and demigod who'd become friends with their pack.

"Maybe it's for fashion advice." His voice was dry.

She nudged him with her hip as they stepped out into the polished wood hallway of the Stavros pack's mansion. She needed to drop her weapons in her room too. "Don't be a jackass."

Solon just smirked, his lips curving up wickedly. Rhea had never felt an ounce of attraction toward the male but she understood why females seemed to fall at his feet.

"I think being a jackass is part of his charm." Victoria's voice made both of them turn as they reached the swinging door to the kitchen.

"Hey." Solon placed a hand over his chest, feigning offense.

"Oh please." Victoria linked her arm through Rhea's. "You'll just have to live without your bestie for a bit. I need to borrow her," she said to Solon, dragging Rhea away from the kitchen.

Normally Rhea had to look up at Victoria, who was a few inches taller, but in her heels they were about even in height today. "How is it that I see you even more now that you've moved to Montana?"

"Because one of my best friends is a demigod who can transport me anywhere in seconds and my mate is a dragon who can fly me anywhere is probably a smart ass answer, but that's how."

Rhea laughed, wrapping her arm around Victoria's shoulders in a quick hug. She wasn't normally big on affection but she made an exception for the healer who she'd always thought of as a little sister. "I'm glad you're here so much. So what do you need to talk to me about?"

Victoria shook her head and pushed open the nearest door—and dragged her into a storage closet filled with bins of Christmas decorations. She flipped on a light, not that they needed it with their supernatural sight, and pointed at Rhea, making a circular motion at her dress. "You look insanely hot. You're the most beautiful woman I know but this puts you into a new category completely. Who's this for?"

Rhea scrubbed a hand over the back of her neck. It was weird having anyone call her beautiful. "What do you mean?"

"The dress, the sorta fuck-me shoes. Who's the guy?"

She frowned at the shoe comment—and the fuck-me one. "When did you start talking like that? And what do you mean sorta?"

"Well, they're a little weak as far as heels go, but compared to your normal combat boots, I figure they count. So, who's the guy?" There was something in Victoria's gaze, something that looked a lot like . . . annoyance.

But that couldn't be right.

"What is wrong with everyone in this pack? I can wear a dress for myself. Last time I checked I'm a grown-ass woman who picks out her own clothes and everything." And okay, yeah, she wanted to look good for a male—who just happened to be Victoria's brother-in-law. Another reason Rhea wasn't going to admit why she was all dressed up. That would just give V and anyone else within hearing distance fodder for the gossip mill of the Stavros pack. No thank you.

"The one and only time I asked you if you wanted to go shopping with me, I'm pretty sure you pulled a blade on me."

"Ha ha." She started to roll her eyes when the closet door flew open.

Their Alpha, Finn, stood there, his ice blue eyes grim. "I don't even want to know what you two are doing in here. Rhea, we've got an issue. Need you to gear up. I'm getting a team to head out in less than five minutes."

She nodded, already going into battle mode. At least she could take these stupid shoes off. "Where's everyone convening?"

"Driveway, by the SUVs."

"I'll be there." She wouldn't even bother asking what the mission would be. He'd tell everyone once they were all together. He was heading down the hallway at a rapid speed before she could ask anyway.

"This conversation isn't over," Victoria muttered.

"What conversation? I thought you wanted to talk to me about wedding stuff anyway."

"Well yeah, I wanted to see if you wanted to be at my table."

That was the kind of question that warranted a phone call or text, not a meeting in a storage closet. "Yeah, sure." Considering how rowdy their pack was she doubted they'd even be sitting for long anyway. And Victoria was giving her that weird look again. "What's going on with you? You're being weird."

Victoria snorted. "I'm not the one dressed like a sex goddess."

For the first time in probably a century, Rhea blushed. Nope, not responding to that. "Gotta go, V." Turning away, she started at a jog down the hallway, cursing her stupid shoes. She had to get changed, get her other weapons and potentially burn this dress. She was being ridiculous anyway. Conall's former betrothed was all delicate and elegant, nothing like Rhea. What was she thinking, dressing up—

"Conall's sitting at our table," Victoria called after her, that weird note in her voice again.

Rhea didn't turn around even if her heart flipped over in her chest at the mere mention of his name. Ugh. Males were way too much trouble. Especially sexy, Alpha dragon shifters.

* * *

Rhea looked at Solon, who pointed up at the first floor of the raised beach house and held up four fingers. The house was about eighteen feet off the ground and they were both familiar with the interior. The Stavros pack owned it and rented it out for income—but no one was supposed to be in it right now.

One of their packmates, who ran a lot of the pack's rental properties, had gotten an alert that one of their alarms had temporarily gone off. So they'd told the security company that it was a false alarm because shifters didn't involve humans any more than necessary in their business. And there was the chance that it was a false alert—until Finn had sent out a scout and discovered four of their places had been compromised.

Hell no.

So now she and Solon were about to breach this residence and find out who the hell was dumb enough to not only invade their pack's territory, but to break into one or more of their properties. If it had been humans they'd have simply called in the authorities, but their scout had seen a male shift to wolf form through a window. This wasn't random.

She held up four fingers, mirroring Solon, and nodded. She scented four specific individuals as well. As a warrior she was well trained, but she also had an exceptional scenting ability. It was one of the reasons she was a tracker, and she knew that four people had been down in the parking and storage area of the rental not long ago.

Next she held up one finger, then signed "woman". Solon was strong, but she was a better tracker and she was almost completely certain that there was one female and three males upstairs. The movements inside had slowed about five minutes ago, but there was an occasional rustling in two of the rooms and the sound of a shower running. Human ears wouldn't be able to pick up on the sounds, not with the insulation, but she could just make them out.

Solon motioned toward the stairs then to himself. She nodded and headed to one of the concrete pillars. She shimmied up it in seconds, moving whisper-quiet over the railing once she reached it. There were automatic sensor lights on all of Finn's rentals, but someone from their computer security team had remotely disabled everything so they wouldn't be given away. He'd also disabled all the magnetic contacts on the windows.

Thank you, technology.

Her heart rate was steady as she crept toward the outer wall of the house. She'd been a warrior for over a century and four wolves were nothing for her and Solon to take on. Not that she wasn't going to be careful. At least it wasn't a full moon this evening. Blending in was that much easier without extra illumination.

All the blinds on the wide windows were drawn, but she needed to find cover and enter through a window. She was planning to breach on the next floor up because it would be unexpected. Solon would be doing the same.

They'd infiltrate, then do what needed to be done. Disable or kill the intruders. Just depended on the reaction of the people inside.

After trying to get a peek into any window, and finding all of them closed tight, she climbed to the next floor using one of the wooden railing posts this time. As she hoisted herself over the railing, she instinctively scanned for signs of life. She could scent that a shifter had been out on the patio earlier, but Solon's scent overpowered it. He was on the opposite side of this floor now.

Moving fast and quiet, she hurried around to find him completely still, his ear turned toward the window. He made a fist, letting her know that no one was inside.

Good.

The rental homes the pack owned all had the same basic layout. On this top floor were three bedrooms and two bathrooms. If no one was in this bedroom, it would be best to use this as the infiltration point.

Since Solon was the better of the two at breaking and entering, she waited while he worked his magic.

Glancing over his shoulder as he bent to lift the heavy pane window, he grinned. When he started to slide it up, they both heard a distinctive click then depression of air.

Shit.

Years of instinct and a deep-seated sisterly love for her packmate had her reacting before she'd realized it.

She grabbed him by the shoulders and used all her supernatural strength to toss him over the balcony ledge. Rhea followed, springing after him as a swell of heat licked at her back.

A booming explosion rent the air as she sailed over the edge, bracing for the impact of the three story fall.

CHAPTER TWO

Rhea grunted under the impact as she slammed to the hard earth. As a wolf shifter her bones were stronger and she was more impervious to injury than humans, but she felt a crack in her ankle even as she rolled into the fall. She growled at the pain, but her wolf took over almost instantaneously, the shift fast even by shifter standards. Her clothes shredded and her blades fell to the ground with a thud.

Wood and debris rained down on her and Solon, but after a quick glance up it didn't appear to have been a fire bomb meant to completely destroy. Just a shock tactic explosion. She'd worry about the minor destruction later.

Her body healed itself as her bones realigned and fur replaced skin. In the seconds it took for her to change form, Solon did as well. Even though he was about fifty years younger than her, the male was strong and would grow even stronger as years passed.

None of that mattered now.

All her wolf knew was that they'd been set up. Which meant her packmates checking the other houses had been set up as well. She wanted to call them, to warn them, but she and Solon had a problem to deal with first.

The scent of other shifters filled the air, agitating her wolf before she even got a visual of the intruders.

Solon started growling moments before four wolves leapt off the first level balcony.

Rhea aimed for the closest wolf, launching herself in a sharp burst of energy. She sank her teeth into his back haunch as she sailed past the huge beast, ripping fur and flesh.

Her wolf cheered at his howl of pain. The shifter she'd injured would heal but she liked drawing first blood. Victoria had once told Rhea that statistically, the person who made the first strike in any fight was more likely to win. Since V wasn't often wrong, Rhea made it a point to attack hard and fast.

She swiveled back quickly to face her attackers. Solon had taken on two and she was going to take on two. She'd been up against worse odds.

Any questions of who these wolves were or what they wanted didn't matter. The only thing that did was eliminating the threat to their pack. In the supernatural world things were savage, brutal. Only power was respected and if they let anyone intrude on their territory it would be taken as a sign of weakness.

And others would come, looking to encroach on their domain. That was how innocents got hurt.

Baring her canines, she snarled at the two shifters. She'd made the first strike and she wanted to see their moves, their flaws.

Drawing out a fight was a good way to get killed. Her Alpha had taught her that over a hundred years ago. Don't taunt your prey.

The first thing Rhea noticed was that the brown and white female shifter favored her right paw—maybe she'd injured herself in the jump—and the all gray male was dragging his back leg from where she'd attacked.

Going with her instinct, she jumped in between the two wolves, taking them off guard. Kicking out with her back leg, she made contact with the female's snout as she lunged at the male.

Teeth bared, she tore at his face, ripping out one of his eyes. With two opponents she needed to maim or injure before she made the killing blow. It would be too difficult otherwise.

The male snarled, snapping his jaws and Rhea felt a vicious tear through her hind leg. She channeled the pain, used it to focus on her task.

As the fire of agony licked up her leg, she slashed out at the male again, using her claws this time. Unlike regular wolves, shifters had retractable claws. She slashed at his face as the female dug her teeth into Rhea's upper leg.

She howled in pain but struck out again, this time snapping her jaw around the male's neck. He clawed at her, his own jaw snapping as she ripped through bone and cartilage until she tore his head free.

Adrenaline pumped through her like lightning as she tossed it to the side.

Claws dug into her back and teeth into her neck as the female pounced.

With a growl, Rhea rolled, slamming the female onto the ground with all her strength.

Immediately the shifter's hold loosened.

Rhea jumped up onto all fours and swiveled to face her attacker. The female charged, jaws open wide.

Avoiding the sharp teeth, she ducked down and rolled to the right. The female couldn't slow the momentum of her charge. Rhea used that to her advantage and struck out, clamping down on the female's throat.

This shifter was smaller, not as strong and the kill was quicker. Breathing hard, her heart pumping wildly in her chest, she let the body slump to the ground and surveyed the four dead shifters.

Solon had made quick work of the other two males as well. As the dead bodies started to return to human form, Rhea forced herself to undergo the change.

The shift back to human wasn't as seamless as her shift to wolf, but it was quick. Her heart rate had started to slow as she stood and looked at the carnage.

Less than ten minutes had passed since they'd attempted to breach the place but it felt like an eternity. Taking a deep breath, she inhaled all the scents around them while listening for any sounds that didn't belong. She couldn't scent any humans or other unknown entities, but that didn't mean anything because someone could have seen the explosion.

Ignoring her bleeding leg and the pain pulsing from the wound, she looked up at the smoldering ruins of the upper balcony bedroom. "We need to call Finn and get rid of these bodies."

From what she could see just the wall and part of the roof had been blown out. "If someone saw that explosion..." They needed the bodies gone just in case the police got called. There wouldn't be a good way to explain four bodies that had been ripped to shreds and decapitated by wild animals.

Solon nodded, moving into action. "I'll grab the SUV."

"I'll call Finn." She grabbed her cell phone from her shredded pants. Her hand shook but she channeled the pain, locked it down. Before she could dial, her phone buzzed in her hand.

"Hey," she said, answering on the first ring.

"We were set up," Finn said immediately.

"Us too. They rigged an explosive. Not sure of what kind yet. Four wolves total. Three male, one female. All dead." She crouched next to one of the bodies and turned it over, looking for any distinctive marks.

When she saw a familiar tattoo on the male's chest, she froze for just a second as ice slid through her veins.

"Explosives at each residence so far, but no others have gone off," Finn said. "We went in non-rigged entrances, just by chance. I killed a couple and so did the other teams. Two got away though."

Rhea swallowed hard, forcing herself to remain calm. Out of instinct, she glanced around, looking for another attacker. "Any markings on the bodies?"

"Yeah, they're all tattooed," he said as Rhea moved to the female body. She was tattooed with an intricate Celtic looking symbol on her inner wrist.

Just like Rhea had been once upon a time. Until she'd literally cut her skin away so that it would grow back without that hideous marking of ownership.

"Don't recognize the tats though," he continued.

She wanted to tell him that she did, but Solon steered into the driveway, his lights off. She'd tell Finn when they were alone. No one else could know. Not unless Finn thought it necessary. "They've got tattoos as well." It went against her instinct to not tell Finn right away, but fear made her hold off. "Solon just pulled up. We're gonna load up the bodies and head back to the mansion. If someone called the fire department about the explosion—"

"I'll take care of it. Just get those bodies and get the hell out of there."

"See you soon." She ended the call as Solon jumped from the driver's seat, fully clothed now.

Wordlessly she hurried to the middle door and yanked it open to grab her duffle bag for a change of spare clothes. All shifters traveled with an extra set or two with them because of stuff like this. Dressed in seconds, she moved quickly to help him load up the dead shifters.

If they got stopped by law enforcement for anything, they'd have a tough time explaining the bodies and heads in the back of the SUV and the blood covering them, but that was something they'd just have to worry about if it happened.

"You okay?" Solon asked as he finally shut the door.

She lifted a shoulder. "Why wouldn't I be?" He couldn't be asking because she'd gotten a little injured during the fight. That was just the shifter way of life.

"You look pale."

At the distant sound of sirens, her heart rate kicked up again. With her shifter senses she knew that she was hearing the sirens long before they'd reach the beach house, but she still wanted to be long gone in case the fire truck and/or police cars were coming this way. "Let me do a quick scan for personal belongings." Neither she nor Solon had brought anything to identify them when they came—they never did on missions—but she wanted to make sure the four dead wolves hadn't left anything else behind.

He nodded and rounded the vehicle to the driver's side as she raced to the house. One quick sweep, then they were getting the hell out of here.

* * *

Rhea allowed herself a sigh of relief as the heavy gate to their mansion compound shut behind their SUV. "I hate driving around with dead bodies," she muttered.

Solon snorted in agreement.

It wasn't as if they couldn't take care of human law enforcement by running then ditching the SUV if it came down to it. None of their vehicles were in their names or linked to their pack, but still, running from the police was a pain in the ass.

"Looks like we're the last ones here," he said as they pulled up behind everyone.

Not only were the teams who'd gone out to hunt the intruders standing around their SUVs, but so were a handful of packmates.

And Conall.

An unexpected burst of pleasure rolled through her at the sight of the impossibly sexy male. She knew he was here to see Victoria, and his brother Drake. But come on, she had to run into him when she was still covered in blood?

"The fates hate me," she muttered.

"He'll still think you're hot." Solon switched off the ignition.

"He who?"

Her best friend snorted. "Play that game all you want, you're not fooling me. And . . . you've got some blood on your nose and cheeks."

"Damn it." She flipped the visor down but when she slid open the mirror she didn't have anything on her face. On her neck, fingernails and okay, one of her ears, but nowhere else. "You're a jackass." She slapped the visor up and got out of the vehicle. Whatever. So she had blood and dirt all over her. She wasn't going to pretend to be something she wasn't. "I might just come down to the club later and cramp your style. Start telling stories about you when you were a cub to some of the ladies."

His dark eyes widened as he rounded the vehicle to meet her. "You're mean."

She just snickered. He was only fifty years younger than her, but she'd gotten to watch him grow up and she never let him forget it. She nodded once at their Alpha as they reached everyone. Conall was standing next to Drake, but Rhea couldn't help but notice two of her prettiest packmates were standing close to Conall as well.

Way too close.

Tall with dark hair and stunning gray eyes, the male was enough to make any woman do a double take. Then come back again for another look. With chiseled cheekbones and that sexy brooding thing down pat, yep, he was a feast for the eyes.

Something her single packmates seemed to have noticed. She had to actually force her wolf not to growl. If she'd been in animal form now, her ears would be pinned back and she'd probably be baring her canines at two females she genuinely liked. Ugh.

"Bodies in the back?" Finn asked.

She nodded once.

"Good. I'm going to start a search on the tattoo in some of our databases. You two go see Ophelia."

"I'm fine," she and Solon said practically in unison. And Rhea needed to tell Finn about the tats anyway. She couldn't wait. "The blood's theirs," she tacked on. Well, not all of it, but since it wasn't a full lie, an acidic scent wouldn't roll off her.

Finn's gaze narrowed. "Is all of it theirs?"

Damn it. "I'm already healed . . . Mostly." The wound on her leg was practically knitted back together. It wasn't like she was bleeding anymore and she wasn't going to waste Ophelia's time.

"I can look at you guys right now," Victoria said.

Before Victoria had moved to Montana she'd been one of their healers too. But now that V had mated a dragon shifter she'd moved in with his clan. "I'm good, V. Promise. I . . . need to talk to you about the tattoos in private," she said quietly, turning her focus on Finn.

His gaze sharpened and she felt Solon's gaze on her. She hadn't said anything to him during their drive and under normal circumstances she told the male pretty much everything. Not this though. Finn was one of her few packmates who'd known her before she'd become a warrior, knew what had happened to her so many years ago. She wanted to keep it that way.

"My office, now." He barked out orders to the rest of the team to start disposing of bodies.

As she fell in step with him, she glanced over at Conall and gave him a half-smile and nod. When he did the same, her traitorous heart flipped over in her chest. There was a hint of concern in his eyes that made her frown. She didn't need anyone worried about her, not after a simple fight. Her jaw tightened when he turned to look at one of her packmates, who was trying to get his attention.

When a prick of pain registered in her palms she realized her claws had extended. Nope. She had to get herself under control. This was not her. With a potential threat from her past on the horizon now was definitely not the time for her to lose it.

When they reached Finn's office, the door was half-open, no surprise. Lyra, Finn's blood-born vampire mate, was stretched out on the chaise lounge, a laptop on her thighs. The blonde smiled when saw them, but her expression quickly morphed into worry. Moving with the speed of her kind, she was up and at her mate's side in seconds.

"I smell blood." She ran her hands up and down Finn's arms, her violet-gray eyes sweeping over him with concern.

The Alpha was more than fine. Rhea didn't even see any scratches or a trace of blood on him, but it was incredibly sweet that she worried about him. He'd always been a good Alpha and deserved the mate he'd ended up with.

Feeling as if she was imposing on an intimate moment, Rhea looked away and stared at one of his bookshelves, scanning over the titles without actually reading them.

"I'm fine," he murmured and Rhea heard the distinct sound of kissing before he growled out, his tone admonishing, "The blood's Rhea's."

She swiveled to find Lyra watching her with concern now. The vampire might be only ninety, but she had that mom look down to an art.

"My wounds are all healed. I swear. I'm just dirty and gross, that's all." Her own parents had been gone a long time and she wasn't afraid to admit she didn't mind a little mothering.

At least not from Lyra.

"Sit," Lyra said, pointing to one of the chairs.

Since it was leather Rhea sat on it, otherwise she'd have gone with the floor. She was too gross to sit on any sort of fabric.

Muttering under her breath about wolves who didn't take care of themselves, Lyra pulled a first aid kit from one of the desk drawers and lifted up both Rhea's pants legs. By now she knew better than to argue with the female so she looked at her Alpha as he sat on the edge of his desk.

"I didn't want to say anything in front of anyone because it has to do with . . . Anson." Even saying that male's name left a bitter taste in her mouth.

Finn's eyes went pure wolf as he looked at her. He just nodded once while Lyra wiped away the dried blood from her legs. She felt a little weird sitting instead of pacing but she needed to get it all out.

"When he took me, he..." Rhea pushed out a harsh, ragged breath. The evil male had done a lot of things, none of which she wanted to think about much less talk about. But one thing she needed to. "He made everyone in his pack get tattooed with a mark of his choosing. It didn't matter that I wasn't there willingly, that I wasn't a pack member, he tattooed me too. In the same place as the female I killed today. Inner wrist for the females, chest for the males."

Finn's gaze flicked down to her tattoo-free wrists.

She ran a hand through her tangled curls. "I cut the skin off as soon as I was free." It had hurt but the pain was worth it to be free of that monster's mark.

"You think it's him?"

"No. He's dead. I know that for a fact. I killed him myself." It hadn't been because of her physical strength back then, just cunning and luck. "I ripped out his heart." She'd also cut off his head just to be sure. "Then I burned the body. He's gone."

His eyebrows raised. "Did my uncle know?"

Nodding, Rhea flicked a glance at Lyra, who'd finished cleaning up her legs. Both Finn and Lyra hated his uncle, Finn more so than anyone.

Lyra half-smiled. "You can talk about him. I didn't even know him."

Rhea cleared her throat and looked back at her Alpha. "Yeah, he knew. He also knew about the tattoos. Said he'd take care of it. He wanted to send a message by destroying everyone from Anson's pack."

"Did Anson have any blood relatives?"

"A couple brothers, but like I said, I thought your uncle killed everyone. When I escaped I told him where Anson's den was and he took out a hunting party. They came back covered in blood and he told me that it was done.

That was it. Other than your uncle, I don't think anyone knew I killed Anson or . . . what happened to me either." Anson's death had been blamed on vampires, which was fine with her. It had taken her years to get over the constant nightmares.

"If some of his packmates survived, this could be a revenge thing."

She nodded, but said, "It's been over a hundred years."

"Which you and I know means nothing. Shifters have long memories." His mouth pulled into a thin line.

"And if someone did want revenge on me or our pack, they'd have to have a strong enough pack to come after us." Which could very well take a hundred years to build up a pack strong and big enough.

"True. Or this could just be some moron who thinks he has the power to take my territory." His words came out more animal than human and Finn's eyes went wolf again, the animal staring back at Rhea with the strength of a true Alpha.

She had to glance down, something she rarely did, but he was her pack leader. The force of his anger right now, thankfully not directed at her, was a powerful thing.

After a few moments he cleared his throat and when she looked at him again his wolf was gone. "Get out of here, get cleaned up. I think some of the pack is headed up to Howlers and some are going to Bo's place. Tomorrow morning I want to meet with all the warriors so be in the training room at eight. We're going to step up the patrols and I'm going to look more into the tattoo."

"What about fingerprints?" They could get them before they burned or buried the dead and run them through any number of databases their pack had access to. Elana, one of their hackers, was very good at getting into places online she wasn't allowed.

Finn's mouth curved up. "Already on that too. Take a break tonight. You look like you need it."

Normally she'd argue, but she needed some downtime and distance from her pack. She nodded and stood. "Thanks." She wouldn't be going to Howlers or Bo's, though. Right now she wasn't in the mood to drink or dance or be social at all. The image of that tattoo had brought up too many nightmares she'd worked hard to keep buried.

Not to mention Conall would likely be at the club if Victoria and Drake were and she didn't have the energy to deal with her confusing emotions toward him. Nope. Her and relationships simply didn't mix. She'd already gotten one male killed. She wouldn't risk doing it again.

CHAPTER THREE

7 months ago

Rhea fell back against her bed, exhausted from a day of training the younger wolves in hand-to-hand combat. "So how was being Alpha today?" she asked Conall, her phone held to her ear.

He snorted. "One of my clan members nearly burned down their kitchen during sex."

She blinked. "What?'

"I still don't know exactly what happened. And I really don't want to know." His voice was dry.

"I can honestly say I don't think we've ever had that issue with my pack." The Stavros pack all lived together in a big mansion. Well, some packmates had their own places around town, but the majority of wolves liked to live together. She knew Conall's clan was different. Dragons were different in general. Their clans lived together in the same vicinity, but everyone had their own home. They liked their privacy.

Conall's laugh was low, gravelly and she felt it all the way to her toes. "I wish I could say it was a first for my clan."

Now she snorted. And people said wolves were crazy. "How's Victoria settling in to life in Montana?"

"Everyone loves her. They dote on her a little too, which I think makes her crazy, but she doesn't complain."

"It's hard not to love her." Rhea had known V since the other female was a cub. She wasn't all that old now, not compared to Rhea's hundred and fifty-plus years. Some days Rhea felt like she was a thousand years old.

"How'd training go today?" His voice had a low, gravelly quality to it tonight and it sent shivers twisting through her even though she had no business being affected by an Alpha dragon who lived in a different territory.

She wasn't even sure how this friendship between them had started. A couple months ago she'd been up in Montana on his clan's land on pack business and they'd fought alongside each other when some rogue dragons had attacked. Well, not directly alongside each other, but still. He'd asked for her phone number and they'd been calling and texting since. Nothing about their conversations was romantic though. Maybe...

No. Maybe nothing. She didn't want to get involved with anyone anyway. She'd already gotten one good male killed; she never wanted to be responsible for something like that again. It had nearly destroyed her the first time. Besides, she thought she was a good outlet for Conall. She figured he didn't have that many people to talk to in his clan, not when he was the Alpha. Alphas always had to have a sort of boundary between them and everyone else.

Clearing her throat, she shoved those thoughts away. "Good. Some of the young ones, especially the males, like to push me, think they can take me on." She laughed darkly.

"Why do I get the feeling you have fun putting them in their place?"

"Uh, because I totally do. They get cocky, think because I'm a female they can underestimate me. Which is beyond stupid on so many levels." Especially since some of the males she was training had incredibly strong mothers. She didn't really understand the mentality but she also didn't have a penis. Or maybe it was a generational thing because the males from her generation weren't so arrogant. At least not about that.

"Anyone who underestimates a female warrior is a fool."

Yeah, she didn't think there was a sexist bone in Conall's very big, very sexy body. Not that she'd noticed how sexy he was. Not much. She had eyes, of course she could see how utterly ripped and lethal the male was. And in dragon form, he was one of the most beautiful things she'd ever seen. Gah, she needed to stop thinking about him like that. They were just friends. "Says the male with the scariest mother I've ever met."

He laughed. "I'll be sure to tell her you said that."

"She'll take it as a compliment."

"I know."

Rhea found herself grinning, relaxed as she stared up at the ceiling of her room. She looked forward to these talks with Conall way more than she should. It had become a weekly thing, with the texts a daily occurrence. Pack life and warrior life was always go-go-go. He was an outlet, someone she could vent to or just be herself with. She trusted him, felt comfortable with him. She started to say more when there was a bang on her door.

"Rhea, gear up, got an emergency!" It was Solon.

"Hell, I gotta go," she said quietly to Conall, already pushing up. So much for having a night off.

"Everything okay?"

"Yeah, probably just a security issue. Talk to you soon?" The millisecond she waited for his answer left her ridiculously riddled with anticipation.

"Definitely. Stay safe."

"Same to you." As they disconnected, she ignored the sense of loss she felt. It was weird. She hadn't known him that long, but every time they talked she realized there was nothing she looked forward to more than talking to him.

And she definitely didn't want to think about why that was.

CHAPTER FOUR

Conall leaned back in his high-top chair as Victoria dragged Drake onto the dance floor at Howlers. Drake looked uncomfortable dancing, but the way he gazed at Victoria was pure love and adoration.

"Never thought I'd say this, but your brother is probably the only male good enough for her," Gabriel said, quiet enough for Conall's ears only as he watched the two of them as well.

Conall wasn't completely sure of the Guardian's relationship with Victoria but knew he viewed her as a sister. "They certainly fit." There was an innocence to the two of them. It didn't matter that his brother had been trapped in Hell for over a thousand years, he'd somehow retained his goodness. And found the perfect mate. It gave Conall peace, knowing his brother was so happy.

He glanced down at his cell phone for what felt like the hundredth time. He'd texted Rhea an hour ago and hadn't heard back. He knew she was talking to her Alpha about something, but after seeing Rhea briefly at the Stavros pack's compound he couldn't get her out of his mind. Okay, he hadn't been able to get her out of his head since the moment he'd met her. He hated that she'd clearly been injured but hadn't gone to see her healer.

Ever since his first meeting with her, his dragon had awakened in a way he was still coming to terms with.

Whenever he thought of her, his beast rippled under the surface, demanding that Conall claim her. Shaking those thoughts away, he took a swig of his beer as a female named Lauren sauntered up to the table. He'd met the blonde earlier outside the Stavros mansion.

She smiled at him just a little too widely and he realized her friendliness from earlier was more than just that. "Come join me on the dance floor?" she asked, practically purring.

He shook his head. "Thank you for asking, but no." He didn't care if it was a caveman mentality, he wanted to pursue a female, not be pursued. But he was from a very different generation. Besides, the thought of dancing with a female who wasn't Rhea offended his dragon half. No, *all* of him.

"I heard Spiro whining earlier that no one can keep up with him on the dance floor. Saw him by one of the bars. Go show him up and put us all out of our misery," Gabriel said before the female could answer.

She pouted prettily before turning away. He looked at his phone again. Frowned. Still no response. God, he felt like . . . okay, he'd never felt like this. He wasn't used to feeling unsure about anything. From the time he'd been a young dragon females had always thrown themselves at him. He'd never cared because he'd been betrothed to a female. Even after they'd parted ways he'd never been insecure where females were concerned.

Because he'd never cared about any of them.

The realization punched into him as Gabriel ordered another round for them. "Just got a text from Finn. Rhea's headed back to her room. I don't think she'll come out tonight. Seems she has a lot on her mind."

Conall glanced at the male. His green eyes were as unreadable as his expression. And damn him, his words were annoyingly cryptic.

"Thought you might want to know," Gabriel continued, his half-smile smug as he nodded a thank you to the server dropping off their new round of beers.

Conall frowned as Gabriel's words settled in. "What kind of stuff on her mind?" He shouldn't be asking, shouldn't show any weakness to anyone, but this male had already proved himself to be trustworthy.

As Alpha of the Petronilla clan, Conall had recently signed a treaty of alliance between his clan and the Stavros pack. And Gabriel was the pack's Guardian, basically the second-in-command after the Alpha's mate.

Gabriel just lifted a shoulder.

Conall slid his beer to the middle of the table. "You can finish this if you want. I'm gonna head out." The truth was, the only reason he'd come out tonight was to see Rhea but if she wasn't coming he was heading back to his place. It was clear Drake and Victoria were going to be leaving soon and he didn't have it in him to be civil in a social setting to anyone else. He threw a few bills on the table, more than enough to cover his and Gabriel's drinks.

Disappointment filtered through him that she hadn't responded to his text. But she was a complicated female, something he'd come to learn in the last eight months. She only let him in as much as she wanted, never revealing any weakness. Not that he wanted to see her weak, but damn, he wanted to find a way past that wall of hers.

"She likes weapons," Gabriel said without looking at him.

Conall paused with his wallet in hand. "What?"

"Rhea. If you plan on courting her, she likes custom made stuff or vintage pieces. Has a whole collection."

Conall immediately thought of something he could make for her, then just as quickly dismissed the idea. He couldn't just give her something like that without giving away his intention. A weapon forged in dragon fire was sacred and rare, something only given to a mate. He knew his brother had given one to Victoria, but he'd never thought he'd want to give one to someone. Hell, he'd thought if he ever got mated it would be to another dragon.

His dragon swiped at him with vicious claws, the sensation as deep as if he'd been physically struck. Clearing his throat, he shoved his wallet in his pocket. "Thanks," he murmured, turning to go.

"If you hurt her, she'll kick your ass. And then Solon and I will finish the job." There was a savage bite to Gabriel's words that made Conall turn around midstride.

He knew his dragon was in his eyes, was barely containing his beast. Not because of the threat, but because he needed to see Rhea. Being in the same city as her and not being in her actual presence was making him edgy.

A little uncontrollable. He'd never felt like that before, not with any female.

And he didn't like that she'd been off on some mission and gotten injured. She'd been so dismissive about it too, but he'd scented her blood above all the other wolves who'd been injured. He wasn't even sure how he'd known it was hers, but it stuck out, sang to all of his senses. He hated that she'd been hurt and he had no right to ask her about it. Or demand she see a healer. Every fiber of him had wanted to insist, or simply take care of her himself, but he'd restrained himself.

Barely.

He quickly made his way through the bar/club attached to Finn's hotel. Out in the parking lot he breathed in the fresh night air.

When his phone buzzed in his pocket his heart rate kicked up. Which just made him feel pathetic. But when he saw Rhea's name on his screen he didn't care.

Hey, heard you were out. I'm headed to the OS public beach. Needed to get some space from the mansion. Will park near the bridge. Come if you're free. Could use the company.

Just like that all the muscles in his body tightened in anticipation. He fired off a response, the need to see her all-consuming. He'd been in the Gulf Coast area a year ago, when his brother had escaped from Hell. Conall and his sister had spent months searching for him so he was familiar with the area and knew where Rhea would be. Anticipation hummed through him as well as relief that she'd reached out to him. He'd never had to work for any female's attention before, not truly, and this . . . he liked this. He liked *her*.

He looked around the parking lot for any other patrons walking to their vehicles. His brother had already told him where he could avoid cameras if he wanted to shift. First he put his phone and wallet in his rental truck.

Using the cover of darkness, he stripped off his clothes then called on his natural camouflage. Dragons were the chameleons of the supernatural world. They were fewer in numbers than vamps or wolves but Mother Nature made up for that with other gifts she'd bestowed on his kind.

Once he was masked from prying eyes, he allowed the change to roll through him, letting his dragon completely take over as he launched himself into the air. He scooped up his clothes in his claw at the last second. He'd been so focused on getting to Rhea he'd almost forgotten.

One of his wings toppled over a car he hadn't seen but he ignored it. Maybe he should feel bad, but all he cared about was getting to Rhea. In his dragon form he was stronger, more in control. His wings flapped harder the higher he rose into the air, up, up, up.

As the cool wind rolled over him and he left the earth behind, his dragon felt that same sense of freedom he always did in flight. Buildings, cars and people grew smaller as he rocketed even higher.

Banking a sharp left, he headed toward the bridge Rhea would be near. It crossed the Intracoastal Waterway and there was limited parking on the other side. He tried to tell himself to calm down, that he was just meeting up with a friend, but he couldn't make himself believe the lie.

Not when fantasies of her had been invading his dreams for eight straight months.

As the bridge came into view he had to remind himself to stay camouflaged, something he'd never had to do in his fifteen hundred years.

Instead of flying over the bridge he banked right and dipped down to the water below. He flew hard and fast, letting his wings expand fully at the last moment. The whipping sound was followed by silence as he glided over the water, heading straight for his destination.

A cluster of sailboats and other water crafts were moored in front of a local yacht club. The two-mile stretch of white beach was quiet this late at night.

With his supernatural vision he immediately spotted Rhea sitting near the shoreline, her legs stretched out in front of her.

Unfortunately she had on clothing. Not that he'd expected her to be naked. Still, a dragon could dream.

Flying over her, he knew she was aware of his presence when the wind ruffled her wild curly hair. He glided to a landing fifty feet behind her, his talons sinking into the soft sand. He'd perfected his landings centuries ago. After shifting to his human form he let his camouflage drop and headed toward her.

Naked.

He held onto his clothes, but didn't bother to put them on as he stalked across the sand. Nudity was no big deal to shifters but normally he clothed himself in front of females in socially appropriate situations. Now, the most primal part of him wanted Rhea to see all of him.

To see what he had to offer her.

Caveman mentality? Yep. He'd never claimed to be civilized though.

She'd turned in the sand and watched him approach, her amber eyes glinting brightly under the moonlight. He wasn't sure if it was a trick of the light or her reaction. He knew she'd be healed by now, but he was glad he couldn't smell her blood anymore.

Her gaze tracked over him in one sweep. She lingered between his legs, but her expression was unreadable before she quickly looked away. "That was fast," she murmured, staring out at the still water.

He held his clothes in front of him, not wanting her to see his now clear reaction to her. "I was leaving Howlers when you texted."

"Oh..." She looked over at him again as he sat next to her in the cool sand. She raised her eyebrows. "You planning on putting any clothes on?"

He lifted a shoulder. "Feels good out. And I don't want to deprive you of seeing all this." The semi-teasing, flirty comment took him off guard as the words left his mouth. The last eight months their communications had been friendly. Not even borderline flirty.

To his surprise, Rhea's head fell back as she laughed. Those wild dark, corkscrew curls bouncing with the movement. Her laugh was full-bodied and beautiful, the sound rolling over him like the sweetest music. "Alphas are the same no matter the species, I think," she finally said, still chuckling.

She was probably right. Alphas were, well, alpha. He could be arrogant, territorial and obnoxious. And he'd made a decision tonight. Okay, he'd made it eight fucking months ago. This female was his. If she'd have him, he was going to claim her. In that moment, if it had been physically possible, his dragon half would have high fived him.

Oh yeah, she was going to be his.

"God, I needed that tonight," she murmured, her laughter fading.

There was a stressed note in her voice that made every part of him take notice. Despite what he'd said, he slid his jeans on, not wanting his junk hanging out while they talked, especially since he seemed to be hard around her more often than not. Something told him she needed a friend right now. He wanted to be the one she turned to. "What happened earlier tonight?" He knew some of it, but wanted to hear it from her.

Sighing, she scooted closer and to his complete surprise, laid her head on his shoulder. He went immobile, not wanting to scare her off, before he slid his arm around her. He savored the feel of her this close. Shifters liked touch as a rule, but he'd noticed she wasn't overt with her affections.

"A group of shifters thought they were strong enough to invade our territory and we showed them otherwise." Her voice was contemplative.

And that vanilla and jasmine scent unique to her wrapped around him, teasing him. "Did you ever see a healer?"

She snorted, but didn't move position. "It was just a few bite marks. I healed during my shift. Mostly."

His dragon swiped at him, hating that helpless feeling. He knew she was a capable female but it didn't mean he had to like her getting injured or running into battle whenever her Alpha ordered it. "What else is bothering you?"

She looked up then, her eyes unreadable. "Why would something be bothering me?"

"Your text said you could use the company." And he could scent a very thin thread of... something he couldn't define rolling off her. Some emotion that had his dragon going a little crazy.

She let out a sigh. "Yeah. It's just stupid stuff. I don't want to talk about it, but I needed a friend tonight. Thanks for coming. And sorry I didn't get to talk or hang out earlier."

He decided to ignore the word friend, even if they were just that. He wanted more. "I understand. You going to the party tomorrow?" Bo and Nyx were doing a week-long celebration before their wedding. Conall wasn't really sure why, but the half-demon wanted to do something big for his mate. Apparently that meant a week of themed parties.

She snorted. "Yeah. Don't know what I'm gonna wear though."

He just grinned and looked out at the water.

She pinched his side. "What's that look?"

"You'd look good in a flapper dress." Or any dress. Or *out* of any dress. He couldn't take his gaze off her, knew all the heat he felt for her was in his eyes now.

To his surprise, she flushed and glanced away. "I don't even understand the themes. There's no rhyme or reason for them. New Orleans from any decade, which okay I actually get that one since Bo's from there. But someone mentioned something about a masquerade ball, and maybe a cowboy theme one night . . . ugh, I can't even remember."

His lips pulled up. "Mated males can be insane." Hell, they weren't close to being mated and Rhea was already making him crazy.

"So are mated females. Nyx is totally on board with everything. I love a good party, but costumes?" She let out a mock shudder.

"We can boycott dressing up together."

"And listen to your sister-in-law complain? No thanks."

"I think because she's been sucked up into the insanity of their wedding she wants everyone else to be." Victoria was one of Nyx's bridesmaids and was taking her job very seriously. He didn't really understand since dragons didn't do weddings. Neither did wolves for that matter. They just got mated and sometimes had a big party to celebrate. As in a single party.

"Apparently we're at the same table for the actual reception after the wedding." Rhea looked away from the quiet water and turned to him.

"Good."

She watched him for a long moment, her amber eyes glinting a little brighter than normal. "How long are you in town? You never said." There was a note of interest in her question, one he'd never heard before.

Yeah, he didn't think she was as unaffected as she wanted him to believe. "At least through the wedding." And as long as it took to convince Rhea to be his.

She looked back out at the water. His gaze trailed up the column of her neck and along her jaw line. Her café au lait skin was smooth, perfect. The urge to bury his face against her neck, to tease and kiss her was damn near overwhelming.

He put a lock on those thoughts and forced himself to look away. He could mask his scent to an extent, but it was growing more difficult to keep his attraction under wraps. And he knew that the second they kissed his mating manifestation would flip on.

All Petronilla dragons put off a bright glow when they were in the mating process. He'd never had it with his former betrothed but he knew it would happen with Rhea as sure as he knew the sun would rise tomorrow.

Unfortunately he knew it would freak her out. She'd been hurt in the past and while he didn't know the details, he'd done enough research—aka, harassing his sister-in-law for information—to know that she hadn't had a serious relationship in a very long time.

If he had anything to say about it, that was going to change very soon. He couldn't overtly court a female like Rhea. She'd shut him down before he'd started.

Nope, he'd just have to be subtle and smart—and get her so addicted to him that she wouldn't want to walk away.

CHAPTER FIVE

Liberty carefully shifted the huge cake so that it was perfectly centered in the middle of the round table.

"It looks great," Rory murmured in that faint Scottish accent as he approached from her right side.

He'd learned months ago not to approach her from behind. She felt like a bit of a freak because of that, but after she'd screamed and nearly attacked him, he'd started making his presence known very clearly.

She didn't look up as she critically eyed the cake. If she did, she'd probably lose her train of thought. The man was walking sex appeal. With just a dusting of facial hair that gave him that rough, brooding look, ridiculously broad shoulders, a wicked smile—and *that* accent she'd get distracted for sure. "I'm not sure if it's big enough." The five-layer purple, black and white cake with intricate designs and miniature Venetian masks made of fondant on each layer was huge, but Bo and Nyx had invited so many people.

She knew it was because Bo didn't want to offend anyone, so naturally the whole Stavros pack was invited, then a huge chunk of the Petronilla dragon clan, and members from yet another dragon clan because . . . Liberty couldn't even keep the reasons straight. Not to mention various supernatural beings who frequented Bo's club. According to Nyx he'd known some of them for almost fifty years and couldn't trim his guest list because he didn't want to offend anyone. There were simply so many people it was hard to comprehend.

And she'd likely be the only human there. A year ago that thought would have been beyond weird to her. She hadn't known beings other than humans even existed. A shudder racked her body as she thought of the hell she'd been through at the hands of half-demons months earlier, but she shrugged it off and locked it up tight in that little box she'd created in her mind. She'd been in a sort of therapy for months, talking with Ophelia weekly to help her deal with everything, but some days were harder than others.

"Nothing would be big enough for the Stavros pack, but considering the menu you've got planned, you're good." He shoved his hands in his pockets as he looked at her, his gorgeous green eyes intense. Wearing jeans and a T-shirt that did nothing to hide all his delicious muscles, she was finding it harder and harder to fight her physical attraction to him. With his hands in his pockets like that, all the tendons in his arms were pulled taut, showing off his sleeves of tattoos. Before Rory she'd never thought tattoos could be so sexy.

After what she'd been through she hadn't thought she'd be able to even *think* about being with a man again. But in the last couple months she'd realized she wanted Rory. She knew he wouldn't hurt her physically and he was incredibly sweet.

"True enough. So what do you think?" Turning, she motioned to the transformed Howlers. For the first party of the week Nyx and Bo had wanted to do a New Orleans theme and Liberty had been busting her ass the last eight months getting everything in order for the seven days of festivities. Finn, also the owner of the hotel and casino attached to Howlers, had reserved the place for an entire week so that only supernatural beings were allowed in the hotel, casino or Howlers.

In her previous life, as she liked to think of it, before she'd been trapped in a Hell realm with true monsters, she'd been a party planner. With a degree in hospitality and business and a whole lot of experience, it was something she knew how to do well. She'd grown up dirt poor so making parties work on a shoestring budget had been a specialty of hers. Of course Bo and Nyx's budget was the sky which made planning this a lot easier.

"It's perfect." He surveyed the place. "Fucking impressive," he continued.

The praise in his voice did something strange to her insides. Now instead of a bar/club, thick purple and gold drapes covered most of the walls and windows and round tables had hand-painted masks for everyone to take home as gifts—and to use at the next themed party, which was a masquerade one. Candelabras and lanterns set the mood lighting and though she'd wanted to schedule a jazz band, Bo and Finn had both nixed the idea. They didn't want any humans in the place—other than her—and the supernatural jazz band Bo would have used was touring on the other side of the country. That was okay though, they had a really good DJ who would be setting up soon as well.

Everything was glittery gold and purple and just waiting for people to come enjoy themselves. The only thing not ready was the buffet tables, but the hotel kitchen staff wouldn't be bringing anything out for another hour when people started arriving.

"The wait staff's going to be walking around serving dirty martinis, champagne and anything anyone wants, really. Including Café Brûlot's."

"Flaming coffees?"

"Bo wants it." Apparently it was a famous drink to come out of New Orleans and it was the one thing the half-demon had requested. Considering how much he was paying her, Liberty would make anything happen for this party. If he decided he wanted a juggling bear, she'd get it done.

"Fire around wolves is usually a bad idea..." Grinning, Rory just shook his head. "My brother has lost his mind."

She cleared her throat, a little nervous. She'd been in crazy planning mode the last month and hadn't had much alone time with Rory, except at night. But he was usually in wolf form then, which made talking harder. She usually lost her nerve anyway, but now that it was just the two of them she needed to get this out.

"Listen, I, uh, I don't think you should sleep over anymore." Saying the words were almost impossible, but she couldn't keep using him as a security blanket. He deserved better than that.

He jerked back as if she'd actually slapped him.

Guilt immediately infused her when she realized he'd misunderstood her intention. She stepped forward, gently touched Rory's forearm. "I appreciate everything you've done for me. If it wasn't for you..." She swallowed hard, but made herself keep his gaze. "I don't know that I'd have ever left Bo's house."

After Rory, Bo, their other brother Ian, and Nyx had saved her from a Hell realm, Liberty hadn't been able to leave Bo's house for two straight months. She'd been too afraid to venture into the real world again. But she'd needed to get access to her bank accounts and to do that she'd had to prove that she wasn't dead or missing. She'd been listed as a missing person by someone she'd worked with, her former condo had been rented out and most of her stuff put in storage.

She was lucky her former landlord had been kind enough to keep her stuff in storage. She'd since picked everything up and moved it to her new place, but after the kidnapping she'd walked away from her former life without a backward glance. Her home was in Biloxi now and she couldn't go back and pretend she didn't know that other beings inhabited the world. Not to mention she wasn't that same woman she was before. Months in a Hell realm had changed all that. Changed her. The old Liberty was dead.

"You'd have gotten to that point on your own with or without me," he said softly, reaching out a big hand to cup her cheek.

But at the last second he pulled back instead of touching her, his green eyes going shuttered. He always did that, acted like he was afraid to hurt her. Not that she blamed him. She'd been a mess when they first met and he'd been sleeping at her side ever since—in wolf form. And she had to stop using him for security. She wanted more than that from him, even if she was too afraid to put exactly what she wanted into words. But the one thing she knew was that he had to stop seeing her as helpless if they could ever move to a different level.

"Maybe, but . . . I can't keep using you as a crutch, Rory. I haven't had a nightmare in weeks." Which was a lie, but she hadn't woken up screaming in the last few weeks so that was progress.

He snorted, disbelief in his gaze.

"What?"

"I can smell when you lie." His voice was tight and all the muscles in his arms were pulled taut as he shoved his hand back into his pocket.

"That's not fair," she muttered. "Look, I need this. You've done so much for me and it's time for me to stand on my own two feet. Speaking of, I've saved enough money to pay you back for—"

"I'm not taking your money," he snapped, actually growling at her. Something he'd never done.

She'd spent enough time with shifters in the last eight months that she knew he wasn't being aggressive toward her, he was just annoyed. She raised her eyebrows. "Um, you will take it, because I owe it to you." She'd needed somewhere to stay when she'd found the courage to move out on her own and he'd helped her find a place that she felt safe in.

Of course he hadn't told her that he'd bought the dang townhome she now lived in or that he was her next door neighbor—or that he owned the whole string of townhomes around them. Not that she minded. Having Rory around made her feel safe, but she wasn't being fair to him. She knew he'd been living in a Hell realm for decades and she didn't want him sticking around the human realm for her, not if he felt obligated.

And if he didn't, she still couldn't have someone taking care of her out of pity or any other reason. Especially not since she wanted . . . more from him. She wasn't quite sure what the more was. She knew she wanted a physical relationship with him, but she didn't know if they would ever have more than that. He'd seen her at her worst and she wasn't sure if he could see her as an equal. And maybe she was overthinking things anyway. He might not want more from her regardless.

"The house is paid for and I don't need the money. If you try to pay me back I'll just tell Bo to give you a raise to cover what you're trying to give me. So really, you'll be taking more money from him."

She blinked. "You . . . can't do that."

"Pretty sure I can."

Liberty gritted her teeth and thumped him on the chest. "You are maddening sometimes."

"Just give up the argument now and save yourself time and energy. If it makes you feel better, donate the damn money to a charity or something. But don't think I'm ever going to take it." His grin was smug and just a little wicked.

Just like that, butterflies took flight in her belly. Even when he annoyed her he had the ability to get her turned on. Some of that had to do with his accent, which just made her melt. She shifted slightly because of the faint ache between her legs. All because of Rory. She felt so safe with him. She just wanted him to start seeing her as a female, not as a helpless victim who needed someone to look after her.

Suddenly his eyes went pure wolf.

She stepped back out of instinct. "Wh—"

But he'd turned on his heel and was striding across the bar before she could finish one word, let alone a whole thought. Aaaand, that was when she remembered that shifters could scent emotions. Feeling her face heat up, she realized he must have smelled her reaction to him. Oh, God, she didn't even know what to do with that.

She hadn't even had the chance to ask him why he'd stopped by Howlers. Not that it mattered now. She wondered if he'd left so abruptly because her scent was offensive to him in some way. She didn't think so, but there was so much about supernaturals she didn't know. A pang slid through her chest that he might not like her scent, might not want her.

"Liberty, you need to get changed pronto."

She turned at the sound of a familiar female voice. Taylor from the Stavros pack. One of the shifter females who helped run Howlers and who was in charge of the catering for tonight. "What, why? We've got an hour before the food is set up and people won't start showing up until at least half an hour after that." Bo and Nyx would be here in an hour but guests shouldn't be here for another ninety minutes.

Snickering, the redhead shook her head. "You've obviously never dealt with wolves before. They know there's gonna be a lot of free food and they know Bo and Nyx will be here in an hour. They will be here as soon as the *food* is out sniffing around like, well, wolves. My office is free or just use one of the hotel bathrooms to change."

"Thanks, just give me ten minutes and I'll be back to help with the setup." Shelving thoughts of Rory—for now—she picked up her duffle bag from one of the bar chairs she'd left it on and hurried toward the kitchen. Taylor's office was small but she'd be able to change into her flapper dress and other costume jewelry and be ready to go.

Tonight would go off without a hitch. It just had to. For months she'd been working toward this wedding celebration, letting the planning consume her. It had been a heck of a lot easier to work than drown in her nightmares. Now that it was here she was terrified of what she'd do after the wedding was over.

But that was a fear for another day. Right now, she was taking things one minute at a time.

She contemplated telling Rory that she was interested in more, but wasn't sure she was ready to be that brave. Making the first move and getting rejected wasn't something she thought she could handle right now.

* * *

"You're acting like a mated male," Bo murmured.

Rory grunted a non-response, took a sip of his beer as he watched Liberty talking to one of the servers helping with the party. He vaguely recognized the female, knew she was part of the Stavros pack.

Liberty's hands were on her hips, the black and gold sequined dress pulling taut across her lush breasts. She'd gained a little weight in the last few months, weight she'd needed to put on, but she was still slender and delicate looking. Her long blonde hair was softly curled tonight and she had on a hair band with feathers on one side to complete her ensemble. She was the picture of confidence.

It was when she wasn't in the 'work zone' as she called it, that he could see her insecurities.

Hell, it had taken her a couple months just to leave the damn house. "She told me she didn't want me staying over anymore at night. Doesn't want me to be her crutch." The confession cost him more than he wanted when he saw the flash of something in Bo's eyes. Maybe pity.

He didn't get her reasoning either. He wasn't her crutch. He just wanted to protect her. It was what mates did. They looked out for each other. But he didn't have much experience with females so maybe he was doing things wrong. He still had trouble adjusting to the human realm. Sometimes he didn't act exactly right in social settings.

Finally his brother spoke, his words careful. "That's not necessarily a bad thing."

Rory looked away from him, scanning the crowd. The place was packed with wolf shifters and dragon shifters. His wolf was okay in this place, but his demon half wasn't loving it. Being back in the human realm had some drawbacks. "Why is that?" he asked.

Bo cleared his throat, looked over to where his mate was. Rory followed his gaze to see Nyx on the dance floor with some females from the Stavros pack tearing it up.

He couldn't help the laugh that bubbled up. "For all her gifts, she's a terrible dancer."

Bo grinned, the adoration on his face ridiculous. "I know."

The first time he'd met his half-brothers, Bo had told Rory and Ian that they would stay twenty feet away from Nyx at all times. He'd been in an insane protective mode. And okay, just plain *insane* over the female. It had been clear that she could do no wrong in his brother's eyes. Even when she looked like she was trying to fight her way out of a blender—and called it dancing.

His brother cleared his throat. "Nyx said Liberty's trying really hard to stand on her own two feet." Bo lifted his eyebrows meaningfully, as if that should explain everything. "You know what I mean?"

No, he didn't fucking understand. He wasn't trying to stop her from that. But he'd gotten used to sleeping near her. He didn't want things to end. Every part of him was content when they were near each other. If someone had tried to explain the feeling to him before he'd met her he wouldn't have come close to understanding.

And . . . she still had nightmares. She could deny it all she wanted, but even if she hadn't been crying out in her sleep lately, she still tossed and turned and woke up in a sweat. She tried to cover it, but she couldn't hide from his supernatural ability to scent her. She'd been repeatedly assaulted by the leader of a band of half-demons. The male hadn't shared her with the others, but it didn't matter.

He'd hurt her in ways that made Rory wish he could bring the male back to life so he could torture him for weeks, months . . . it would never be enough. At least she was getting help from Ophelia. Every time Liberty saw the healer she seemed stronger.

"I'll take that surly growl for a no..." Bo trailed off, watching as Nyx knocked over a tray of glasses from a passing server. He stopped the glasses midair using his demon-half's gift.

A few of the shifters stared but most had seen Rory's brother in action before. "Go be with your mate, ignore my grumpy ass. This is your week and I'm happy for you." He clapped Bo on the shoulder, glad his brother had found true happiness.

Rory couldn't believe that less than a year ago he and Ian didn't know they had other siblings. So far they knew they had Bo and Cynara . . . their half-sister who was around here somewhere. With her shocking purple hair it was hard to miss her so she must have stepped out. But considering what a douche their father was, they all figured they had more siblings they might never know about.

As Bo moved toward his mate with a heated look, Rory knew they'd be leaving their own party soon. Or at least using one of the rooms upstairs.

Sweet heaven, he hoped they used a freaking room. He'd lived with them for a couple months and those two were not quiet. Turning back, he scanned the room again, his gaze immediately drawn to Liberty.

He wanted her with a desperation that made it hard to think some days. His wolf and demon halves had been going crazy not being able to touch her, claim her. But he had to hold back because she wasn't ready and he didn't want to scare her.

When he saw her talking to Solon, his wolf snarled and clawed at the sight of her smiling up at the male. His demon half just wanted to attack, which he knew on every level of normalcy was insane. But his demon side had never wanted anything the way he wanted Liberty.

Without conscious thought, Rory set his bottle down on a tray of one of the passing servers and maneuvered his way through a cluster of high-top tables.

He heard someone calling his name, but he ignored them as he reached Liberty and Solon. Liberty blushed but smiled when she saw him. "Hey, are you having a good time?"

"Yeah, this party's amazing. You did a great job."

The pink in her cheeks deepened, giving him dirty, dirty thoughts. Which made him feel like a dick. She was still healing, she couldn't possibly want him the way he wanted her. Rory turned to Solon, not bothering to paste on a fake smile. "Some female was asking for you. Said you promised to show her a good time upstairs or something."

Solon blinked once in complete surprise—at Rory's obvious lie—before his eyes narrowed. "Thanks," he muttered, and stalked off.

Liberty raised her eyebrows. "I heard he was a player," she murmured, laughing lightly.

Rory didn't know if the guy was or not and didn't care. He didn't like the male talking to Liberty and he felt no guilt. "Listen, since I'm not staying over..." He cleared his throat, trying to find the right words. "I wanted to know if you wanted to unwind with a movie later."

He planned to stay and help clean up too. Anything to spend more time with her. She needed to see that he was in this for the long haul.

"Um, yeah. Are you sure? I might be here late." Her brow furrowed and he resisted the urge to smooth it out, to touch her. He clenched his fingers at his sides, smothering the need to bend down, settle his lips against hers. He couldn't count how many times he'd fantasized about doing just that.

The party was only until ten so by the time they got the place back to normal—and the team of shifters working cleanup would be fast—he'd still be able to spend time with her before he had to leave. He nearly snarled at the thought of not being able to spend the night with her, but reined it in. This time he wouldn't be in his wolf form either. She needed to stop seeing him as just a guard dog, but a male who wanted her. He'd assumed he'd been taking things at the right pace but maybe . . . she could want more. "I'm sure. You look beautiful tonight, by the way. In case I didn't say it earlier."

Her cheeks went full-on red as she watched him and his dick went even harder. He shifted slightly but it did nothing to help. He just hoped she didn't notice.

"Thanks. I borrowed it from one of the pack but it fits well enough."

"It does," he murmured. On instinct his gaze fell to the soft swell of her cleavage. It barely showed any skin, but what he wouldn't give to bury his head between her breasts.

The thought brought him back to reality though. He'd been keeping all his hunger on lockdown since they'd met because no way in hell did she need him or any male coming on to her until she was ready. She deserved someone who wasn't out of control. But when he looked up at her face he saw raw need in her dark brown eyes. And the scent rolling off her was the same one he'd scented a few hours ago. Definite arousal. This time it was stronger, more defined.

The sight and smell caught him as off guard as it had earlier. His throat clenched as he struggled to draw in another breath, resisted the urge to tug her close, to bury his face against her neck and rake his canines against her soft skin, to nibble at her sweet lips. Earlier today he'd been so surprised by the scent he'd left without a word. She'd let him off the hook though, hadn't questioned him about his insane behavior. But hell, she'd shocked him.

Before he could respond, she looked away. "I've gotta check on the..." She mumbled something so nonsensical even his shifter hearing couldn't pick out the actual words as she hurried away.

Rory watched her go, devoured the way the dress pulled against the curve of her ass, the way her calf muscles tightened with each step. She was at work so he would let her go. For now. But tonight things were going to change. Now that he knew she definitely wanted him, he wouldn't be holding back. She was his.

A hard hand gripping his shoulder made the warrior inside him flare to life. His demon's claws extended and he was sure his wolf was in his eyes as he turned to face the male.

Solon flashed his canines and squeezed again before letting go. "So that was a dick move."

There was no doubt what he was referring to. Rory shrugged, not the least bit sorry. "Don't hold your breath waiting for an apology. Stay away from my female." Hell, he was barely civilized. Being in the human realm again was taking some adjustment. The fact that he hadn't attacked the male for talking to Liberty was about as civilized as he was going to get.

Solon rolled his eyes. "First, she's not your female." When Rory flashed his own canines, the male's mouth pulled into a line. "Second, everyone in the pack knows how you feel about her. I wasn't making a move. I was just being friendly. That's it. She's a sweet female. It's called talking, being civilized."

What the fuck ever. He shrugged again. "Okay."

"That your version of an apology?"

Rory snorted and looked away, scanning the crowd again. Liberty was near one of the buffet tables arranging shot glass desserts. There wasn't enough food in them to appease anyone, but she said they were micro desserts and apparently trending. Whatever the heck that meant. He'd seen one of the Stavros pack members go through the line and take ten of the things. "You're lucky you're still walking."

To his surprise, Solon laughed. "God, you and Bo really are cut from the same cloth."

The way he laughed eased the pressure in Rory's chest. He knew he didn't have a claim on Liberty, that she could talk to any male she wanted. While that drove him nuts, he didn't want to take that away from her, but he didn't have to like that she was surrounded by all these . . . threats.

And that was exactly how his demon half viewed all these shifters. Threats and yeah, competition. He wanted to kiss her, claim her in front of everyone so they knew who she belonged to. And that he belonged to her. He didn't want to own her, but he did want to mate her so that the whole supernatural world knew she was off limits.

It didn't matter that Finn Stavros, the pack's Alpha, had asked Rory if he wanted to join the pack, he still viewed everyone as more or less a danger. He was constantly on alert, making sure no harm came to Liberty. She'd been through so much, he didn't want anything to hurt her ever again. The need to protect her made him obsessive and . . . a dick, apparently. "The mating call is intense," he muttered, a twinge of remorse hitting him.

"I do *not* envy you." Solon clapped him on the shoulder again, this time lighter and clearly friendly.

"No shit—" An explosion tore through one of the covered windows, incinerating the drapes and showering everyone in glass and fire.

Shouts of alarm rose up, but Rory ignored everyone as he jumped into action.

He had to get to Liberty. He saw a flash of her blonde hair before she disappeared from sight. He let out a savage growl.

Liberty was human, the only person in the entire room who was truly vulnerable. He wasn't concerned about who'd attacked, he just needed to get her to safety.

Not caring who got in his way, he raced toward her.

CHAPTER SIX

Rory was barely aware of moving, but he sprang into action, racing across the dance floor and launching over a table of miniature cakes. He'd seen Liberty duck down at the first explosion. He wasn't waiting for a second.

People were a blur around him as he cleared another table in one jump. With fear driving him, he dodged a couple crouched next to it. He skidded to a halt near where he'd seen Liberty last.

When he lifted up the silver table cloth he found her huddled under it, her eyes wide. Relief slammed into him to see her alive.

She lunged at him on a silent cry, tears tracking down her face. He scooped her up, hating the terror in her dark gaze. On a burst of speed, he had her back in the kitchen and out of relative danger in seconds.

One of the Stavros packmates burst out of a cooler, buttoning up his pants. "What happened?" He was followed by a female buttoning up her shirt.

"Explosion near one of the front windows. That's all I know." He kept moving through the kitchen until they were near one of the exit doors. Though it went against all his instincts not to stay and fight the threat, he wanted to get her to safety more.

"No," Liberty said, clutching onto his upper arm as he would have pushed the exit door open. "And you can put me down. I'm okay."

Ignoring the last part, he ducked into a nearby office which was the size of a freaking matchbox. With his free hand, he pulled out the only chair in the room and sat her on it. Crouching in front of her, he ran his hands up and down her arms, checking her for injuries. His heart was pounding out of control and he belatedly realized he was in his demon form.

Explained the insane speed he'd used to get her here. But he'd never shifted like this before, without conscious thought.

"Sorry, I didn't mean to shift," he muttered, scooting back an inch as he continued scanning her. He didn't want to scare her in this form. He worried it might trigger a panic attack.

There was a small tear in her dress near the bottom hem, but that was probably from when she'd dove under the table. He couldn't scent any blood. She'd been far enough away from that explosion that she wouldn't have even been touched by glass.

The rational part of his brain knew that, but the possessive, protective male in him wasn't thinking clearly.

"It's fine and I'm fine, promise." She cupped his cheek gently so that he'd look at her.

Her touch froze him. If she'd wanted to surprise him more she couldn't have. She'd seen him in his true form in a Hell realm before but in this one he never shifted to his demon form. Just his wolf. After what had been done to her by a half-demon, he never wanted to remind her of his bloodline even inadvertently. He couldn't believe she was touching him at all. He was pale blue, seven feet tall and covered in tattoos symbolizing his lineage. At least he didn't have horns, unlike his cursed father.

He scented someone before he heard the person enter the kitchen. A female. Turning, he stood and blocked Liberty as soft footfalls sounded. His claws automatically extended. When Rhea stopped in the doorway his claws immediately retracted.

Her eyes widened as she took in his form but she quickly regained her composure. "Is Liberty okay? I heard you guys ran back here."

"I'm fine." Liberty nudged him out of the way and even though he didn't want to move, he stepped aside.

When she went to step forward, he held out an arm, which earned him a glare. He ignored it, focused on Rhea. "What happened?"

"We're not sure yet. An explosive device was set on one of the exterior windows but it wasn't strong enough to do any structural damage. Ian is doing an aerial recon with Drake right now to see if they spot anything and we've got teams scouring inside and out for more explosives. I need to get back, but—"

"What about Bo, Nyx, and Cynara?"

"All fine. No one was actually injured. This bomb was weak, more of a shock tactic than anything."

Rory knew there had been an issue the night before with the Stavros pack and wondered if this was related to that attack. "I can help with searching for explosives but I want to get Liberty out of here."

"I'm not going anywhere." She ducked out from under his arm, her stubborn expression surprising him.

He frowned. "You shouldn't be here."

"Is the threat over?" she asked Rhea.

"We're not a hundred percent sure of anything, but no one's scented any other explosives inside and the team hunting is fast—we'd have known long before now if there had been any inside the party. But it might not hurt for you to leave—"

"I'm going to check on my friends and help with the cleanup. I'm not helpless," she snapped, a myriad of emotions popping off her before she turned and slid past Rhea.

He stepped forward, intending to follow, only to be stopped by Rhea's hand. It didn't matter that the female was wearing a dress and heels, she looked every inch the warrior as she pushed him back. The strength there surprised him, not that he'd ever admit it.

"If you try to take away her control or run her life, you'll lose her in the end. I don't know exactly what happened to her but I can guess. She needs *control* in her life. Remember that."

He hadn't been thinking in those terms at all. He'd just been focused on making her safe. Though the most primal part of him wanted to knock Rhea out of the way and go after his mate-to-be, he knew he couldn't. Rhea was right. He'd lose Liberty that way.

He scrubbed a hand over the back of his neck. He wished he knew more about females, but he'd spent decades living in a Hell realm. And he'd never been with a sweet, human female like Liberty. All his wolf and demon knew was that for eight long months they'd been denied claiming the female they knew was their mate. His most primal side didn't understand why.

"Thank you. I'll remember that." Or he'd try to. "Where do you need me?" Because this was his brother's party and he needed to help. Guilt pervaded him that he hadn't immediately worried about his brothers, sister or even Nyx. He'd been consumed with getting Liberty to safety.

"Outside. But first we've gotta find you some clothes. You look like a blue Hulk. And I'm getting out of this damn dress," she muttered, turning away.

He followed after her, eager to keep Liberty in his line of sight. Just because he wouldn't be dragging her out of here like he wanted didn't mean he wouldn't be keeping watch over her. She was his to protect.

* * *

Liberty stood with the cluster of Stavros packmates as they all listened to Finn Stavros talk. "Everything is under control and no more explosives have been found. Even so I want the majority of you guys back at the mansion. I need you all safe while we finish cleaning up and securing this place. The less people here the easier it'll be for me. Anyone have questions?"

When no one said anything he nodded. "Good. Whoever did this will pay." The savage bite to his words sent a chill down her spine.

Occasionally it was easy to forget she was working with people who could literally rip her throat out and not break a sweat.

As the packmates dispersed and started to head for the exit, she saw Rhea duck into the kitchen. Liberty broke away from everyone and hurried after her. Inside the industrial room she found Rhea lifting a tray of sandwiches.

"Do you need help?" she asked automatically, even though it was clear Rhea would never need help with something so light.

"Ah, no. Just grabbing some food for the team staying. You heading out?"

"Yeah, I just, uh . . . a while ago Keelin told me you trained her in weapons and self-defense. Said you were really good at that kind of stuff." And Keelin was a freaking dragon. If she'd wanted Rhea to train her, then there was no one better for Liberty. Sure she could ask Rory but she knew he'd be too much of a distraction and she needed to learn.

Rhea cleared her throat. "Look, I trained Keelin for a bit, but you're human. I don't know, I don't think it would be a good idea." Something flickered in Rhea's eyes as she watched Liberty.

Pity.

The sight pissed her off. "Don't you feel sorry for me," Liberty snapped, surprising herself. She hadn't meant to lose her temper, almost never did anymore, but she couldn't take the way people looked at her, like she was a victim. She'd been through a hell of a lot and she simply wanted to learn to defend herself.

She'd been talking to Ophelia weekly—more than once—and the therapy had helped, but still, learning to deal with something emotionally wasn't the same as being able to defend herself if she was attacked again. Not that she thought she could take on a supernatural being but she could defend herself against humans and at least learn to fend someone off long enough to run. But she wouldn't beg for help. "I'll find someone else to train me," she muttered, turning away.

"I'll do it." Rhea's words made her turn back.

"What?"

"Right now things are crazy, as you well know. I don't know what kind of patrols my Alpha is going to have me on or what I'll be doing in the next couple weeks but we'll make something work. Just let me figure out my schedule, okay?"

"You're really going to help me?" She hoped Rhea wasn't just saying this and planning to blow her off later.

Rhea paused, nodded. "Yeah. You remind me of myself," she said, her smile wry.

She blinked. Rhea was the ultimate badass. Liberty had heard enough stories about her in the last eight months. Seriously, the female had killed a dragon and very recently had fallen off a three story house only to kill two shifters moments later. But she wasn't going to correct the female and risk her changing her mind. Not that she thought Rhea actually would, but just in case. "Thank you. Just tell me when and where and I'll be there."

"I've got your number and I'm sure I'll see you around over the next week anyway. Why didn't you ask Rory?"

Liberty didn't want to be honest, but knew she couldn't lie, not when shifters could smell it. She wasn't sure if they could scent half-truths either, though she made a mental note to find out from Victoria or Keelin. She wished Keelin was in Biloxi, but she hadn't arrived from Oregon yet and wouldn't be in town until the actual wedding. Her and her mate had their own clan business to deal with right now. Or something to that effect.

"He's distracting and..." She swallowed hard. "I'm worried to train with a male." She was afraid it might trigger a panic attack and she didn't want Rory to see her freak out.

Rhea gave a sharp nod. "I'll be in touch then. Now clear out, we need to get this place locked down." The commanding note in her voice made it clear that Rhea was used to giving orders and having them followed.

Liberty wasn't ready to leave because it meant she and Rory would be alone, but knew there was no way around it. He would have smelled her reaction to him earlier and she wasn't sure what he thought, what he wanted. Who was she kidding? She wasn't sure what she wanted from Rory other than something physical. And she was terrified that she wasn't even capable of that at this point. After what she'd gone through she was afraid that she was totally broken. It didn't matter what Ophelia said, that she'd get through everything and lead a normal life and have normal, healthy relationships.

Liberty wasn't sure at all.

* * *

From the safety of his stolen SUV, he watched the live video feed on his laptop as shifters from the Stavros pack scrambled around the parking lot of Howlers, looking for more bombs.

"Keep driving until I say stop," he said without looking up at his driver. He'd hired a human to chauffeur him around, not wanting to be near his pack right now.

He'd lost fourteen of his people last night and some of his packmates were angry, wanted to strike out. They hadn't expected the loss of life, but he had. It was why he'd sent in his youngest pack members for the attack. Hell, two of them had survived and gotten away. That was something. The female hadn't even wanted to be there, to fight for him, so losing her was nothing. He'd needed to see how swiftly Finn Stavros' wolves would react and he hadn't been willing to sacrifice his older warriors.

Now he got to see the arrogant Finn on screen, shouting out orders to those around him. They moved like a cohesive unit and unfortunately they were working with other supernatural beings in addition to their pack.

He'd known about Bo Broussard, the half-demon, and tonight he'd figured out the pack was friendly with at least a couple dragons. He'd never seen a dragon actually shift—had always wondered if they were truly extinct—but he'd seen two males on the screen disappear before his eyes, then a blur of motion. Since dragons were the only creature he knew of that could do that, he had to assume they were working with the pack.

Which created a complication. He hadn't realized the Stavros pack had other allies. Well, other than vampires. He sniffed at that thought. The Stavros Alpha had mated with a vampire. Interspecies mingling was revolting, but especially to one of those creatures.

Vampires were beneath shifters.

When Rhea came on screen he straightened as he watched her move lithely across the parking lot. The camera he had in place was small, unobtrusive and secured high enough on a light pole that almost no one would notice it unless they were looking specifically for it.

The stunning female had her hands on her hips as she spoke to two males he recognized from his recon over the last month. His pack had been watching the Stavros pack covertly, invading their territory right under everyone's noses. It wasn't as if the pack had eyes everywhere along the Gulf Coast and his people had been very careful. He'd even bought property in the territory. Not under his name of course.

Tonight had been another test to see how they reacted to a simple bomb. One that couldn't be traced to him or any of his people. He hadn't told his pack about it. No, he liked to keep all his plans close to the chest before revealing anything. After he'd lost his brothers and all his family members, trust didn't come easy to him.

A growl built in his throat as he watched a male walk up to Rhea, place his hand at the small of her back in a subtle, but possessive gesture. That was very interesting. Maybe he could use it against her.

Aware of the human driver looking at him in the rearview mirror, he snapped, "Keep your eyes on the fucking road."

Not recognizing the male next to Rhea, he zoomed in on his face and froze the image. He looked very similar to one of the males he suspected was a dragon. Dark hair, deadly gray eyes and a large build.

With his fingers flying across his keyboard, he uploaded the picture into a database. If this male was important to Rhea, maybe he'd found a way to get to her. To hurt her. And hurt her he would.

Ultimately he planned to take over the Stavros territory completely, keep it for his own. He and his pack would settle here and if he had to go to war to do it, then so be it. But killing her—and torturing her before he did—was his number one priority.

The bitch had taken everything from him and he would take everything from her.

CHAPTER SEVEN

"What is it?" Conall asked, placing his hand at the small of Rhea's back.

She wanted to move into that touch, savor it, even if the timing was inappropriate. It was hard to care about the timing though as she looked into those gray eyes. It had been so damn long since she'd been with a male and Conall wasn't like anyone she'd ever met.

Shaking off the thought, she looked up at the hotel and casino, eyeing it critically. They'd moved everyone non-essential out of the parking lot and hotel so just warriors and trackers were here. Thankfully no humans had seen what happened and called the police so the scene was contained. Things could have been so much worse tonight.

No one had been injured. Not really. A few packmates had gotten cut from the glass, one male suffered first degree burns that were already healing, and a few females had torn dresses from diving out of the way of the explosion.

She frowned at herself. She should be happy that no one had been injured. And she was. Still, she couldn't shake the feeling that everything about this was wrong. "Whoever did this could have made a much bigger statement. Easily. The placement of the bomb was . . . weak."

Though easily accessible, she realized, as she looked at the position of the video cameras around the area. Security should have seen whoever had done this moving around in the parking lot and near Howlers, but the place the bomb had been left was at an odd angle. Because it was out of range from the cameras.

"I know."

Getting a bomb inside the actual hotel would have been hard, considering shifter senses. Or at least a much bigger risk since any number of the pack could have scented explosives. Placing a bomb outside, where their security had been admittedly weak tonight was relatively easier. Still, she looked upward, moving in a slow circle, taking everything in.

Drake and Ian were doing aerial recon but... "Son of a bitch," she muttered when her gaze snagged on something that didn't belong.

As a shifter she had heightened senses, but her exceptional eyesight was one of her tracker gifts.

"What?" Conall asked, falling in step with her as she stalked across the parking lot to a light pole about fifty feet away.

"A video camera. Could be nothing, but I'm gonna check it out." She was aware that Solon and Gabriel had started following them as well but she ignored everyone as she shimmied up the light pole.

The column was on the corner of the east side parking lot and would give the viewer a clear visual of the comings and goings of the whole sector. She also noted that the bomb had been on a part of the hotel facing the back of the property. Not the front, where there was a lot more traffic. It didn't matter that Finn had shut the place down to anyone but supernaturals for the festivities, claiming that the hotel was undergoing renovations and that a private party had booked Howlers for the week. Plenty of tourists could have pulled into the parking lot or seen an explosion from the main drag.

By placing that bomb at Howlers, it reduced the chance that it was seen by humans. Something she found very interesting. As she reached the top, she let out a low growl of triumph. The small circular device was definitely a video camera. High tech, too, if she had to guess.

She gave the camera the middle finger before yanking it down. It had been secured by an adhesive and was probably still live. She knew enough about technology to be proficient in this modern age, but tracking where this thing came from was out of her realm of expertise. Luckily she had packmates who'd have no problem hunting for the source of the viewer. Of course if someone was currently watching they'd seen her and would likely cut the feed, but maybe her packmates could find something anyway.

Halfway down the pole, she let go, dropping to the ground silently. Solon, Gabriel and Conall stood there waiting. It was a little weird having Conall in the mix, but she found she liked him being there. She seemed to like everything about the male. He was a solid presence, a male she knew she could trust, but she didn't want to get used to him being around. She'd already lost one male, she couldn't stomach the thought of losing another she cared about.

She held out her hand. "It's a camera."

Gabriel plucked it from her palm. "I'll get this to Elana, see if she can figure out anything about it." He looked at Solon, nodded sharply. "Grab a team of three, do a full sweep for more of these." Solon had turned on his heel before Gabriel turned back to Rhea and Conall. "Finn just radioed, he's on his way outside, wants to see you both."

"We'll head his way." Finn had gone to review the security feeds so she knew what exit he'd be coming out of. She was surprised that he'd requested Conall come with her, but masked it.

Conall was silent as they rounded the building to find Finn and Lyra heading their way. A cool breeze picked up, ruffling Rhea's hair, but she barely felt it. She was way too aware of the male next to her. Dragon shifters seemed to be bigger in general and Conall was definitely no different. But it wasn't his size so much as his presence. There was something about him that just brushed against all her senses, made her exceptionally aware of him. The distraction was a little maddening.

She straightened when she saw the look on her Alpha's face, a shot of adrenaline pumping through her. She recognized it well.

He'd found something.

"Walk with me," he ordered, nodding respectfully at Conall. "I'd like your assistance if you're willing?"

"Just tell me what you need."

Finn didn't break stride as they hurried toward an idling SUV. She could see Chloe sitting behind the wheel. "Got two individuals on screen, human I believe, planting the bomb. Both male. They snuck onto our property on foot and did a good job of keeping their faces hidden—

until they left the parking lot. Got a clear shot of both their faces from one of my extra cameras."

Rhea knew her Alpha had a lot on and around his property, which made the addition of the new security camera and the bomb itself troubling. "You know who they are?"

"Yep. Both have criminal records. Got their address and I want you coming with me, Lyra and Chloe. Gonna hit them now."

Which meant he'd probably had Elana hack into some database or just used one of their own for facial recognition. "Who was running security?" she asked as they reached the SUV. Normally she was up to date on stuff like that, but she hadn't been at the party as part of security. She'd been there tonight as a guest.

Lyra got in the back seat, but Rhea stayed where she was since Finn hadn't made a move to get in.

His wolf flashed in his icy blue gaze as a rush of power rolled off him. "It's being taken care of."

Which wasn't an answer at all. But Finn was a fair Alpha. Whoever had been manning security had clearly screwed up and would pay for it. She'd hear soon enough who'd been the one to screw up and since it wasn't important for right now, she didn't push for an answer. "Good."

He looked at Conall. "I've got an address for these humans. We're going to hit their place hard. Will you do aerial recon for us?"

Rhea found it interesting that Finn was asking at all. Ian was Bo's brother so it made sense he was helping out.

And Drake would always be considered one of their people no matter what. It was nice that Finn was including Conall though, even if she was surprised by her Alpha.

Conall nodded. "I'll follow overhead and scan the entire area."

"Thank you. It's about twenty minutes driving from here." Finn slid into the back seat with his mate and shut the door.

"I'll hold your cell phone and stuff if you want," Rhea said to Conall.

"Thanks." He stripped off his shirt and when he handed it to her she resisted the urge to press it to her nose and inhale. Because that was definitely inappropriate behavior. Friends did not do that.

Even though she tried to stop herself, her gaze raked over his massive chest and the cut lines and striations of his pecs and abs. Shifters as a whole were simply bigger than humans, at least wolves, but dragons . . . they were something else altogether.

God, thinking about starting something with him was ridiculous, unless . . . maybe they could indulge in a little affair. It had been so damn long since she'd been with anyone. Who said she couldn't have fun? He was Alpha of another clan, wouldn't be looking to mate a wolf. Or she doubted he would. And he'd never said a word about mating regardless. But just maybe . . . she looked up to find that his gaze had gone supernova as he watched her.

Heat flooded between her legs as she stared into that bright gaze so full of hunger.

Silently he unbuckled his pants, keeping his gaze pinned to hers. She should look away. Yep, she really, really should. But she couldn't force herself to do it. Not after she'd gotten a view of him last night. She was used to shifter nudity. After over a hundred and fifty years on the planet she'd seen her share of naked bodies. It seemed her packmates were always in a state of undress.

But this was like watching a piece of art being unveiled. She'd seen what was between his legs and she wasn't ashamed to admit she wanted to see it again. More than just see it. Touch and taste would be a good start.

She tried to cover her scent, and did a pretty good job of it, but another rush of heat flooded between her legs as he inched his pants down lower, lower…

At the last minute he turned, giving her a perfect view of a perfect ass. She bit back her growl of frustration as he half-turned to face her, the most wicked, knowing grin on his face as he handed her his shoes and the rest of his clothes.

She gritted her teeth as he walked away to gain some distance before his shift. Somehow she forced herself to get into the front seat and not stare at the way his ass and leg muscles flexed. Unfortunately she knew her pheromones were out of control when Chloe snickered.

"Oh, girl, that male is—"

"Do not finish that sentence." Her wolf clawed at her, annoyed that her friend and packmate had even noticed Conall. Didn't matter that the male was sexy and of course any single female would check him out; Rhea didn't have to like it.

From the backseat, Lyra smothered a giggle, but Rhea refused to turn and look at either her or her Alpha as Chloe kicked the vehicle into gear. An address was already plugged into the GPS.

Rhea didn't look out the window to see if Conall had shifted or cloaked himself. Looking at him made her brain go haywire and right now she needed to be in full-on warrior mode if they were going after an unknown threat. Didn't matter that it was only a couple humans. It was likely they were working with a shifter. Or maybe a vampire with a grudge. Either way, she had to be ready.

"All I was going to say is that he's delicious," Chloe continued as she steered to the exit of the parking lot.

"I know what you were going to say," Rhea snapped, frowning at the grinning profile of her friend. She didn't want to hear it.

"I certainly wouldn't kick him out of bed." Though Chloe's voice was only slightly taunting, there was a hint of truth in her words.

"If I ever find him in your bed I'll rip your face off." The words were out before she could stop herself. She'd pretty much just admitted in front of three members of her pack—one who had a big mouth—that she was interested in Conall. More than interested in him.

To Rhea's annoyance, Chloe just snickered again.

* * *

"Thanks for driving me home," Liberty murmured as Rory steered into her driveway. He'd insisted on driving and had asked one of the Stavros pack members to bring her car later.

He simply grunted and pulled into her garage. He had her extra garage door opener and a key to her place. And he'd insisted on a top of the line security system. Her townhome was in a high-end area. When she'd first found it she'd been ecstatic that it had been available to rent for such a great price. Of course by the time she realized it belonged to Rory, and that he owned the one next door and a whole string of them—sneaky man—it had been too late to back out. Not that she'd wanted to. She needed to feel safe, but also have a sense of independence. Moving here had been a big step in that direction.

"Can we talk?" she asked as she shut her door behind her.

The garage door was closing behind them. He looked at her across the hood, his expression unreadable. But he nodded. "Yeah. Let's get inside first."

Inside the insistent beeping of her alarm immediately went off but he moved to the panel and punched in the code. With his back to her she took a moment to drink in the sight of him. When she'd first met him she'd been aware on an intellectual level that he was attractive but men and sex hadn't registered on her radar. He'd been such a force of nature though, moving his way into her life that she hadn't thought to stop him. She didn't want to. He'd given her back a sense of safety and she cared for him so deeply it scared her.

Before he turned back to her, she looked away, not wanting to be caught staring. She slipped her pea coat off and hung it on the rack where she kept her keys. The four hooks curved into fleur-de-lis'. Rory had bought it for her and hung it up a week after she'd moved in, saying she needed it because she always misplaced her keys.

A sad truth.

The man was always so thoughtful. She wondered what she even had to offer to him. She was human; he was a powerful half-demon wolf shifter. He was wealthy, though he didn't talk much about how he and Ian had come to be that way. Not to mention jaw-droppingly sexy. Feeling suddenly nervous about what she had to say, she leaned against the nearest counter in her kitchen and met his gaze.

And found him watching her with a heated intensity that made her breath catch. For a moment she completely lost her train of thought.

"What did you want to talk about?" His deep voice cut through the silence, sending another shock of awareness through her.

She wasn't sure how to even voice what she wanted. He'd obviously scented her attraction to him and she'd seen him checking her out at the party earlier. She wondered if maybe . . . Ugh, if she couldn't put it into words in her own head, no way could she say it out loud. "Did you still want to do a movie night?"

He blinked once, took a step closer to her so that he was in the middle of her kitchen. For a townhome it was large. All top of the line stuff too, thanks to him. None of that mattered now. Only a few feet separated them. "That's what you want to talk about?"

"Picking the right movie is a serious decision, especially if you want to watch one of those awful foreign films." She tried to inject a light, teasing note into her voice but couldn't manage it. Her attempt at humor was lame but she was grasping at straws now. She shouldn't have said anything at all.

His mossy green eyes went pure wolf for a moment before flickering back to human. He took another step toward her until he was inches from her. Though he didn't touch her, his presence was all-consuming. His spicy scent teased her, invaded her senses.

"I don't want to talk about a stupid movie. Why'd you run out on me in that office?" He sounded almost hurt.

She frowned. *That* was what he wanted to talk about? "I just wanted to help out and you were trying to rush me out of there." To take control of her actions. Even if he hadn't intended that, it was how it had felt. Like she was helpless, incapable of looking after herself.

"I wanted to keep you safe. Not control you," he snapped, as if he'd read her mind. "Rhea said something earlier and . . . I just wanted you safe. That's it!"

"No, you think I'm helpless because I'm human!"

His eyes widened but he didn't back down. "That's bullshit. You're the strongest female I've ever met."

Surprise ricocheted through her at his words. She didn't feel strong most of the time. She felt like a hot mess just trying to keep it together.

"Then why'd you run out on me in Howlers earlier this afternoon when you scented...?" She'd raised her voice even higher, almost against her will, but she still couldn't finish the thought. She hadn't meant to ask him about *that.* Wasn't sure she'd even wanted the answer. But now the question was out there and damn it, she *did* want to know. Even if she was afraid of not only the answer, but what the consequences might be if things changed between them.

Growling, he pivoted, turning his back to her, but didn't step away. Just rubbed the back of his neck in a gesture she'd seen him do more than once when frustrated. "I don't want to hurt you."

"Oh." *Oh, God.* She'd misread everything. Pain pierced her straight through the chest. Of course he didn't want to hurt her. He was a decent male. He'd saved her from a Hell realm and he'd been looking out for her ever since. But she had to be a burden. Eight months was a long time to look out for someone. And she'd confessed to him what had happened to her at the hands of that half-demon leader; the constant rapes and practical starvation. Maybe Rory had just felt too bad to walk away from her.

She'd thought she'd seen an awareness from him tonight at the party, for just a moment he'd seemed to be checking her out, but…

Embarrassment burned her cheeks. So what if he found her attractive? That didn't mean anything. "Look, we can just forget this then." To her horror, her voice cracked on the last word.

He swiveled, his eyes wide. "Don't cry." It was a panicked order.

When he said that it was too much. She'd told herself not to get used to having him around. Eight months ago she'd even told him that if he started to view her as an obligation to walk away, no hard feelings. But now that he was trying to let her down easy, it freaking hurt.

"Sorry," she muttered, stupid tears streaming down her cheeks.

He had his arms around her before she'd blinked away the blurriness, his tight embrace making it better and worse at the same time. "Please don't cry," he murmured, rubbing a steady hand up and down her spine.

"I'm not," she sniffled into his chest. "I'm just embarrassed. I thought maybe you wanted something to happen between us..." Letting out a nervous, watery laugh, she stepped back and swiped away the wetness. "I'm just being stupid."

Rory frowned down at her, not giving her an inch of space. She loved the way he smelled, like a cold winter night in the forest. Confusion emanated from him and though she might not have any supernatural abilities it wasn't hard to see it in the tense lines of his body and in his expression. "I *do* want you. More than my next breath." The deep timbre of his voice made her freeze as much as the raspy admission itself.

Suddenly his earlier statement about not wanting to hurt her made sense. Or she hoped it did. "When you said you didn't want to hurt me, did you mean . . . physically? Or were you trying to let me down easily?"

His eyes went pure wolf. "Physically."

"Oh." Well that changed everything. She'd thought he hadn't wanted to her hurt her emotionally. Feeling a whole lot braver, she shed some of her worries and stepped closer, placing both hands on his chest.

His breathing was erratic, his eyes changing wildly as he looked at her. Human, wolf, demon. They all looked back at her, hunger bright there. "I'm terrified of hurting you." His voice was a raspy growl.

The truth in his gaze eased any lingering fear she had. Rory would never hurt her. That was a truth she felt to her core. After seeing true monsters, this was a man who simply couldn't hurt a female. It wasn't in his DNA. "That's the last thing I'm worried about, but I don't know what I'm ready for. One day at a time is all I'm capable of focusing on right now."

He nodded once, as if he understood.

She hoped he did but wanted to make things perfectly clear. "You deserve better than me." He frowned, started to protest so she placed a finger over his lips.

To her surprise he nipped at it. Heat flooded between her thighs at the simple action. Even he looked a little surprised by what he'd done. Until raw heat bled into his gaze.

She couldn't remember what she'd wanted to say. Even more, she didn't want to talk. Not when Rory was looking down at her as if she was the most precious thing in the world.

She slid her hands up higher, dug her fingers into his shoulders, holding onto him to steady herself. She hadn't been sure she'd ever get to the point where she was capable of wanting to be with someone else again, but she knew she wanted Rory.

In a swift move, he lifted her up onto the counter so that they were closer in eye level. Because of the fit of her dress she couldn't spread her legs far, but with him caging her in like this, it felt impossibly intimate. Especially when he was staring at her as if he could consume her.

It didn't scare her either, it just thrilled her. It had been so long since she'd felt pleasure with a male. Even though she was still a little scared, she was dying to feel Rory's mouth on her.

Moving slowly, he bent his head, giving her enough time to back away if she wanted. She didn't. Her entire body vibrated with the need for him.

Feeling nervous and excited at the same time, she leaned forward into his kiss, desperate to taste him.

When his lips met hers, she melted into him, flicking her tongue against his a little hesitantly. She wasn't sure how far she wanted to go, how much she could even handle right now but kissing was good. Kissing with Rory was perfect. She just hoped he'd understand if she wanted to stop.

He groaned, his big body trembling underneath her fingertips. He didn't touch her anywhere else though, just kept his hands on the counter next to her as his tongue stroked against hers. His teasing grew hungrier by the second.

She met him stroke for stroke, her entire body reacting to the taste of him. Her nipples beaded tightly against the fabric of her bra and the juncture between her thighs grew slick. When she leaned in harder, wanting more, linking her fingers together behind his neck, he pulled back.

Breathing hard, he looked down at her with a mix of too many emotions for her to decipher. "I'd like to stay here tonight." The words seemed to be torn from him. And he still wasn't touching her, she noted.

She swallowed hard, the rejection on the tip of her tongue. She didn't want him to stay because he thought she needed the protection.

"Adjusting to being in the human realm has been difficult for me. I know you think you've been using me as a crutch, but . . . I like being with you at night. It helps me sleep too."

Surprised, she stared at him, searching his eyes for the truth. She'd gotten pretty good at reading the male since they'd met and she didn't think he was lying. "Really?"

He nodded once. "Yeah. It's . . . different here. More peaceful. Quieter. It's an adjustment."

She could believe that, especially since he'd been in a Hell realm for decades. "Will you stay in human form?"

He swallowed hard. "If you want."

"I do want." Way too much, probably.

CHAPTER EIGHT

Rory felt like an inexperienced cub as he stepped into Liberty's bedroom. He'd been sleeping with her in his wolf form for the last eight months so he was familiar with her bedroom, but it was very different being in here like this.

He could hear water running in the bathroom so he knew she'd be a few minutes. He sometimes watched her little rituals of taking off her makeup and washing her face and all the little things she did at night. It had always felt intimate to watch her but in his wolf form she was always so relaxed. He'd taken advantage of that to simply drink her in.

Because he wasn't a threat to her. Not that he viewed himself as one or would ever be one, but tonight was going to be different.

Especially after that kiss and his admission that he wanted her more than his next breath. It was true and he didn't regret it. He was just glad she hadn't been scared away by him.

His gaze skimmed over the pale purple and white comforter she'd spent hours agonizing over whether to buy or not. Everything in her room was soft and feminine. Like her. Before her, he'd thought humans were weak, but he loved her softness. Hell, he loved everything about her.

When the bathroom door opened, he nearly jumped, then cursed himself. He wasn't some untrained cub. But the women he'd been with had all been shifters of one kind or another. And always one-night-stands. Sometimes two-day things, but he'd spent the last fifty years in and out of the Hell realm, only going to the human one for occasional sex.

Besides, just because he was staying with her didn't mean anything would happen between them.

He'd been more turned on than he could ever remember being when they'd kissed, but he'd pulled back, for both their sakes. The last thing she needed was him getting too worked up. He had to be in complete control over himself where she was concerned. She'd told him a little of what had happened to her and it had been enough for him to worry about her and sex.

Wearing a long-sleeved pajama set with pink little dogs covering a blue background, she smiled when she saw him. "It's a little weird with you being in human form. And those words are pretty weird to say out loud." The lightness in her voice eased something inside him.

If she was okay with this, he would be okay with it too. Sleeping next to her and not being naked sucked, but if it took a while for her to get to that point, he was okay with that too. Even if it was making his wolf and demon edgy. So he decided to keep things as normal as possible.

"What time do you have to be at Bo's place tomorrow?" Even though he already knew the answer since his brother had told him, he wanted to keep a benign conversation going as he moved to the left side of her bed. He didn't think they should even continue the parties after that bombing, but apparently Bo—and Finn—insisted. They had to appear strong and cancelling something because of an attack would make them appear weak in the supernatural world.

"The party won't start until the evening but probably around noon. I want to start getting stuff set up and triple check everything." She pulled back the covers on her side and gave a shaky laugh. "I'm just going to say I'm nervous, okay?"

He pushed out a sigh of relief. "Me too."

Her dark eyes widened. "Really?"

"Yeah." Things were changing between them and while he knew what he wanted, he also understood she wasn't ready for forever. Not even close. He hated the unsettled feeling inside him, that desire to mark her, to claim her, to let everyone know she was his. He hated that when they were out in public she was considered available to any supernatural being who wanted to talk to her. It made him restless twenty-four-seven.

"Can we try kissing again?" she asked as she slid onto her side of the bed.

Her question and the burst of lust that rolled off her nearly bowled him over. He hadn't been expecting that at all. He'd thought . . . who the hell cared what he'd thought. Not trusting his voice, he nodded as he got into her bed.

He cleared his throat. "If I do anything you don't like, just tell me to stop and we will. And we don't have to kiss at all." His wolf and demon slashed at him, telling him to shut the hell up, to take what she was offering. But he couldn't.

She nodded, her breathing slightly erratic as she watched him lean against the headboard. She surprised him again when she moved closer then straddled him.

He froze as she settled down over him. His instinct was to grab her hips, to tug her close, but he stopped himself. Instead he clenched his fists against the sheet. They were both fully clothed so there were plenty of barriers between them, but his cock was hard and throbbing for her. His natural instinct was to take over, to flip her under him so that he was in complete control.

But he knew things would be different with Liberty. She'd suffered too much trauma and he wouldn't forget that.

He was more than okay with letting her be in control now. Even his most primal side was quiet, at peace. Because Liberty was here with him.

"I've never been so nervous in my life," she whispered, dark eyes wide.

"What are you nervous about?" He kept his voice low too, not wanting to do anything to dispel the intimate moment. He thought he knew the answer but wanted to make sure he was on the same page.

"I . . . don't know if I'll ever be ready for more than this. Kissing."

"Okay."

She shook her head, frustration flashing in her eyes. "You say that now, but—"

"No *but.* We're going to take this one day at a time. I don't care how long it takes." As the words left him, he knew it was true. Yeah he wished he was naked with her right now, buried deep inside her, but he cared about this woman on an intrinsic level. His wolf had recognized her as his mate long before he'd gotten to actually know her, but the last eight months he'd seen what a strong female she was and knew the woman at her core. She was truly beautiful, inside and out.

She pushed out a breath and though he could see the insecurity simmering in her dark gaze, she gently placed her hands on his shoulders.

Almost against his will, his hips rolled once, his cock pushing between her thighs. He froze until her eyes went heavy-lidded and the unmistakable scent of lust rolled off her. But he let her make the first move even if he had to shove back all his instincts to do it.

Slowly, she leaned forward until her lips brushed over his.

He didn't bite back his groan as she nipped his bottom lip. Even though he wanted to hold her, tug her closer, he kept his hands at his side, clutching onto her sheets as she slid her breasts against his chest.

Didn't matter that they had clothing in the way, he could still feel her beaded nipples brushing against him as she gently rocked into him. Her movements were sweet, sensual, and he wondered if she was even aware of the way she was basically riding him.

He teased his tongue against hers, stroke for stroke, her sweet taste embedded in his brain. When she moaned into him, he slid one of his hands up and gently held her hip as she moved against him.

Their kiss seemed to go on forever. The longer their tongues teased each other, the more relaxed he could feel her growing—and the harder his cock grew. It bordered on painful, but he'd deal with it as long as it took.

When she pulled back, breathing hard, he groaned at the lust blazing in her eyes. "I'm not ready for anything else but I'm incredibly turned on."

He wanted to go down on her, to taste all of her, but knew it was too soon. Still… "You could touch yourself," he murmured, growing hot at the thought of her doing just that. "Slide your hand right down your pajama bottoms and stroke yourself while I watch." All his muscles tightened as he waited for her reaction.

If the way her scent sweetened was any indication, she liked the idea of it too. But she remained still, her fingers digging into his shoulders as she watched him with those penetrating, dark eyes he swore could see straight to the heart of him.

When one of her hands loosened the death grip on him and oh so slowly slid down between their bodies, he realized he was holding his breath, waiting for her to do more. He wished he was the one who got to touch her, but this held an appeal all its own.

She teased the elastic of her pajama bottoms, but he knew she wasn't doing it to tease him. Her neck muscles were corded tight as her hand hovered in between her flat stomach and the stretchy material. He saw the moment she made the decision.

Her gaze snapped to his, her eyes bright as she slipped her hand down and out of his sight.

With their clothes on he couldn't see what she was doing, not really, but his imagination was going wild. He kept his gaze on hers anyway, watching the way her mouth parted slightly as she began to stroke herself.

He wished he could see exactly how she touched herself, the pressure she used, but he would learn all that one day. He had to believe it would happen. She trusted him enough to do this and that humbled him in a way he'd never imagined.

He wasn't a good male, had never thought to find a woman like Liberty. For years he'd been in that Hell realm, just hiding, he realized. Because he'd become so damn disillusioned by everything. He'd never fit in anywhere, not as a being with mixed blood. Neither he nor his brother had. It was why they'd settled away from the human realm so easily. Now the thought of staying in this realm forever wasn't even a choice. He'd live anywhere as long as Liberty was there.

Her breathing ratcheted up the slightest fraction as she bit her bottom lip. Her cheeks were flushed and from her scent, he guessed it was a mix of lust and self-consciousness.

This was incredibly intimate and though he wanted to see her expression while she came, he wanted her comfortable. His cock throbbed between his legs, the pulsing ache definitely painful now, but he leaned upward, buried his face against her neck.

Apparently it was the right thing to do because she shuddered, let out a soft moan of pleasure as she slid her fingers through his hair with her free hand.

He kissed the soft column of her neck, raked his teeth along her pulse point as she shuddered again.

"Imagine it's my tongue on your clit right now," he murmured. He'd never been one for dirty talk, but right now something told him she needed words. Needed something. If he couldn't touch her, he'd damn well help push her over the edge another way.

She jerked at his words, her breathing even harder, her movements a little faster. He nibbled at her neck again before pressing her earlobe between his teeth. Everything about her tasted sweet. Taking him by surprise she cried out so softly but he knew she was coming as her body jerked, her hips rolling against his in harsh, uneven movements. He wanted to touch her, to slide his hands up her shirt, cup her breasts, but he held back.

He kept his face buried against her neck, inhaled the scent of her orgasm. It surrounded him, made his wolf and demon edgier than he'd expected, but he locked that side of him down as she relaxed completely against him.

When she withdrew her hand, he grasped her wrist and pulled back to look at her. Too many emotions bombarded him.

He lifted her hand, and, knowing it was a primal, raw gesture, sucked her first two fingers into his mouth. His taste buds exploded with the essence of her. Though her cheeks burned crimson as she watched him, he scented that she liked what he was doing.

Since he was pretty sure there wasn't anything appropriate to say now, he just lightly kissed her before settling them under the covers. He pulled her back so that she was tucked right up against his chest.

For the first time since he'd known her, she fell asleep in less than a minute, her breathing as steady as her heartbeat.

His dick still ached, but too bad. He'd deal with it later, once he was certain she was asleep for good. For now he wanted to savor simply holding her. What they'd just done was huge. She'd trusted him enough to be completely vulnerable in front of him and it gave him hope that he'd be able to claim her soon.

CHAPTER NINE

5 months ago

"Why do you look so happy?" Victoria asked as she sat on one of the stools next to Conall's kitchen island.

They'd come over to talk about building plans for a new . . . something to do with the ski lodge. Hell, he didn't know. Didn't really care at the moment.

"Huh..." He looked up from his phone to see Drake and Victoria watching him curiously. "Oh, this is nothing. Just clan business." A total lie. He'd been texting with Rhea, something he seemed to do more and more of lately. Talking to her was an addiction. He was tired of just talking though. His fantasies of her were out of control. He couldn't think about other women, didn't look at them. Didn't want to. But he wasn't sure what she felt for him, other than friendship. She was a complex female.

Drake's head tilted to the side ever so slightly. "I can sense when you're lying."

Victoria just snickered and shook her head. "You're being all secretive with your phone lately. It's a woman, I know it! Who have you been talking to?"

His phone pinged again. "Give me a sec, gotta respond to this," he murmured.

He was vaguely aware of Drake and Victoria talking quietly to each other as he looked down at the screen to see another message from Rhea, but he tuned them out. He knew he was being rude and if anyone had done this to him he'd be annoyed. But he was Alpha. He could use work as an excuse any time he wanted. Right now, he definitely wanted to.

Solon almost got his ass kicked by a couple felines tonight. Had to save his ass at Bo's club. Seriously, that male is never gonna grow up.

A very small part of Conall hated that Rhea's best friend was male, but he squashed that feeling. He'd seen the two of them together, knew they were more like brother and sister than some blood siblings. His fingers flew across the screen. *He will when he meets the right female.*

She texted him back an emoticon rolling its eyes, then; *We'll see. Until then I'm stuck saving his ass from crazy females.*

You love it, he texted back. And he loved that about her. He'd talked to her enough to know that she did love looking out for her packmates. It was part of her DNA and one of the reasons he admired her. She was loyal to her people.

Lol, it's true. Keeping him alive is a favorite pastime. What are you up to tonight?

Clan meeting with V and Drake about building permits.

I'd rather be doing that than stuck here at this club.

Yeah, he'd rather she be right here with him too. His dragon rippled beneath the surface, beyond pissed that he wasn't in the same vicinity as Rhea. Far too many miles separated them. Months had gone by since he'd seen her last and it was making him edgy. Their daily communication was one of the only things that kept him sane. Right now his dragon wanted to shed this human form and take flight, head straight down to Biloxi and see his female.

His? He rolled his shoulders once. He needed to get himself under control. She wasn't remotely his. They were just friends. For now. He was just biding his time.

His fingers flew across the screen again. *Pack your bags and head up here.*

There was a longer than normal pause then; *One day I'm gonna take you up on your offer.*

You're always welcome here. And he meant it. If he got her up here again, he'd never let her go. That much he knew.

Maybe I'll come up this winter and ski. Last time I didn't get a chance to enjoy myself much.

That was because they'd all been busy dealing with a threat. A traitorous now dead cousin of his. Not to mention violent dragons from a warring clan attacking. *We've always got an open guest house. And V would love to have another wolf here.* He nearly snorted to himself at the lie. Sure, V would love it if she came up here, but he would love it way more.

I'm going to look at my schedule and make it happen . . . crap, gotta go. I think Solon's bitten off more than he can chew. Again. Call you later?

Yeah. I'll be up. And he'd be waiting for her call. Which made him feel just a little pathetic.

Conall shoved his phone back in his pants pocket. Anything else clan related could wait. When he looked up he found Drake watching him with a knowing expression. Victoria must have left and he hadn't even realized. Shit.

He really was distracted. The knowledge made a thin thread of ice slide through his veins. He was never, ever distracted. Not to the point he didn't notice someone leaving a damn room.

"How's Rhea?" Drake asked quietly.

Conall blinked once, then schooled his expression into a blank mask. He loved his brother more than anything, but he didn't want anyone to know about his conversations with Rhea. Not yet. In his clan everyone knew everything about everybody. And as Alpha he was usually involved in everything, even when he didn't want to be. He liked having something that was just his. Not to mention he had no idea if she was even attracted to him. She kept up such tight walls it was impossible to tell. "How would I know?"

Drake just snorted and turned the tablet he and Victoria had been looking at so Conall could see the plans they'd been reviewing.

"If you ever want to talk about . . . anything. I'm here. Not that I'm an expert on females, but I am mated to a wolf." Drake's voice was stilted, just a little awkward.

His older brother had been trapped in Hell for over a millennium and in many ways was still adjusting to this new world. He could be socially awkward, but Conall knew that wasn't what this was about. Drake had been the best big brother when they'd been children and Conall was still getting used to having him around again.

Drake should have been Alpha and had the ability to start his own clan if he wanted. Hell, Conall had tried to let him take over this one once he'd returned from Hell, but Drake had no desire to be in charge of their people. He simply wanted to be with his mate.

It was . . . nice having an older sibling. But still foreign. For so long he'd taken on that role and still was an older brother to Keelin, but hell, maybe he *should* talk to his brother.

He cleared his throat. "My dragon knows what he wants." He didn't have to say Rhea, the implication was clear enough.

Drake nodded once, as if he completely understood. "It was the same for me. I knew before I even saw Victoria. Her scent was..."

"Perfect?" Just like Rhea's was to him.

"Yes. So what are you waiting for?"

Conall rubbed the back of his neck. He wasn't used to asking anyone for advice. He was always the one in charge, putting out fires, literally and figuratively. "We're just friends." Because he wasn't sure if she wanted more. Normally he'd charge after what he wanted, but Rhea was different, special. He couldn't go all Alpha caveman on a warrior like her. He had to be more subtle. And the truth was, the past few months of getting to know her had been some of the best of his very long life. Even if he was frustrated that he couldn't see her, touch her, on a daily basis.

"Hmm." Drake simply nodded but didn't push.

Which Conall appreciated. He was too on edge now. The longer he was away from Rhea, the harder it became to keep his dragon side appeased. He knew he had to see her soon.

And when he did, he was going to find a way to make her his.

* * *

Present day

Wearing the pants he'd grabbed from Finn's SUV, Conall slipped into the house Rhea and the three others had recently infiltrated using a back window. He'd been basically sidelined for the break-in and even though it grated on all his nerves, he understood.

This wasn't his territory. He was just a guest.

Before he'd made it to where the others were, he scented blood. A lot of it. None of it Rhea's, of that he was certain.

Not to mention he could hear the faint murmuring from the wolves. No panic, just annoyance. So the humans were dead.

As he stepped into the sparsely furnished living room of the two bedroom home, all four wolves turned to look at him. Finn with annoyance, Rhea with a half-smile and the other two females dismissed him entirely before turning back to the bloodbath.

"Don't touch anything," Finn growled as Conall stepped further into the room.

He just snorted. He didn't need to be told, but figured the Alpha was establishing dominance. Conall didn't care about that though. He didn't want this territory. He just wanted Rhea.

Scanning the room, he saw a human hand in an empty fish tank, a leg on a ceiling fan, and two sets of body parts strewn all around the room. "Is the violence contained to this room?" he asked, more out of curiosity than anything. Since he and Finn had recently created a pact of sorts declaring their alliance to each other he did have an interest but this was just two dead humans who'd likely been involved in the bombing.

"Yes," Finn answered.

"Any tattoos on them?" he asked, watching Rhea for a reaction. Last night he'd heard her tell Finn she needed to talk to him about a tattoo and something had been off about her body language. She'd been too rigid. When he'd asked Drake and Victoria about it, neither of them had known much other than the shifters who'd attacked the Stavros pack had all had matching tattoos. He wanted to know the damn significance since it appeared to matter to Rhea.

Finn shook his head. "Not that we can see." He cleared his throat, looked *almost* apologetic. "I need to talk to my packmates alone. I'd like to see you in the morning though if you're free. My office. I know your parents will be in town then. I'm going to ask them to come as well."

Ah, so he was being dismissed. It rankled, mainly because he wanted to stay near Rhea, but he nodded. This wasn't his business. He looked at Rhea. "Walk me out?"

Her eyebrows raised ever so slightly, but she nodded and followed him. Instead of using one of the windows, he headed for the backdoor, careful to grab a hand towel to open it. He didn't doubt the pack would wipe the place down, but he still didn't want to leave any DNA behind.

"Sorry about that," Rhea murmured as they stepped out into the crisp, cool night air.

The homes in this neighborhood were close enough together that he could hear a television blaring from next door and a dog barking from the yard of the neighbor behind. At least there was a privacy fence blocking them from potentially prying human eyes.

"I understand. He's got to investigate with his pack. I'm an outsider."

Rhea looked as if she wanted to say more, but nodded instead before glancing around. "I think you're good to leave from here." Meaning the backyard. "But I can call someone to pick you up."

"Thank you for the offer, but no. Any idea who killed them?" He'd done the aerial recon, scanning the place before they'd infiltrated. There'd been no unusual movements. Of course from the scent of that blood and the way most of it had been dried onto various surfaces, the humans had been dead more than a few hours.

"Not yet. We're going to do a full sweep of the house, see if there are any connections to any supernatural beings but I'm not hopeful."

He nodded, understanding. Whoever had come in here tonight had been cleaning house, had likely known Finn and his pack would trace the humans who'd planted the bombs back here. Collateral damage. Whoever was behind the attack had probably always planned to kill these humans. Hiring them had been smart if the humans had no supernatural ties. It'd make it that much harder to trace whoever was really behind the bombing. "If there's anything I can do, let me know."

"I will." Her gaze dipped to his mouth for a moment before she looked at him again. That unmistakable heat was there, making everything inside him flare to life. The need to claim her was consuming, but he knew he had to play things right with her. He had to move in subtly so that she never saw him coming. He knew she'd almost been mated, but didn't know the details. Damn it, he needed to find out what had gone wrong, needed to know because he didn't want to lose her.

Because winning Rhea was a battle he would never lose. He refused to let that happen.

"You plan on sticking around to watch me strip again? I should start charging you admission—or ask for a strip show in return," he murmured, watching her carefully. He kept his voice light.

Her cheeks flushed but she met his gaze head on. "I'll give you a show, if you think you can handle it." And on that note, she turned and headed back into the house.

The soft sway of her hips and ass got him hard. Again. Around her that seemed to be a permanent issue. Forcing himself to look away from her retreating form, he did another scan of the surrounding area before stripping. Time to leave his human form behind.

Rhea's heart pounded just a little bit harder as she headed back into the house. Things between her and Conall had definitely shifted. Overnight, it seemed. Okay, not exactly overnight if she was being honest with herself.

She wasn't sure how she felt about it, but she was pretty positive that very soon she was going to see him naked and flat on his back underneath her. Or on top of her. Didn't matter which. It almost seemed inevitable.

"Give your male a goodbye kiss?" Chloe asked, practically purring as Rhea stepped back into the room. Finn wasn't anywhere to be seen but she scented him nearby.

"Man, you really must want to lose that pretty face."

Chloe just grinned. "Come on. I need details. I've been celibate way too long. Is he a good kisser?"

Rhea stilled a moment at the thought of his lips on her. She'd certainly imagined what he would taste like, would feel like pressed up against her.

"You two realize we're standing in the middle of a gruesome crime scene?" Lyra asked, her voice dry.

Rhea lifted a shoulder. If she'd been human she'd probably be puking her guts up right now but she'd seen enough scenes like this over the decades. Worse ones, even. "These two morons planted a bomb at Howlers."

Lyra's mouth lifted a fraction. "True. So let's get down to business. Finn's already started searching the garage. Chloe and I are going to hit the other two rooms and move inward to search for anything that might link them to anyone who could be behind the bombing. Rhea, I want you to start cataloguing scents for anyone you might recognize. You know what to do. Start with the living room."

She nodded, going into warrior mode as her Alpha's mate laid out the orders. It was time to get to work.

As a tracker she was exceptionally good at sifting through specific scents. Even if she didn't recognize it, if she scented something specific she'd know it if she scented it again later.

Even though she didn't want to, she shelved thoughts of her very sexy dragon and got down to work. Someone thought they could mess with her pack? Very soon they'd find out how very wrong they were.

CHAPTER TEN

A full moon hung high overhead, with a smattering of stars splashed across the night sky. Conall slid a hand behind his head as he stared up at it. The lounge chair on the second level deck of his house was so comfortable he was thinking about sleeping outside. Not that he'd be getting rest any time soon. Hours had passed since he'd left Rhea in that house full of blood and death and as usual, she consumed his thoughts.

He'd hated leaving her, hated not being part of the investigation. He wasn't exactly worried about her safety, not when she was so capable, but he was so damn used to taking over situations. Being sidelined because he was in another Alpha's territory, was . . . frustrating. And he just hated being apart from her.

But he liked that Rhea was attracted to him for who he was, not because of his position in his clan. If anything, he thought his Alpha status might be a strike against him in her books. He couldn't be sure though because the frustrating female was so closed off. It didn't matter how much they talked, it was like she always had a wall up between them.

When his phone buzzed he glanced at it, expecting it to be one of his parents since they were arriving in Biloxi tonight. Or one of his many clan members. They'd been checking in the last few days with one issue or another, which was to be expected. But when he saw Rhea's name his heart went into overdrive again.

Back at the mansion, no leads so far. You make it to your place? Her text was benign, but he liked that she'd texted him regardless. It meant she was thinking about him.

Some part of him he didn't want to evaluate too deeply wouldn't have let him sleep without knowing she'd made it back to the mansion. He swiped his thumb across the screen. *Yeah, nice night for a run if you want to head over here.*

Though he hadn't told anyone—except Finn since it was his territory—Conall had bought a place in Biloxi almost a year ago. He'd told himself it was so his brother could use the house whenever he came down here to visit with Victoria. But the truth was, he'd bought it because deep down, after he'd met Rhea, he'd known he'd be following her to Biloxi. His dragon half wouldn't let him rest otherwise.

If I wasn't so exhausted I would. There was a pause in her text, then, *What are you wearing?*

The question took him off guard. He sat up on the lounge chair and typed back, *nothing*. Even if it was a lie. He had on loose cotton pants. But he wanted to give her the right visual. He was tired of the slow burn between them, tired of waiting to claim her. As a fifteen-hundred-year old dragon, he had a lot of patience, but he ached for this female. *What about you?*

She texted him back an image. His heart pounded in his chest as a picture of her pretty feet in strappy black heels downloaded. He forgot to breathe for a moment. *Nothing else?* he texted back.

Nope.

He paused, his heart still racing out of control at her flirty text. His dick was rock hard, aching for her. Something had shifted between them earlier. It was subtle, but he'd sensed it when she'd stared at him while he'd been undressing before he shifted forms; sensed she wanted more from him. With Rhea it was damn near impossible to tell if she just wanted something physical. He'd take that—for now. But he would have everything from her eventually.

Groaning, he scrubbed a hand over his face, imagining her in those sexy shoes and nothing else, spread out on his bed for him to feast on. Her wild corkscrew curls fanned out on his pillow, her lean warrior's body his to devour.

Give me something more, he texted, liking this new dynamic between them.

The wait seemed to go on forever. When she sent another picture, this time of her . . . bare knee, he grinned.

That's weak, he texted.

You want to see more, you've gotta give me more.

You've already seen me. More than once, he thought.

True enough.

So?

So what? I'm not sexting you pictures.

Why not? He waited, staring at the screen, practically holding his breath for her answer.

You'll have to wait to see the real thing.

His body jerked once at the response. Oh yeah, things had definitely changed for them tonight. *Does that mean*

I'll get to see the real thing? His fingers flew across the screen as he responded. Dear God, yes please, he thought.

Maybe.

You're killing me.

Good. That's what you get for walking around naked. He could practically hear her sultry voice, hear her muted laughter.

You liked it. A statement, not a question.

Also true.

He groaned again. All the muscles in his body were pulled taut. This woman was determined to kill him. He wanted to know what had brought on this change in her, but he wasn't going to question anything.

You sure you don't want to come over for a run tonight? he texted, even though running was the last thing they'd do and they both knew it. If she came over, he'd have her naked and flat on her back before she could blink.

There was another long pause, then, *Not tonight, but soon.*

Well, fuck him sideways. Things were definitely about to change between them. He knew what he wanted; Rhea. Unfortunately he wasn't sure if she wanted more than just a roll in the sheets.

And he couldn't settle for just that. He wanted to claim all of her.

* * *

Edgy and beyond sexually frustrated, Rhea shoved the kitchen door open. Finn had asked her to meet him in his office half an hour before everyone this morning and she needed coffee.

And sex.

But coffee would do for now. Last night she had no idea what had come over her with those texts to Conall. Okay, that was a lie. She wanted Conall and she'd made a decision. He'd be leaving soon, probably in a week or so. There was absolutely no reason she couldn't have a little fun with him.

Anything to get the male out her system. Then they'd go back to being friends.

She'd gotten one male killed and she wouldn't risk doing it ever again. It was why she'd never get mated, but she could still have fun. That was what she kept telling herself anyway.

Rhea had scented the two females before pushing the door open, but seeing Taylor and Lauren sitting at the long granite-topped island drinking coffee only annoyed her more. She loved both her packmates, adored them actually. But Lauren had been looking at Conall as if she wanted to jump him the other night.

"Hey, Rhea, you got an early shift?" Taylor, a striking redhead, asked as she headed for the industrial sized, stainless steel refrigerator. Their pack definitely ate a lot.

"Not sure. Most of security has a meeting in a bit." But she figured she would, considering the bombing and the attack. Everyone was on high alert right now. She pulled a travel mug down from one of the cabinets and poured the hot liquid into it. The scent of coffee in the morning always made her smile.

"Here," Taylor said, sliding over a bottle of flavored creamer.

They'd all lived together long enough that they knew a lot about their packmates. "Thanks," she murmured, adding it to her mug.

"So," Taylor leaned her hip against the counter, faced Rhea. "I heard that fine dragon Alpha got naked last night in front of you and we missed it. Is he as hot as Chloe says?"

Yep, Rhea was gonna kick her friend's ass later. She shrugged. "He looks alright."

"Hmm. Not what I heard. And Lauren is dying to get a piece of that. Not that I blame her."

Rhea snarled at her, her canines dropping without warning. That hadn't happened since she was a cub and couldn't control herself.

Before she could say anything, Taylor simply grinned and turned to Lauren. "Pay up, sucker!"

Groaning, pretty, petite, blonde Lauren pulled out a twenty and slapped it on the counter. "I hate it when you gloat."

"What the hell is this?" Rhea demanded, even though she had a pretty good idea.

Taylor's grin remained in place. "I knew you liked him and Lauren didn't believe me. She hit on him the other night at Howlers—"

Lauren held up her hands when Rhea turned to her, snarling again. Jeez, what was wrong with her?

"I didn't know you were in to him. I swear. I'd never hit on someone taken," she said before glaring at Taylor. "Taylor told me but I thought she was crazy."

He wasn't taken but Rhea wasn't going to correct her. "You're such a bitch," she muttered to Taylor, fighting a smile.

"Tell me something I don't already know." Her packmate waved her twenty dollar bill around like she'd won the damn lottery. "Come on! I've literally never seen you with a guy. You've given the pack something to gossip about, at least for a few weeks. You and a sexy dragon! You better not leave us like Victoria though."

"I'm not going anywhere, but . . . spread the word that he's off limits." Saying that out loud soothed her inner wolf in a way she didn't want to evaluate. Not now, not ever. It had been a long time since she'd felt territorial over a male. And she couldn't ever remember feeling this possessive over one, not even the male she'd almost mated...

She shook herself mentally. Some days she could forget she'd been such a weak female, that she hadn't always been a warrior. It was like the before and after versions of herself. And the old Rhea was long dead. She sure didn't miss her.

"I will if you tell me what it's like with a dragon. Victoria's such a prude, she won't give any details on Drake," Taylor grumbled, shaking Rhea out of her thoughts.

"God, you're such a perv."

"Again, tell me something I don't know. Hmm, I wonder what I'll spend my winnings on?" She continued waving the bill at Lauren.

Rhea just shook her head, laughing. "I've gotta go, freak. I'll see y'all later though. Hey . . . be careful if you're out this week. And make sure you always tell someone where you're going." Taylor and Lauren were strong, as shifters were, but they weren't warriors and with the bombing and that attack Rhea worried about her pack. "In fact, use the buddy system—"

Taylor lifted an eyebrow. "Dude, we already know. Finn's already told all of us we're pretty much on lock-down."

Oh, right, of course he would have. "You better listen then or you'll answer to me." The thought of anything happening to any of her packmates shredded her. She never wanted to let anyone down again; it was why she trained so hard, fought so hard to defeat any threat to her pack.

"We will. Now get out of here. I saw Conall headed up to Finn's office," Lauren said, a grin lighting up her face.

There was no acidic scent rolling off her so Rhea knew her packmate wasn't messing with her. Her heart rate kicked up just a bit faster at the thought of seeing him, especially after those texts from last night. She hadn't even expected him here this morning. She'd secretly hoped she'd have a few hours before she saw him again. The male had gotten under her skin and now she felt all flushed and excited, something she wouldn't be able to hide from anyone.

After exiting the kitchen she picked up her pace, not caring that she was pretty much jogging to her Alpha's office because she wanted to see Conall. Upstairs she caught the earthy scent of him in the hallway outside Finn's office. Conall's scent always reminded her of the forest in spring.

Taking a deep breath, she forced herself to remain calm and collected as she pushed open the door, but she wasn't sure she'd be able to fool anyone. Finn was sitting on the edge of his desk, arms crossed over his chest while Conall leaned against a bookshelf, his hands shoved into his pockets.

The male had on dark gray cargo pants, a light gray T-shirt and black boots. All that gray just made his eyes even more stunning—something she shouldn't be noticing right now. If she was affected by him, he'd scent it. Her gaze dipped to his mouth and she fought a shudder, imagining what it would feel like to—

"Glad you're here," Finn said, pushing up from his desk.

Thankful for the interruption to her wayward thoughts, she looked at her Alpha. "What's going on?"

"I want you and Conall to team up for some hunts today. I'm grouping up most of my warriors, except the ones who'll stay on patrol here, and you know the city well."

"You don't want me with Solon?" She certainly wasn't complaining to be working with Conall but she and Solon almost always worked as a team.

Conall let out a low growl, surprising her, but when she looked at him, his expression was perfectly neutral.

"Not today," Finn said. "I've got him with Chloe and they're taking one of the younger warriors out hunting."

"Who?"

"Silas."

She nodded once, glad Finn was letting the male go on an op with trained warriors. Though he was thirty, Silas was still young and relatively inexperienced. "Good. So what are our targets?"

He picked up his tablet from his desk, held it out. She was surprised he hadn't printed a list out. Finn tended to go old school most of the time.

"Most of these stops will be for pure questioning. You have a calmer head than almost everyone so I want you and Conall to take the first three stops, see if you can find out about any packs trying to move into our territory."

She scanned the entire list he had and realized why he'd given her the first three names. She was on good terms with the two felines and one wolf shifter on the list. All packless, but all living in Finn's territory under the condition that they respected his rules.

But something made the nape of her neck prickle. She steeled herself before asking her question. "Are you reaching out to people who might have known Anson?"

Somehow she managed say the name without giving away a reaction. She knew she'd probably opened herself up to questions from Conall later about who the male was, but she needed to know what Finn was doing. Especially because of that damn tattoo.

It had brought up too many memories of the female she'd been before, of that bastard Anson who'd killed her almost-mate, had taken her captive and tried to force her to be his. He'd even tattooed her with that symbol of his lineage, branding her as his. He'd seen her as his property. His slave. The day she'd carved it from her skin was the day she'd killed him. She'd never felt more free.

"Scroll to the next page," he murmured without answering her question.

When she did she saw a list of ten individuals. "What about Knox?" Another Alpha who lived in Alabama. Over a thousand years old and from an old Germanic land, he'd also mated with a vampire. "He's one of the oldest shifters on the planet."

Conall cleared his throat. When she looked at him, his eyebrows were raised.

"One of the oldest *wolf* shifters," she added, since Conall and many of his clan members were far older than her pack and even Knox. As in, centuries or millennia older. "He had some land issues with Anson's old pack." Which would have been when Finn was barely older than a cub. "That male never forgets a dispute and from what I hear, can hold a grudge. He might know something."

Finn looked surprised, but nodded. "I didn't even think of him. I don't want to be far from the pack now, but I'll contact him, tell him you and Conall are coming." He glanced at Conall. "Unless you object?"

"No."

He nodded again. "Good, then the names on your list can wait for this afternoon. I think an in-person visit for this is best. If Knox is available now, I'll contact our pilot. Be ready to leave in an hour unless I tell you otherwise," he said as the door opened.

She'd heard and scented her packmates in the hall, but was surprised when a dozen of them strode in, including Lyra, Gabriel, Bo, Nyx, Victoria, Drake—and Drake and Conall's parents, Dragos and Arya.

Arya's face lit up when she saw Rhea and the ancient dragon patted her on the shoulder gently. "Good to see you again."

Over the last eight months Arya had called her a couple times a month, seemingly for no reason at all other than to talk, usually about weapons. Rhea had asked Victoria what was up with the ancient female but V just said Arya did what Arya wanted and there was no rhyme or reason to what the female did. The truth was, she liked the phone calls, even if Arya was a little intimidating.

"You too," she murmured, nodding at everyone else. Then to Finn, "I'll have my phone on me. We'll head to the airport now." After getting a cache of weapons, of course. Not that she planned to use them against Knox's pack, but with an unknown threat targeting their pack she was going to be prepared.

After Conall spoke quietly to his parents and brother, they headed out. Once they were downstairs and alone, she glanced at Conall to find him watching her. "I want to grab some weapons before we leave. Did we need to stop by your place too?" she asked, proud of herself for talking in a normal voice when her heart rate kicked up by merely being in his presence.

His eyes were slightly brighter than normal, more silver than gray as he watched her. Intently.

"What?" she asked when he didn't answer her question.

"Just wondering what color your panties are." He said it so matter-of-fact as they turned into another hallway, headed to the training room.

She felt her cheeks heat up, but didn't respond. Wasn't sure *what* to say. She was the one who'd started the flirty texts last night, but now, being alone with Conall, she was wondering if she'd bitten off more than she could handle. The male was an Alpha with a capital A.

"Or maybe you're not wearing any at all," he murmured as they reached the open training room door.

"Lacy purple with a black bow right . . . here." She pointed to a spot right above her butt.

He simply growled, his eyes going supernova as they stepped inside. "I'm going to see them soon." It was a statement of fact, not a question.

Maybe that should offend her, but all it did was get her even hotter. Her nipples beaded against her matching purple bra—and the fact that she'd worn something other than her normal tank-bra made it pretty obvious she'd planned for something to happen with him today on the off chance that she saw him.

They had a busy day, she shouldn't be thinking about the two of them naked, tangled together. Unfortunately for her sexually frustrated self, in spite of the threat hanging over them all, that was *all* she could think about.

CHAPTER ELEVEN

"Bet Lyra hated missing this," Gabriel murmured to Finn as they crept down the quiet alley.

"Yeah, but I promised her a hunt tonight." Finn's mate was a blood-born and powerful, but couldn't walk in daylight. But some things he simply couldn't wait for. "I don't think she minded too much though. She's helping Vega fill out college applications today."

Gabriel's mouth flattened, but he didn't respond. Lately whenever Finn brought up Vega his Guardian simply frowned.

"What? You think I shouldn't let her go away?" Because the truth was, he didn't want to. She wasn't even looking to go far; Tulane was her top choice and that was only an hour and a half. Still, he'd only found out about his daughter's existence a little over a year ago. And she was barely eighteen. He didn't want to let her go yet.

"I think she'll need to live off campus and with packmates—meaning guards," he said. "She's powerful, but she's young. And she would be a very valuable bargaining chip to someone who wanted to hurt you, Lyra or the pack. But you've already thought of all that," Gabriel murmured.

Yes, he definitely had. She wouldn't start school until the summer, seven or eight months away, so he had time to figure everything out. Until then he'd just pretend that she wasn't leaving.

Gabriel went still as they reached the end of the alley.

It opened up into another alley that crossed over this one. A string of warehouses lined the industrial block. He'd heard that a vampire nest had moved in a few days ago. Under other circumstances he might have given them a warning, but as it was, he wouldn't now.

He couldn't appear weak. Ever. It was why the wedding festivities would go on as planned. No one screwed with his pack or his friends. And vampires, any vampires, would know better than to move into his territory without talking to him first. There simply was no excuse for this. It wasn't an oversight, it was blatant disrespect.

Inhaling deeply, he frowned. He smelled blood. Human blood. When he looked back at Gabriel, his Guardian had clearly scented it too.

Gabriel's expression was dark as Finn used hand signals to indicate the plan. They'd worked together enough that he likely didn't even need to communicate, but he did anyway.

His Guardian nodded and crossed over to the other side of their current alley. Daylight was their friend right now. Vamps tended to sleep during the day, especially those who nested outside of established covens.

But that didn't mean they wouldn't be vigilant.

Finn peered out into the alley that crossed over theirs, nodded once and they both sprinted across it with supernatural speed.

If humans were nearby watching, it was doubtful they'd even see them with the naked eye. Finn veered right and Gabriel went left, as they both skirted the outside of the nearest warehouse. They'd gotten a tip that the nest was here, but the human blood was a dead giveaway.

Without pausing, he raced around the edge of the building, knowing Gabriel was doing the same on the other side. They were going to infiltrate on different sides and take out any intruders they came across.

A simple plan.

He had two short blades, but he planned to use his claws or just go full wolf if necessary. Depended on what the situation called for.

As he reached a side door, he tested it. Locked.

One quick pull using his strength took care of that. The door opened silently. He slipped inside and because of his supernatural sight he didn't need time to adjust to the darkness as he moved into the shadows.

In a quick scan he saw the place was nearly empty except for a cluster of what looked like bodies in one corner. Dead humans, if he scented right. The bastards had bled the humans out and just left them.

A collection of cots and mattresses were in the middle of the warehouse with vampires stretched out on them. If they'd binged on blood it made sense they were sleeping so hard. A dozen vampires, by the looks of it. He glanced up and saw crisscrossing steel beams high above him.

There could be enemies waiting in the rafters but he didn't think so. Not with how early in the morning it was. No, they'd all be sleeping, content in their beds while their victims' bodies lay yards away.

He let his wolf off the leash, let his animal side take over as he stripped off his clothes and underwent the change. Moving lithely, he circled the entire warehouse, looking for more vampires lurking in the shadows but found none.

He sensed Gabriel more than saw him. His Guardian was a dark mass of stealth moving toward the sleeping enemies on silent feet.

They approached from opposite sides. When Finn was within striking distance, he let out a savage growl and attacked the nearest one, ripping the male's head clean off. Ash filled his mouth seconds later as the vamp disintegrated.

Screams and cries filled the air as the vampires tried to scatter. It was too late for them now.

The most primal part of Finn, the part that was all animal, relished the killing of these monsters. They'd brought humans here, killed them, discarded them like garbage. Yeah, he felt no guilt. His wolf side never did.

A male went for a blade. Finn lunged, tore into the male's arm as another male jumped on his back. He felt claws dig into his sides but ignored the bite of pain as he swiped at the male he had pinned, used his own claws to slice the vamp's head off.

Pain punched through his belly as the male sliced at him again—apparently the vamp couldn't figure out where his heart was. Finn rolled onto his back, dislodging the vampire before turning and making quick work of him, severing his head in a clean kill.

In less than two minutes, all the vamps but one were nothing but ash.

Breathing hard, ignoring the pain from his battle wounds, Finn underwent the change. Skin replaced fur as he let his human side take over, most of his wounds healing in the process. Gabriel had shifted back as well, had his hand around the last vampire's throat as he held him up in the air.

The male was tall, lanky, his eyes wide and terrified. The scents coming off him told Finn he was very young, probably only turned in the last year or so. "You kill all those humans?" he growled low in his throat as he approached.

"They're nobody," the male whispered, looking back and forth between him and Gabriel. "Just homeless people. Why'd you do this?" He sounded truly shocked.

Finn grabbed the male by the throat, taking over for Gabriel. "Because you're in my fucking territory."

"You're Finn." A statement, not a question. One filled with terror.

"No shit. Give me one reason why I shouldn't kill you." He wanted to know more about why this vampire and his friends had nested here because it truly made no sense unless they had a death wish. Moving into Stavros pack territory without permission was just plain stupid.

The vamp swallowed hard. "He said . . . he said we'd be safe here."

"Who?"

The male shook his head. "I don't know his name. He's like a ghost, but he's building a huge shifter pack. An army. Said things would be different, vamps could live here too once he took over from..."

Finn wasn't going to get into the fact that vampires and many other beings lived in his territory—as long as they lived by his rules. Which included not killing or harming innocents. It would be lost on this dumbass. "From who, me?"

The male's silence was the only answer he needed.

"So some ghost is going to take over my territory, huh? What's his name?" he asked again.

"I don't know."

Finn didn't sense a lie rolling off the male. "Is there anything special about this pack?"

"No, no . . . wait, they're all tattooed. All of them. That's all I know, I swear!"

"I believe you." Finn severed the vamp's head with a single slice of his claws, stepping back as a wave of ash rolled over him. "Damn it," he muttered, looking at the pile of dust covering the floor. "Let's do a sweep, see if there are any survivors, then get out of here." Though he was almost certain there weren't any. He couldn't hear any heartbeats and dead bodies had a very distinctive scent.

He had to make an anonymous call to the cops too, but only once they were long gone from here. And if the dead humans truly were homeless, he'd discretely pay for all their funeral expenses. They'd been murdered in his territory and that was unacceptable.

Some fool thought he could move into his territory, could tell others they could do the same? Whoever was behind this was going to find out very soon how wrong he was.

* * *

"So who's Anson?" Conall asked as the plane raced down the runway.

She cleared her throat, not wanting to answer right away. After gathering weapons and a slightly awkward, sexual tension-filled drive to the private airport, they'd boarded the plane. The flight was only forty-five minutes but driving would have taken about four hours and she doubted Conall wanted to fly there and back in dragon form with her riding on him.

She'd expected the question since she'd mentioned the dead male in relation to Knox not too long ago, but it didn't mean she was ready to answer. She turned to look at him. He'd chosen to sit directly next to her in the private plane when there were a dozen other seats. Something that pleased her very much.

Like a siren's song, his eyes drew her in. Almost no one in her pack knew what had happened to her, not even Solon. Many of the older packmates who'd been around when Finn's uncle was Alpha had either left the pack or been killed after challenging Finn. "He was an Alpha of a wolf pack."

"Was?"

"He's dead. I . . . killed him." Some part of her felt compelled to tell him everything. Well, almost everything. Even this much went against her very private nature, but the most primal part of her simply trusted Conall. It was an innate reaction. Her wolf wanted to rub up against him all the time.

"Why?"

She turned away from him and stared out the window, but she could feel his gaze on her. It made it easier to talk this way. "Because he was a monster. I told you I was almost mated before," she said, finding the strength to meet his gaze once more.

He nodded once, a frown on his face. Yeah, he didn't seem to like that at all.

"Anson killed Damien. That was my betrothed's name." It didn't hurt as much to say Damien's name as it had once upon a time. Not even close. She wasn't that person she'd been a hundred years ago. Even if she did still carry guilt over Damien's death, she'd buried him and her former self.

She cleared her throat. "Anson was a powerful wolf and greedy for anything that wasn't his. He was like a child. A very psychotic one. He was part of a neighboring pack and things were different a hundred years ago. The stronger tended to rule with an iron fist." Still did for the most part, but they were more civilized as a whole compared to what they'd been back then.

He nodded in understanding. Even if dragons had more or less been in the closet to most supernatural beings up until very recently, she knew dragons had had their own skirmishes with each other. And they too had been violent. "It was the same for my kind in years past. More bloodshed and a 'kill now and ask questions never' kind of attitude."

A wry smile tugged at her lips. Yeah, that was exactly how things had been for other shifters and vamps years ago. Only in the last couple decades had they started working to make lasting peace between their own species and across other ones. They couldn't afford to start wars anymore. Not with humans and their invasive technology. The risk of getting caught was too great.

"Well, Anson wanted me and was angry he couldn't have me. He came to my Alpha, had the balls to try to *buy* me. Something neither my Alpha nor my mate-to-be liked. Don't get me wrong, my Alpha was old school, believed females should take on a more submissive role no matter what, but his pack was his pack. No one messed with us. Anson left and didn't bother us for almost six months. I'd forgotten about the annoying male." She still felt like a fool for not seeing the depth of Anson's insanity.

Years ago she'd questioned herself constantly, wondering how she'd missed seeing that something was truly wrong with the male until it was too late. She rubbed her damp palms over her pants, feeling awkward telling him all this.

"You don't have to tell me anymore," he murmured, as if he'd read her mind. "You'd mentioned him in Finn's office and I thought he might be important to who we're hunting."

She took a steadying breath. "Thank you, but I want to tell you. And there *is* a possibility he's somehow tied to what's going on." Or one of his old packmates were tied to it, because that sick male was dead and gone.

Her cheeks and neck felt clammy as she forced the next words out. She wasn't sure what even compelled her to tell Conall all this. He didn't need *all* the details. He simply needed to know that someone related to Anson was likely targeting her pack because she'd killed the male. But... "He cornered Damien and me in the woods when we were out running. He killed my mate, raped me, then dragged me back to his den." She paused, trying to keep her voice steady as she continued.

"The male was obsessed and insane. He had everyone in his pack tattooed with the same symbol we found on the wolves we killed the other night. It's why I recognized it."

Conall was growling low in his throat, his dragon clear in his gaze as he visibly struggled to talk. "You're certain he's dead?"

"I ripped out his heart and beheaded him for good measure." That had been the first time she'd ever killed another person. She was definitely certain of his death. It was the only way she'd been able to move on with her life. She cleared her throat. "Then I set him on fire. Anyway, he kept me for weeks until I killed him." Something she tried not to think about.

She turned away to look out the window again, was surprised but glad when he took one of her hands, gripped it tight. The male was such a soothing presence. "I escaped back to my pack and my old Alpha hunted down and slaughtered Anson's pack. He didn't tell anyone what had happened to me, but said they were avenging Damien's death. And he let everyone other than our pack believe that vampires had killed them. I've never heard of any of his packmates resurfacing again. I believed my Alpha when he said they were all dead, but maybe some of them got away..."

"And you think this Knox might know more about Anson's dead packmates? Or living packmates, as it seems it might be."

When she forced her gaze back to Conall, his dragon still remained lurking in his eyes, too many emotions shimmering there, but no pity. She was thankful for that; she didn't think she could bear this male pitying her. It had taken her years to get to where she was and she didn't want anyone feeling sorry for her.

Breathing easier, she nodded. "Knox can hold a grudge. The male is seriously old and a bit autocratic."

His lips quirked up. "What Alpha isn't?"

She smiled at that. "True enough. But yes, according to Finn's last text Knox knows something and he's ready to meet with us. His mate is a day walker by the way, so just be prepared."

Conall's eyes flickered with brief surprise. "I've never met one before."

"I've never actually met her either, but she was part of Titus's coven—who is Lyra's brother. Lyra hates her brother though so don't bring up that connection or anything," she added.

He half-smiled. "I won't."

She watched him for a long moment, mesmerized by his silver eyes even as the strangest weight seemed to be lifted from her chest. Telling him had been surprisingly therapeutic.

His expression become intense as he held her gaze. "The words are weak and pathetic, but I'm truly sorry about what happened to you."

She swallowed once, hard. "It was a very long time ago, but thank you. So . . . are you still in love with Fia?" He wasn't the only one who got answers today. And screw it, she desperately needed to know. The question had been bothering her for months. It didn't matter that she'd convinced herself things between her and Conall would be casual, that he'd be leaving in a week or so. She couldn't sleep with him if he was in love with someone else. She simply couldn't. And Rhea had met the female, his former betrothed in person, months ago. So she knew the woman was sort of in Conall's life.

He jerked back slightly, definitely surprised by her question if the way his eyes went back to human were any indication. "No. God, *no*. I . . . never really loved her."

Rhea's eyebrows raised. "You sure about that?"

"Yes. I thought I did but we would have made each other miserable."

"She is a lovely female." The female was all grace and elegance. It was a little annoying.

He gave her a wry smile. "Yes, but she's very dependent on her mate. She likes being helpless. And I thought I wanted that in a mate, someone to take care of, someone who needed me for everything." He shook his head, seemingly at himself.

"And you don't now?"

He pinned her with the force of his supernova stare. "I would take care of a mate, don't misjudge my words, but I want a partner. A warrior. *You*."

As the weight of his words settled in, her throat tightened. He couldn't mean he wanted her for a *mate*. She was a freaking wolf and he was the Alpha of a dragon clan. But—

She jolted forward as the plane dipped suddenly, her stomach dropping with the turbulence.

"Just a bit of turbulence," the pilot said over the intercom, his voice calm. "We'll be landing in fifteen minutes and, right on schedule."

Jeez, the trip really was short.

Wordlessly Conall linked his fingers through hers, pulled her hand into his lap and just held it.

She squeezed his hand, fighting all the emotions punching through her. Why had she ever thought she could do casual with this male?

Too many emotions ripped her up inside. She *couldn't* have more with him. It had nothing to do with what she wanted, but everything to do with keeping him safe. If they mated he would become more vulnerable, could die if she died. No, she couldn't let that happen. She wouldn't.

CHAPTER TWELVE

Conall was surprised when the Alpha, Knox, and his vampire mate were already waiting on the tarmac for them. The female leaned against an SUV, looking at her phone while the male stood as if he was ready to attack at any moment. His arms were crossed over his chest, his expression unreadable, but it was clear he was poised for anything.

Scanning the surrounding area, the action instinctively borne out of millennia of habit, Conall wasn't exactly surprised that the private airport seemed to be cleared out. He did the same thing with his own private airport when necessary, but he wasn't certain he liked how quiet this one was. With the plane silent and no other apparent flights taking off or landing nearby, the whistling wind was the only real sound.

"If we're attacked, I'll shift. You will ride me out of here," he said quiet enough for Rhea's ears only as they stepped out onto the rolling set of stairs. Normally he'd fight any danger head on, but depending on the threat he would get Rhea to safety first—though something told him that would be an impossible feat, considering she'd want to stay and fight a threat.

Her cheeks flushed a sexy shade of pink and he belatedly realized how that sounded. "That sounded shockingly like an order," she murmured.

He turned away as he felt his cock growing hard. He couldn't meet with this Alpha with a raging hard on. "You like it."

He heard a soft inhalation behind him as he stepped down first. Males always went in front of their mates regardless of the situation, to check for potential danger. Or to take the hit if someone attacked. Rhea wasn't his mate yet, but she would be, and in the meantime he considered her his.

When they reached the bottom of the stairs both Knox and his mate approached, welcoming expressions on their faces. Well, on the female's face. She was about five-feet-six, the same height as Rhea, with pale ivory skin and choppy black hair that fell around her face in a bob. Her eyes were gray, very similar to his own, and her cheekbones sharp. Knox was muscled and huge, where she was the opposite.

"Knox," Rhea said in greeting as she came to stand next to Conall.

He allowed his instinct to rule him as he placed a hand at the small of her back. Fuck civility and everything else. After their conversation on the plane ride he felt as if years of so-called civilization had fallen away. The darkest part of him wanted to throw her over his shoulder and find someplace for them to be alone. Dragons loved treasure, that was not a myth about his kind, and Rhea was the greatest treasure of all. He didn't want to share her with anyone and he didn't care that this male was mated, or that Knox's mate was right next to him. The most possessive part of Conall didn't want another male to even look at Rhea.

Which . . . was completely insane.

He realized Knox was watching him with predatory eyes, his stance rigid. That was when Conall also realized his dragon was most definitely in his eyes. Using willpower he didn't know he had, he managed to shove his beast back. Barely. He managed a small, sort of smile. "I'm Conall Petronilla. Thank you for allowing us into your territory." His dragon sneered at the words. No one *allowed* him to do anything. He was a fucking dragon. He did what he wanted.

The other Alpha seemed to sense his thoughts, gave a half-nod but his stance didn't change much. "I'm Knox."

"I'm Angela. And holy balls, can we tone down the testosterone here?" she asked.

Rhea snorted and nudged Conall in the ribs, her expression as admonishing as the vampire's. "They're here to help us," she murmured.

And he was letting his dick take over because he was feeling territorial of Rhea. He cleared his throat, nodded at the vampire politely. "It's a pleasure to meet you."

She smiled, held out a hand to him, then to Rhea before turning back to him. "What are you? Your heat signature is weird."

He stilled at her question.

"Ah..." Rhea looked as surprised as he felt.

"You can read my heat signature?"

Angela nodded. "Yep. One of my vampire gifts."

"A dragon," Knox muttered, surprising Conall even more. "Finn told me Rhea was bringing another Alpha, but I assumed he meant a wolf. Your last name though, I know it. I've met your parents. Many, many centuries ago," he added when all three of them looked at him.

"How terrifying is Arya?" Rhea asked, her voice light, breaking up the tension.

Knox just grunted, but Conall thought he saw a flash of agreement on the male's face. "Is it okay if we just talk here?" he asked.

"Normally we'd invite you back to our compound but it's a bit of a drive and we know you're pressed for time," Angela added.

"We just appreciate your time," Rhea said. "What did Finn tell you so far?"

"That he thinks someone from that fucker Anson's old pack might be trying to take over his territory. That guy was always trying to take what wasn't his." Knox shook his head and pulled out a folder he must have had tucked in the back of his pants. "I was glad when some vampires took that male and his pack out, but one of his brothers—who I thought was dead—popped up on my radar a few years ago." He handed the file to Rhea. "That's everything I have on him."

Rhea opened it, paled a bit when she saw the picture of a male. Conall didn't know if there was more to what she'd told him in the plane considering her reaction to the picture. He frowned and looked back at Knox. "Can you give us a rundown of who he is?"

"Ezra Meyer. Was a cub when his pack was killed. Maybe the vamps let him go because he was so young. Who knows?" Knox lifted a shoulder. "Couple years ago he tried to move into the territory of an Alpha I'm friendly with out west. He tried to play it off like he didn't know the territory was claimed."

Next to him Rhea snorted and Knox simply nodded. "Total bullshit, but he didn't harm anyone so my friend let him and his pack go. A few weeks later there was some property damage to a few of his companies. The actual buildings. It was petty shit and while he could never prove it, the scent of Ezra's wolves lingered near some of the damage. After that I started asking around about him, building a file. His brother was bad news so I wanted to be prepared if that fucker Ezra ever came sniffing around my territory."

God, Rhea had been right. Knox really did hold a grudge.

Rhea looked up from the file. "He's into illegal underground fighting?"

Knox nodded. "Yeah. Keep reading though. He's been involved in running drugs and people. Allegedly. There's a lot of information on the male, but he keeps moving every few years. Everything I know is in that file. If you need to follow up about any of it, just call me. I'd prefer not to discuss any of this over email or any other online method. I only have hard copies of that," he said, nodding at the file in Rhea's hand. "Nothing saved electronically."

Conall bet the male had more files like that on countless other supernatural beings.

"Thank you, we appreciate it." Rhea flipped the file closed, held it at her side.

"It's no problem. I trust Finn to keep this in a safe place. Just don't save that information online. I've spent years building it up and I don't want him to get a hint I've been keeping tabs on him. And . . . I don't want the government to ever see it either."

"My paranoid mate," Angela murmured, nudging him with her hip.

The male wrapped his arm around her shoulders, shrugged. "Better paranoid than dead."

Conall nodded in agreement. With the invasive government surveillance on a global scale, it was smart to keep certain things offline.

After they all said their goodbyes, Conall and Rhea returned to the plane. The trip had been short, something he was glad for. Now he had another forty-five minutes alone with Rhea. Though he knew she'd be reviewing the file during the flight, he still savored their time together. After what she'd told him about her time in captivity, he had an even stronger urge to keep her close, to imprint himself on her. He knew she could take care of herself, but that didn't diminish his need to keep her safe. Protected.

The pilot and co-pilot had them taxiing in record time.

"So you think my mother is terrifying?" Conall asked as the plane raced down the runway. On instinct, he reached for her hand, was glad when she linked her fingers through his.

She snorted. "Anyone who thinks otherwise is a fool. It's not an insult," she quickly added, looking at him as if worried about his reaction.

"I know. I think she'd be insulted if people *weren't* afraid of her."

"She calls me, you know," Rhea murmured. "A couple times a month."

"I . . . did not know that." He gritted his teeth. He was an Alpha, almost fifteen hundred years old. Maybe he was jumping to conclusions but it sounded a lot like his mother was meddling.

Rhea shrugged. "Yeah, she's funny. She always calls to talk about different weapons."

He frowned. Maybe he was wrong about the meddling. "That's it?"

"Yeah. She thinks humans are freaks for developing so many, but she's still curious about them. She called me once to talk about the schematics of an RPG and how hard I thought it would be to *build* one."

"That makes my head hurt," he murmured.

"No kidding."

He didn't want to talk about his mother anyway. "How much did you read in the file?"

"Enough to know this guy has a habit of creating havoc wherever he goes. He doesn't respect human laws or our own, it seems." Pulling her hand from his, she opened the folder again, flipped a couple pages inward. "In some of the cities he's stopped in, female shifters have gone missing when he and his pack leave. All packless females with no one to protect them."

"They could have joined his pack willingly."

She lifted a shoulder. "Yeah, maybe. But if he's like his brother, he won't care if a female is willing."

He growled, making her pause so he forced himself to rein it in.

She cleared her throat. "And some of these . . . the ones who went missing had good jobs, were established in their communities. The main thing they have in common is they're wolves and Ezra was in their city when they went missing."

"Want to split the reading up?" he asked, wanting to help with the burden. It didn't matter that he wanted to finish what they'd almost started on the plane ride here, this was important to her pack's safety and more important to him, Rhea's safety. He wanted to hunt the bastard Ezra down and anyone else ever linked to Anson.

She nodded, opened the file. "Thanks."

His jaw flexed once before he spoke again. "The male. Did he hurt you too?"

Rhea stiffened, then ran a hand through her wild hair. "No. He was too young, but he looks a lot like Anson did. Seeing that face again after so many years was just jarring."

He wanted to reach for her, to pull her into his arms, but didn't know if he had that right—didn't know if she'd welcome it right now. "I'm sorry this is hard on you."

She looked at him almost in surprise. "Thank you."

"Why does that surprise you?"

"It doesn't, it . . . it's just nice to be working with you, is all."

He felt like she was holding back, but now wasn't the time to push. Not when she'd already opened up to him about her past. Instead he took half the papers from the file and set them in his lap. It was time to get to work. His dragon half loved puzzles and one way or another he was going to hunt down and kill that male Ezra. Whether he was involved in the bombing or not, Conall planned kill the male regardless after he started reading the file Knox had given them.

This male needed to die.

* * *

"Gray is a little . . . eccentric," Rhea murmured as Conall steered down the long gravel driveway.

This was the last person on their list to question and Conall was looking forward to being done for the day. After they'd returned from Birmingham they'd handed all the information over to Elana so she could dig deeper into the file Knox had given them. Then they'd started on the list of people Finn wanted them to talk to.

Spending time with Rhea was a bonus but she'd been in pure work mode since they'd landed. Which he understood, but he didn't have to like it. He wanted to take her away, hole up somewhere for weeks. "How so?"

"Maybe that's the wrong word, but he's a lone wolf. Which is kinda odd for our kind."

He nodded, understanding. Wolves especially needed packs. It was part of their nature. "Finn doesn't care that he lives in his territory?"

"Nah. The guy's an artist. Wood carvings mostly. He's apparently a big deal in the art world," she said.

Conall eyed the small cabin and huge workshop next to it as they approached. "What's his last name?"

"Don't think he has one. Not that I know of anyway. Or it could just be part of his artist persona just being known by one name."

"He know we're coming?" he asked as he parked in the driveway. All the lights in the house appeared to be off but he saw light spilling out from the workshop and could hear the faint sound of a chainsaw.

"No. But as part of living in Finn's territory, either Finn or a representative from the pack has the right to stop by anytime unannounced. We never actually do, we always call, but not this time."

Conall nodded. He'd figured that, since the others they'd visited today had been surprised by Rhea and him stopping by. When they got out of the SUV, the sound of the chainsaw stopped, which meant the male wolf likely knew someone was on his property.

Inhaling deeply, Conall scented for individuals, only found one distinctive one. Probably the male who lived here. The place was on fifty acres of forest, according to Rhea, and they'd had to drive about thirty minutes to get here. He'd have preferred to simply fly them, had wondered what it would feel like to have Rhea riding him in his dragon form, but they didn't need to risk letting an outsider know what he was. And he wasn't sure she'd want to regardless. It involved a certain amount of trust from both parties. He trusted her on the deepest level, but knew that flying wasn't for everyone. "You scent anything off?" he asked.

She shook her head. "No. He knows we're here though."

Before she'd finished the statement, the sliding door to the workshop opened and a male walked out. He wore a long, dirty apron, thick-looking gloves that went up to his elbows and a welding helmet shoved back on his head.

He appeared to be in his early thirties, but with shifters you could never tell their actual age. He also looked surly.

"What the hell are you doing on my property?" he snarled, stomping across the grass and gravel as he made his way toward them on the driveway.

On instinct Conall growled, his Alpha nature shoving to the forefront as he stepped forward. The only thing that stopped him, barely, was Rhea's gentle touch on his forearm.

"Don't be a dick, Gray," she said. "We're here to talk."

The male blinked as he came to stand a few feet in front of them. He was covered in sawdust shavings. "Oh, didn't realize it was you. Who's this guy?" he tilted his chin in Conall's direction, but didn't bother looking at him.

Conall growled at the insult. Normally he let stuff slide, but today he was particularly edgy thanks to the sexy she-wolf standing next to him with her hand still on his forearm. He loved the feel of her slightly callused fingers touching him. He knew it was from weapons and her warrior status and found it sexy as hell. He didn't want a soft female. Once upon a time he thought he did. Now he knew what a fool he'd been.

"Gray, this is Conall, he's a friend of my pack. Be nice." Her tone was more admonishing than anything, almost as if she was scolding a cub.

The male looked at him with sharp green eyes, assessing him in a quick sweep. Conall bared his canines and to his surprise the other male did the same. Gray didn't back down an inch as his wolf flared in his gaze. Conall knew instantly this was another Alpha, wondered if Finn knew that too. It was even weirder that the male lived alone.

"Both of you stop, this is ridiculous," Rhea snapped. "Stop it now or I will stab you both."

He didn't think she really would, but Conall stopped snarling and retracted his canines. But he didn't take his eyes off the other male. It was obvious Rhea trusted him to some extent, but Conall didn't. Gray followed suit.

"What are you doing on my property?" he asked again, looking back at Rhea.

"We need to ask you a few questions."

He crossed his arms over his chest. "Fine, talk."

"You're not gonna ask us in?" she asked with a bite of sarcasm.

"I'm on a deadline, so no," he snapped.

Conall moved forward lightning fast, gripped the other male's throat and lifted him off the ground. "Talk to her with respect."

Gray latched onto his forearm, held tight, but didn't outright attack with his claws. Just nodded once, his eyes burning with resentment.

When Conall let him go Gray flashed his canines once, then looked at Rhea again. "Sorry, I'm in a shit mood and you two just interrupted my project. Can we just get over whatever this is?"

"You ever hear of an Ezra Meyer?" she asked, getting right to the point.

He paused and Conall could tell the guy was thinking, not trying to come up with a lie—which would be pointless with their ability to scent out untruths. Finally, Gray shook his head. "I've got a lot of customers but that doesn't sound familiar. I can't be sure without checking my files though. Why?"

"You hear of anything strange going on in the area lately? Anything to do with rogue vamps or shifters moving into the area?"

"No . . . well, a couple months ago I was at a dive bar over in Pass Christian and these two females–wolves–were hitting on me pretty hard." His lips pulled into a thin line. "They were rubbing all over me, telling me how they were part of this new, strong pack and wanted to know if I wanted to join. They were rubbing my dick as they asked." He snorted, shook his head. "It was like a cult recruitment or some shit."

"What'd you do?" Rhea asked.

The male shrugged. "Told them to get off me and they left."

"You follow them?"

"I trailed them a few miles, but they were headed west toward New Orleans so I figured they were headed out of this territory."

"Why didn't you tell Finn?"

The male lifted a shoulder. "He's not my Alpha."

Conall growled again, the disrespect chafing at him.

The male rolled his eyes as he looked at Conall. "This is my polite mode. I'm trying here." He looked back at Rhea, his expression a little softer. "I didn't tell him because I forgot until just now. I hooked up with a female later that night and . . . for the week after. I'd just finished a big project and was taking some downtime."

"You remember the name of the bar?"

"Yeah." He rattled off a name and address then said, "It's a dive. I doubt they have video surveillance there if that's what you're asking for."

Rhea just smiled politely at him, but didn't respond directly. "Can you tell me what they looked like?"

"Pretty wolves, average height for both, a little undernourished I thought, as if they weren't eating enough. But they could have just been really slender. Ah, white. Dark brown hair for both. One had brown eyes, the other blue. And . . . oh, they both had Celtic-looking tattoos on their wrists. Noticed when they were rubbing up on me. That combined with the fact that I could tell they weren't into me at all, even though they were trying to get me going, is why I drew that cult conclusion."

Rhea didn't respond, but Conall could tell she was digesting all the information. He wondered if the females were being treated as Rhea had by their new pack. His dragon slashed at him, wanting to hunt this Ezra down right now.

"You're an artist, right?" he asked Gray.

The male just grunted in what sounded like an affirmative.

"Think you can draw sketches of the females?" Conall continued, forcing himself to remain polite when he just wanted to punch this guy.

Gray's jaw tightened, but he nodded. "Yeah, just give me a few minutes," he growled before stomping off in the direction of his workshop.

As he walked away Rhea turned to Conall. "Want to head up to Pass Christian now? It's only forty minutes from here. Or I can drop you off and—"

"I'm going with you. We were assigned this as a team." And he wasn't letting her out of his sight. Though his bullshit assignment had nothing to do with it. He was here with Rhea because she was his. Simple as that.

Her lips quirked up. "Yeah, because you actually *let* another Alpha tell you what to do. You're here because you want to be."

"That's very true." He took a step closer, crowding all her personal space and not caring. His gaze dipped to her mouth and all he wanted to do was devour her right then and there.

She swallowed hard, one of her hands trailing up his chest, settling there in what felt like a very proprietary move. He shuddered at the simple feel of her fingertips on his shirt, wanted to burn all their clothes away so there was no barrier between them.

The thought of her naked and under him—or riding him, didn't matter—had him loosening his control. His dick grew even harder with her so close, her scent making him crazy. The wild, erotic fragrance that was all Rhea made him insane and made it hard to think straight. He needed to taste her. Make her understand he saw her as his.

Without second-guessing himself or giving her a chance to pull away he crushed his mouth to hers, taking what he wanted.

Moaning, she leaned into him, her hand digging into his chest as he slid a hand behind her head, holding her tight. He wasn't letting her go. What he wouldn't give to push her right up against the SUV and take all of her.

Her tongue flicked against his in erotic, frantic strokes as her other hand wrapped around his waist. He felt her nails dig into his back, savored the feel of her losing control too.

Now wasn't the time or place to get naked, but fuck it. Fuck everything. She owned him. He fisted one of her hips, nipped her bottom lip.

When she made a soft growling sound he felt it all the way to his core. Too many emotions pumped through him, mainly the need to claim, claim, *claim*. It was why he'd been so damn patient, careful with her. He'd known once he had a taste he'd need to mark her, make her his. And damn it, he wasn't sure she was ready for that.

"Whoa." Gray's voice jerked him back to the reality of where he was standing.

Conall pulled back, pissed at himself for not paying attention to his surroundings. He never got distracted. Never. Now, however, another dragon could have swooped down from the sky and he'd have never heard him coming.

He looked down at Rhea to see her staring up at him in a sort of horror. Her pupils were dilated and her beautiful lips slightly swollen. And that was when he realized he was glowing.

Shit.

"No, no, no." She shook her head, took another step back. "Nope, nope..." Trailing off, she turned to Gray—who was staring at Conall in surprise.

Conall bared his canines and grabbed the sketches from the male. The way she was blatantly rejecting his mating manifestation cut him deep. Sliced him up so hard he was surprised he wasn't bleeding out all over the driveway. Apparently he wasn't good enough for a mate. "Is this it?" he snarled, his voice more animal than man.

Gray just nodded, not looking surly at all anymore, just sort of fascinated. Which annoyed Conall. Not bothering to say thanks or anything else he turned and stomped back to the SUV. Rhea could say goodbye or whatever to the male.

He slid into the driver's seat though all he wanted to do now was shed his human form and take to the sky. To put distance between them. Her flat out rejection of him as a mate shredded him. Yep, he needed to get out of here and flying always soothed the ragged edges.

Less than a minute later Rhea slid into the passenger seat, the emotions rolling off her too many for him to sift through. He didn't start the vehicle, just turned to face her. "Is it really so fucking bad that I want to mate with you?" he snapped. Because it was clear she knew what the glowing meant. Every dragon manifested their need to mate in a unique way. His family put off a bright glow that kicked into gear whenever a Petronilla became intimate with their intended mate. It only went away once they were truly mated. And if they didn't get mated—he wasn't even going to go there.

"No! I . . . it's not that. I just . . . didn't realize that's what you wanted. You're an Alpha, and..." She trailed off, rubbing her hand against the back of her neck. Distress rolled off her now, both in her scent and body language.

The tension inside him ratcheted higher. "And what?"

"I can't mate you," she whispered, expression stricken.

Anger slammed through him until the word *can't* registered. "Can't, or won't?"

"*Can't.*"

He thought of everything she'd told him on the plane, felt some of his anger diminish but not all of it. "Is it because of what happened to you? I'd never let anyone hurt you, Rhea."

She swallowed hard, shook her head. "That's not it. You're a dragon. I know from Victoria that you guys mate for life in the literal sense, so if I die..." she trailed off again, looking miserable.

She didn't need to finish. If she died, he would too. Dragons were the only shifters whose bond wasn't severed even by death. "I'll make you weaker, make you a constant target. If someone wants to target you, they'll just come after me. I'd be your greatest weakness. You're an Alpha, you have to have a lot of enemies. I could literally get you killed just by being mated to you!"

He shook his head, refusing to accept it. "I don't give a shit about that, Rhea. At least let me make that decision. Give us a chance to see if there's something real—"

"No! I won't risk your life like that. I already let one male down. God, I could literally get you killed. I'm a warrior, I fight other supernatural beings all the time. Anything could happen to me." That same horror was on her face as before and he realized her fear was for him.

Which didn't dull the edge of his anger any. He was glad she cared about him and wanted to protect him, but his animal side was not rational when it came to his mate. All his dragon knew was that his mate didn't want him.

Knowing that anything he said in the next minute would be full of rage, he shoved the door open and jumped out. "I'll follow you to Pass Christian." While he stripped, she didn't say anything, just watched him miserably as she slid into the driver's seat.

His jaw clenched and he wanted nothing more than to shake sense into her. Or just kiss her and give her as many damn orgasms as it took for her to see reason. Her reason was total bullshit and while he understood it, he wasn't letting her get away. He would never stop fighting for her.

He tossed his clothes into the back seat and after a quick glance at the workshop, he let his cloaking fall into place and shifted with a roar. His dragon took over in an instant, launching into the air before he had time to fully process any thoughts.

Right now he needed space from Rhea before he did something stupid. His dragon was ancient and primal. And right now it demanded to claim her, regardless of what she wanted.

CHAPTER THIRTEEN

Liberty glanced around Bo and Nyx's club, a little surprised by the transformation even though she'd been part of making it happen.

Supernatural people were so freaking weird. Tonight was supposed to be the masquerade ball but because of everything that had happened, the party had been postponed indefinitely—because no one was allowed to hide who they were. Instead, tonight was now the western-themed party, which basically meant everyone was dressed as cowboys and cowgirls.

It was like a bunch of grown-ups—who could also change into various animals or drank blood from people—thought it was hilarious to dress up and act like four-year-olds. A female wolf shifter was currently dancing on a tabletop and swinging a lasso.

"Oh, honey, this is perfect!" Nyx appeared as if out of nowhere and threw an arm around Liberty's shoulders.

Grinning, Liberty looked at her friend who was dressed as a saloon girl in a crimson dress with black ruffles everywhere. "Yeah?"

"Yes! I had no idea how you'd make this work but it looks like the interior of a saloon." Nyx, the half-fae/demigod, practically squealed with delight. "Even though I grew up in another realm I still had access to things from the human realm, including television. I went through this phase when I was about six where I wanted a cowgirl-themed birthday party. Of course I never told my mother because well, I just didn't. But I mentioned it to Bo, and..." She shook her head, looking around, a hint of tears glistening in her eyes. "I love that male," she murmured.

"Well he loves you back." Liberty squeezed Nyx tight and looked out at her handiwork.

She had oil lamps—faux ones—on most of the tables, hay bales and wooden crates to replace a lot of the former seating. The beer bottles were being served from giant bins with cattle horns branded on the front. And any other drink was being served in glass cowboy boots. She'd replaced all the art with replica vintage-looking posters advertising steamboat rides or cattle trail maps and a few 'Wanted' posters featuring Bo, Nyx, Cynara and other employees from the club. Combined with the wagon wheels, wooden barrels, faux barbed wire, rope and other western-themed décor around the place, it had a most definite western feel to it.

"If you want to get your picture taken with Bo," Liberty said, motioning to a big photo booth near one of the bars, "there are four different western themes to choose from."

Nyx squealed again, gave her a smacking kiss on the cheek before rushing off to—who knew where. Most likely to find her mate.

While Liberty had taken charge of a lot of parties before . . . well, in her prior life, she'd never worked with clients who were so laid back about everything. Bo definitely wanted everything done right and basically just wanted Nyx happy, but he didn't micromanage and never complained about how much anything cost. If anything, it was like he wasn't sure that he was spending enough on Nyx.

"I've got an emergency in the kitchen, Liberty." Taylor's panicked voice came over her earpiece, making her nearly jump.

Taylor, one of the Stavros packmates, was one of the managers at Howlers and since the party had moved to Bo's club, she'd agreed to help out over here as a contract employee. Which was good because Liberty had gotten used to coordinating with the female. "I'll be right there," she murmured, turning to make her way around the crowded dance floor where people were attempting some kind of country line dance.

She spotted Rory at the bar talking to purple-haired Cynara—and Liberty's heart rate kicked up like usual. Even though they were half-siblings she could see similarities in the way they talked with their hands. That wasn't even a genetic thing, just something they seemed to have in common. It was adorable, though she didn't think Rory would appreciate her calling him adorable.

Liberty was still reeling from last night. She'd never masturbated in front of anyone before, not even in her "former" life when she'd had normal human friends and human boyfriends. But she'd felt so safe with him, so . . . cherished. The male was almost too perfect to be true. Which scared the heck out of her. She wasn't even sure what she wanted or could handle at this point and she was terrified that by the time she got herself together it would be too late. That Rory would have moved on to greener pastures.

When a female from the Stavros pack joined Rory and Cynara, looking at Rory as if she could eat him up, a sharp spike of jealousy streaked through Liberty's chest. He wasn't flirting or anything and she didn't blame the female for looking at Rory.

But deep down she had to wonder what she could even offer Rory. She was still so damn broken. Frowning, she turned away and pushed through the swinging door to the kitchen and storage area—to find Taylor struggling with a corset-style saloon girl dress.

"What's the emergency?" Liberty asked, setting her clipboard down on one of the industrial counters.

The redhead let out a frustrated growl and swiveled so that her back was to Liberty. "This!"

Laughing, Liberty grasped the ties of the loosened corset and started lacing it up. "This isn't an actual emergency."

"It will be if my boobs pop out while I'm serving food."

"Oh, please. I've seen more naked people from your pack than I ever care to think about." Shifters were so unabashed about their nudity. It was something she wasn't sure she'd ever get used to. She'd actually seen Rory naked when they'd first come back from that Hell realm, but she'd been way too messed up then to appreciate it. She'd barely been able to look at him or his brothers.

"Doesn't mean I like to show off the goods to everyone."

"Fair enough." Liberty pulled the top tight and tied it. "How's this? Too tight?"

"Perfect, thanks." Taylor turned, her vibrant red hair piled on her head in a complicated looking twist. "How do I look?"

"Gorgeous. Now how about you get out there and do some real work?"

Taylor laughed. "All right. I'll go make the rounds, see what we're getting low on."

"Thanks." As Taylor left, Liberty headed for one of the coolers. She'd noticed the first cake—yes, the first—was already devoured. So it was time to bring out another one, a giant chocolatey wagon wheel confection.

When she stepped into one of the walk-in fridges, she shivered slightly. She'd worn a simple black sheath dress with three-quarter length sleeves, turquoise jewelry and cowboy boots. The dress didn't offer much in the way of warmth. She realized how huge the cake was when she saw it on one of the metal shelves. "Gonna need another set of hands," she murmured.

"I can help," a female voice said from behind her, making Liberty nearly jump out of her skin.

She swiveled to find Arya, Drake's mother, standing inside the closed cooler. Holy crap that woman was quiet. Liberty's heart raced in her chest as she looked at the tall, blonde female who was beyond beautiful—and totally terrifying. Liberty had seen her share of predators, more than she wanted, and this female was definitely the scariest. With the exception of maybe her mate, Dragos.

Wearing an elegant dress that wrapped around her like a silky waterfall, Arya could have been a supermodel with that height and those cheekbones. But something in her coffee-colored eyes was . . . God, there was no word for it. When she looked at you, it was as if she saw straight through to your soul, and was maybe thinking about eating you for an appetizer. The thing was, Liberty didn't think the woman did it on purpose, it was just who she was.

Apparently she didn't dress up for themed parties, which didn't surprise Liberty at all. This woman did what she wanted, when she wanted. Liberty cleared her throat. "That's okay. I've got people on staff to help out." She wasn't sure why the woman was even back here. This area was for staff only. Not that she was going to tell Arya that.

Arya tapped her chin thoughtfully, ignoring Liberty's words as she looked around the freezer with apparent disinterest. "I was worshipped as a goddess many, many years ago."

It was such an odd thing to say, though Liberty didn't doubt the female *had* been worshiped. But . . . she wondered why the heck the woman was telling her this.

"I don't mean it as an insult," Arya continued, her gaze flickering so that her dragon looked out at Liberty. "But I doubt you can comprehend how very long ago that was. A few of the real goddesses didn't like that I was being worshipped as a deity." She snorted indelicately.

Everything inside Liberty stilled at the sight of the dragon peering out at her. That was one thing she still hadn't come to terms with. It didn't matter that she was friendly with Drake and Keelin—who she really wished was in town right about now. Dragons weren't like wolves or even half-demons. They were the size of small houses and could shoot fire from their mouths.

"Why are you telling me this?" It seemed a safe enough question for the female who'd cornered her in a freezer. Though the word safe and Arya Petronilla did *not* go hand in hand.

"Because in my long existence, love is the only thing worth anything. Everything else is fleeting. *Everything.* And I see the way that half-demon/wolf male looks at you. He would die for you. I see it clearly in his gaze in a way that moves me. People would die for many things though." Her scary dragon eyes blurred, as if she wasn't seeing Liberty at all for a moment. "But this one would sacrifice everything for you and that's different. Don't doubt him."

Liberty wouldn't pretend to misunderstand, even if she didn't know why this predator was talking to her. "I won't." It was herself that she doubted. Almost on a constant basis. Rory was perfection and she was . . . ugh, she didn't know what she was.

Arya petted her cheek as if she were a child. Even though it was an odd gesture, Liberty figured that to Arya she *was* a child. She also didn't think the dragon was seeing her at all. It was clear why she'd been worshipped. The power rolling off her was palpable, as if the small freezer couldn't contain her. And Liberty was only human. She wondered if supernatural beings had a better sense of her power.

Suddenly Arya gripped Liberty's cheeks. "Open your mouth." Her voice was soft, yet commanding.

Even though she had no freaking idea why this female wanted her to do that, she opened her mouth. Arya did the same and with only inches between them, a soft, white light passed from Arya to Liberty's mouth.

A warmth infused Liberty from the inside out and she smelled . . . spring rain and cinnamon permeating the air—from *her.* Practically frozen in shock as her entire body seemed to sing with new life, she could only blink when Arya pulled back.

Liberty couldn't put into words what had just happened but a deep sense of knowing filled her as she stared into the dragon female's eyes. Shock punched through her as she tried to grasp how different she felt. "I'm immortal now?" Actually asking the question out loud made her feel stupid but whatever Arya had done to her made her feel different. Stronger.

Arya lifted a shoulder. "For the most part. You won't survive a beheading or losing your heart, if that's what you mean, but you'll have a longer lifespan. And you're stronger now. Physically, anyway. Your life essence is already sweet and strong, especially for a human. For anyone really. I find that interesting." Her head tilted to the side a fraction as she watched Liberty with curiosity.

She made Liberty feel like a bug under a microscope with the way she said 'interesting'.

"Why didn't you ask me first?" The question popped out before she could stop herself. Seriously, questioning an insanely powerful being in a small room with only one exit after the female had just given her a gift beyond measure probably wasn't smart.

Arya lifted a blonde eyebrow, a mix of amusement and smugness in her expression. "You wanted to be stronger. I felt it."

She blinked. It was true.

"I can take it back if you'd like." Now she was all smug and knowing.

"No," Liberty said quickly. She wasn't sure about the whole longer lifespan thing, but to be stronger was something she desperately wanted. Rhea had promised to train her but with everything going on, who knew how long that could take. Now she didn't feel so weak. "And thank you."

"Now you can make the decision if you want Rory for himself, and not because he can make you stronger."

Liberty frowned as the female's words sank in, but she wasn't sure she totally understood. "What do you mean?"

Arya's gaze narrowed slightly. "When shifters mate with humans, humans automatically get stronger and have longer lifespans to match their mates. It's a gift from nature."

"Oh." There really was so much about supernaturals she didn't know. She wrapped her arms around herself, surprised she wasn't colder in here than she had been only minutes ago. "I'm grateful for this, but why did you do it?" Because she couldn't imagine the dragon doing this sort of thing all the time. Heck, Liberty could barely wrap her mind around what had just happened.

Arya gave a soft, half-smile. That was when Liberty realized that was all the answer she'd ever get from the woman. Because the answer didn't matter. Arya did it simply because she could. A sort of humming power surrounded the female. "Whatever the reason, thank you."

Arya nodded, regally, every inch the queen Liberty imagined she'd once been. Or for all she knew, still was for her people. "Just don't hurt him," Arya continued. "Half-demons, oddly enough, have much in common with my kind. If you don't want forever, let him go now."

No! The vehement denial formed instantly in her head, but she kept silent. She didn't want to let Rory go, even if she still didn't feel good enough for him. She wondered if it was selfish to want him so much when she knew he could find someone better, someone whole. She might be stronger physically now, but she was still a mess inside. Liberty wasn't sure what to say so she went with, "I could never hurt him."

Which seemed good enough for Arya if her smile was any indication. "Good. Now open the cooler door for me."

She blinked at the command, but did it. Maybe she liked to have doors opened for her or something? Only once she'd opened it did she realize Arya had lifted the huge cake, balancing it with one hand as she exited. "I know where to put this."

Feeling more than a little stunned by everything that had just transpired, she watched in awe as Arya left the kitchen in a flourish, carrying the massive cake in one hand.

Liberty rubbed a hand over her forehead, trying to wrap her mind around what had just happened. She wasn't sure if she was supposed to even tell anyone. Was that against some sort of rules? What would she say anyway, "the scary ancient dragon gifted me with some sort of immortality"? Because that sounded totally sane. She was going to tell Rory at least, but not until they were alone.

She mentally shook herself as Taylor's voice came through her earpiece, asking for help out on the main floor. It was time to get to work. She'd think more about whatever had happened later.

Before she'd taken a step, the kitchen door swung open again.

Ian stepped in, much to her dismay. As Rory's half-brother, she'd hoped they might become friends, but Ian kept her at a very firm distance. She was pretty sure he didn't like her. Or trust her. But she wasn't sure why. Maybe she just disgusted him because she was a weak human who had been used by his kind. He'd been part of her rescue.

That thought made her stomach turn sour. Forcing a smile that she knew came off as fake, she nodded politely at him. "Nice to see you, Ian," she murmured as she plucked her clipboard full of notes from the counter. Belatedly she realized he'd be able to smell her lie because it wasn't actually nice to see him. Annoying shifter senses.

"You got a sec?" His Irish-laced voice was raspier than Rory and Bo's, as if he had a continual sore throat.

He'd never singled her out before. "Oh, uh, sure. Is there a problem out there?"

"It's not about the party." He scrubbed a hand over his espresso-colored hair, his amber eyes flashing with what looked like frustration. "I . . . I'm just gonna say it. Don't break my brother's heart," he snapped.

The words were whiplash harsh, making her take a step back. "I would never hurt Rory."

"Not intentionally you wouldn't, but . . . he's not human, Liberty." She was pretty sure it was the first time he'd ever used her name. "When shifters mate, it's for life."

She knew that both he and Rory were also half-demons and wondered if it was the same for their demon side also.

As if he read her mind, he stepped closer. "Half-demons are territorial and possessive and if you hurt him, he'll never get over you, never move on." There was so much pain and agony in his voice she wondered if he was speaking from personal experience. "He's been rejected by almost everyone in his life, we both have. You can't—" He jerked upright, stared down at her as if she'd grown another head.

"What?"

"You smell."

"Are you freaking kidding me?" She wasn't going to hurt Rory and she wasn't going to listen to Ian right now. Not when she was in charge of this party, and especially after he'd just insulted her. "I don't have time for this," she muttered. When she went to move past him, he grasped her upper arm.

He leaned down and actually sniffed her. "You smell . . . different."

She went to jerk away from him when Rory stepped into the kitchen—and let out a roar of rage before rushing at Ian.

Liberty barely stepped out of the way before he barreled into his brother, slamming him against the ground as if they were playing football.

"Stop it!" she shouted, but they ignored her as they rolled around, punching and kicking—and biting—like complete savages.

Her heart twisted at the sight of Ian slamming a fist across Rory's jaw.

Bo and a few shifters from the Stavros pack raced in, but then stopped and just watched. She raced over to Bo. "Can you stop them?" She cringed at the sound of bone breaking, hoped it wasn't Rory.

Bo's amber eyes flashed once as he shook his head. "No way am I getting in the middle of that. This is good for them, just let them work their anger out. It's been building for a few months."

"But—"

He shook his head and the other shifters just crowded around watching, as if this was entertaining. The thought pissed her off. Watching the male she cared about get hurt wasn't entertainment! Since jumping into the middle of two powerful males fighting was beyond stupid, she frantically searched the kitchen, looking for a way to stop them. The sprayer from the sink wasn't long enough to reach them.

Shoving a male out of the way when she saw what she needed, she snapped up two squirt bottles filled with buttercream icing.

Still keeping a few feet of distance between her and the two insane males, she pressed the release button on both bottles, spraying both of them in a mix of blue and yellow. It took almost a solid thirty seconds before they both stopped punching each other to look up at her—as if she was the crazy one.

Rory's left eye was swelling, his canines were bared and blood trickled from his nose. Ian didn't look any better as he stared up at her, covered in icing.

"What the hell was that for?" Ian demanded.

Rory punched him in the face. "Don't talk to her like that."

When Ian went to hit him back, she held up the bottles. "Stop acting like maniacs! This is your brother's party and look at you two. You're like . . . you're worse than children." And she had no idea what had precipitated this level of violence between them. Building for a few months? What the hell did that mean?

"It's not a party 'til someone gets their nose broken, someone's naked and someone calls the fire department," a male from the crowd said, making everyone laugh.

She'd grown up in the South so the fighting wasn't actually that far out of the realm of normalcy at a party, especially a redneck one, but Rory and Ian had been actually hurting each other.

"Bo, can you make everyone get out?" she asked without turning around.

Moments later the kitchen was empty except for Ian, Rory and her. Both males shoved to their feet, covered in icing and blood. She aimed a hard look at Rory. "What just happened?"

"He had his hand on you and was smelling you." He said it so matter-of-fact, as if that explained everything. As if he hadn't just been trying to kill his brother.

"Why *were* you smelling me?" she asked Ian.

"You smell different, but it's not an excuse," he tacked on, looking at Rory. "I wasn't thinking, I just leaned in, but I wasn't trying to move in on your female."

"I know that. If you had been, you wouldn't be walking." The savage edge to Rory's voice sent a shiver down her spine.

"So smelling me is a bad thing?" she asked.

Rory nodded, his wolf in his gaze when he looked back at her. "No one can scent another male's..." He cleared his throat, trailing off.

"I was being a dick and Rory was right to call me on it. I'm sorry, Liberty." Ian looked perfectly chastised but she remembered everything he'd said to her before Rory had stormed in. How she better not break his brother's heart.

Now wasn't the time to bring all that up though. Not in front of Rory anyway. There was so much about shifters and half-demons and well, the whole supernatural world she still didn't understand. But she'd talk to Ian later. Not about the way she smelled though. That definitely had something to do with what Arya had done to her and she was only going to tell Rory about that for now.

She turned back to Rory. "Are you okay?" she asked softly. She was still stunned by his territorial behavior but found she liked it.

He nodded stiffly, almost as if her question was insulting, but she didn't think he was actually insulted. "I'm fine. These are just a few scratches. Ian and I will clean up ourselves and this," he said, motioning to the icing smeared all over the floor. "I apologize for this. It's not an excuse, but my demon side just took over—my wolf too. I know this party is important to you."

Well yeah, it was important, this was her first real job since returning to the world of the living. But… "You're more important. You're sure you're okay?" She looked him over from head to toe, annoyed with herself for noticing how delicious he looked even with all the buttercream and blood on him.

He'd worn jeans, boots and a button down flannel shirt that he'd rolled up to his elbows, showing off strong, muscular forearms she wanted to trace her fingertips over. When he cleared his throat she realized she'd been staring at him. She also realized he must scent how much she wanted him because his eyes were all raw lust.

Ian just looked away, as if uncomfortable. Oh yeah, she was going to have a talk with him later. Whatever he thought about her, they'd have to work it out because she cared for Rory. And even if she wasn't sure what she could offer him or even how she was going to make it from one day to the next, she knew in the deepest part of herself that her future included Rory.

She refused to accept any other reality.

"Hey, this is good shit," Ian muttered, licking icing off his hand, earning an exasperated nudge from Rory. But it was clear things were okay with the brothers now.

Sighing, Liberty set the half-empty bottles on the counter. As much as she wanted to stay and talk to Rory, she had a job to do. She'd been hired for this party and it was clear he was fine. But as soon as the party was over they were going to find somewhere private to talk.

Maybe more than talk.

CHAPTER FOURTEEN

"You waiting for her to get off work?" Ian asked, sipping his beer next to Rory on a neighboring barstool.

"What do you think?" Rory didn't look at Liberty as she moved around Bo's bar, ordering people to break down different things. He'd already offered to help—half a dozen times—but she'd practically shooed him away. Almost everyone had gone, including Bo and Nyx, but the shifters Liberty had hired for the weeklong parties were still here, as well as some of the club's staff.

"How long are you gonna be pissed at me?" Ian grumbled.

"As long as it takes for me to get the image of you smelling my female out of my head."

"Oh for fuck's sake—"

"I'm not pissed." Not really. It had just jarred him to see his brother touching Liberty. It had brought both his wolf and demon to the surface with a vengeance he hadn't been able to control. He'd never reacted like that, never felt such a loss of control over himself. It probably should have alarmed him, but he knew what it was. He wanted to mate her and any male that got in his way, in the real sense or just perceived, was an enemy.

"So . . . we ever going to talk about the difference in her scent?"

Rory frowned, looked over his shoulder to see Liberty disappear through the kitchen door. He didn't want to talk about it. "Come on, let's start helping." With her out of sight they could actually do some good around here. And the faster everything was cleaned up, the faster they got out of there so he could get her alone.

"I'll take that as a no," Ian muttered.

Good, because Rory wasn't talking to anyone about the change until he talked to Liberty. She'd always had a sweet, enticing scent but something was definitely different about her. He hadn't registered it until after he and Ian had gotten up from their fight. She now smelled like spring rain and cinnamon. It was something natural, coming directly from her, not a perfume.

Considering he'd been obsessed with the female for the last eight months he knew every little change in her scents, when her emotions changed. This, well, he didn't know what to make of it.

"Put us to work," Rory said to Taylor who gave them a wicked grin.

"So glad you boys volunteered. You can take the hay bales outside."

He nodded. "Not a problem."

Liberty came out of the kitchen carrying a bin and frowned when she saw him and Ian lifting bales of hay. She opened her pretty mouth to say something, probably to tell them to stop helping, but Taylor interjected.

"Let them do the grunt work. They deserve it after acting like cubs earlier," she added.

The female was right, but he wanted to help regardless. Anything for Liberty.

Liberty just shook her head, but he saw her grin when she turned toward the bar to start stacking the cowboy shaped glasses into bins.

He tried and failed not to stare at the way her thin dress hugged the curve of her ass perfectly. It was hard not to notice that kind of perfection, especially when it was his. *She* was his. Even if she didn't know it yet. Not fully anyway.

After last night he knew they had a chance at more. She'd trusted him enough to touch herself in front of him, to make herself vulnerable. Tonight he hoped they took it a step further.

The thought of tasting her, bringing her to orgasm with his mouth and tongue—

"Dude, whatever you're thinking about, please stop," Ian muttered, throwing a big bale of hay at him. "I can smell those pheromones."

He caught the hay midair and forced his thoughts on lockdown. For now.

In an hour or so he'd finally be alone again with Liberty. He was counting down the seconds. He knew nothing was a certainty in life, but he was really, really hoping for a replay of the night before. Maybe even more. Tonight he wanted to taste her as she came, not just watch as she stroked herself to orgasm.

* * *

"Are you ready?" Ezra asked into his cell phone. Even though it was close to two in the morning he had on sunglasses as well as a ball cap. He wasn't sure what kind of technological capabilities Finn Stavros's pack had as far as doing facial recognition searches so he wasn't taking a risk he was picked up from a CCTV. Sunglasses would mask his facial features enough and he had a wig under his hat that covered his ears.

It was already risky enough for him to be in the heart of Stavros territory, only blocks from Bo Broussard's club.

But that bastard Finn had decided to let the half-demon continue his wedding celebrations. Which meant he wasn't afraid that someone was in his territory.

Soon enough he would be. Finn would realize how powerful Ezra was, that he was a male to be feared, respected. He was going to strike fear into the heart of the male's pack and he knew exactly how to do it. Slow, create a panic until everyone was afraid, wondering who would be taken next.

"I see headlights," the female said. May, a packless wolf he'd found in Minneapolis at a dead end job. She should be thankful he was giving her this opportunity to be part of his pack. Instead all she tried to do was run away. Until he'd found her weakness. All he had to do was threaten another female in the pack and May fell right in line.

"That's her," he said, referring to a redhead from the Stavros pack. He didn't know her name, but some of his scouts had gotten pictures of her working at Howlers last month and tonight she'd been one of the last people to leave Bo Broussard's club.

She was a target of convenience and he was going to take advantage.

"Just . . . jump in front of her car?" May's voice trembled.

"Yes," he snapped. "She'll stop for you." And if she didn't then May would just have to deal with a few broken bones. Not his problem. The bitch would heal quick enough anyway. He was so tired of her whining. "Everyone else check in."

When three of his men responded via his earpiece, he let out a breath of relief. His men were positioned at various intervals from the club to where May was waiting. In his own SUV, he kept his distance, about a block behind the Stavros female as she turned down a side road of a quiet residential street—a shortcut he knew the packmates sometimes took. They all thought they were being so careful. He'd watched from afar as everyone had been walked to their vehicles at that club. No one was alone—until now.

Just like he'd planned, he watched as May's slender figure darted out into the middle of the road. The vehicle ahead of him jerked to a halt, skidding under the force of the brakes.

He watched as the driver's side door opened and the redhead stepped out. His headlights illuminated her as he approached. His heart rate jumped up. He was only fifty feet away now. She frowned, looking back at him, then she looked forward in May's direction. The redhead's body stiffened and she started to get back into her car.

"Roland, now!" he shouted as he gunned the engine. He knew where each of his males was positioned and Roland was the closest to the female.

Roland lumbered out of the shadows, his gun raised.

Ezra slammed on the brakes, his tires skidding as he threw it into park. He jumped from his SUV. He heard the soft whoosh as the tranquilizer darts left Roland's gun.

The driver's side door was still open. When he reached it he saw the female, in wolf form, unconscious, her clothing shredded around her. He growled in satisfaction, scanning the street to see if anyone had noticed. All the houses were still quiet, but that didn't mean someone hadn't seen from their windows. "Everyone report," he said quietly.

"All good on my end," came one reply, then another said, "Clear here."

Good. He looked back at the reddish-brown wolf draped across the driver's and passenger side seats. He hated that she'd shifted. They wouldn't be able to have as much fun with her now, but she'd still be a good captive. Leaning in, he killed the lights and turned off the ignition.

He'd been prepared for this. "Pick her up," he ordered to Roland. "Take her to the back of my SUV. He didn't bother saying anything to May who still stood in front of the car, shaking. That bitch would just fall in line and get in the vehicle. Without giving her a backward glance he headed to his vehicle and joined Roland at the back.

Ezra slipped on thick gloves then pulled out one of many silver spiked collars he'd had made. The spikes were inward instead of facing outward. He snapped it around the unconscious female's neck. When she came to she wouldn't be able to shift back without killing herself. And anytime she moved she'd be pricked with silver, consistently weakening her. She'd be the perfect hostage.

"Everyone meet back at base," he ordered quietly, slipping into the driver's seat. Roland and May both got in after him and though he sensed May's distress she didn't say a word. Just sat meekly in the backseat, fear rolling off her in waves.

He scented the fear, savored it. It was one of the best scents in the world. It meant the bitch would do anything he said or face the consequences. Keeping his pack in line through fear and rewards was the right way to run a pack. Not like that weak Alpha Finn. The fool had mated a vampire. Now his bloodline would be weak and he'd probably lost the respect of his own pack.

Taking over this territory was the best thing to do. Hell, he was doing Finn's pack a favor. The weak couldn't be allowed to rule.

CHAPTER FIFTEEN

Liberty had been feeling off-kilter ever since her run-in with Arya in that cooler. It was like a new sort of energy hummed through her that she couldn't quite get a handle on. Sitting in the passenger seat of Rory's truck as he drove them from Bo's club, she felt almost too confined by the space. "Can I say something and have you not freak out?" she asked as he steered into her driveway.

"Is it about the way you smell now?" His words were blunt as he put the truck into park.

"Wait, *what*?" Ian had said the same thing to her earlier and she knew what it was—but she wasn't ready to talk about that yet. Not tonight. She needed to get a handle on what had happened before she told someone else. And it hadn't changed who she was. Before he could answer, she continued. "No, I don't want to talk about the way I smell. Unless it's unpleasant?"

His eyes went wolf as he watched her. He shook his head. "Definitely not unpleasant." The sensual note to his voice wrapped around her, made her lightheaded for a moment.

"Well, good," she murmured. They were going to go back to that whole smell thing later, but she needed to get this out before she lost her nerve. "Let me finish before you get annoyed. Okay?"

He nodded once, his mouth a hard, slashing line across his face.

That would have to be good enough. "I want to sleep alone tonight." When he opened his mouth to likely argue, she shook her head. "Not because I don't want you with me. I do, more than anything. That's not what this is about. I just need a night to be by myself. Before . . . I got stuck in that Hell realm, I lived on my own from the time I was seventeen. Spending a night by myself was no big deal. I haven't been alone since you found me. And I need to do that. For me. To know that I can. You and I are moving forward with this relationship and I know we'll be spending a lot of nights together." She felt herself blush, figuring that was an understatement.

His expression lightened a fraction as he nodded. "Yes, we will."

"You deserve someone who has her shit together. I just . . . I need this, Rory. Maybe more than one night," she added. Even if she didn't want to be alone, she knew it was important that she could be alone again. There was no guarantee he would always be around. That she wouldn't end up alone again.

"So, I just need to know I can be alone, in case, you know..." She trailed off, deciding not to finish when he growled. But the truth was if things didn't work out with them, if he got tired of waiting for her to adjust or whatever, she needed to be able to stand on her own two feet.

It was so clear he wanted to argue with her. His jaw clenched tight, but he gave her a sharp nod. "Fine," he gritted out.

She blinked in surprise. "That's it?"

"I can argue if you want." His voice was wry.

"No, I just expected you to, that's all." The man could be so stubborn. Something she really adored about him, even if it drove her a little crazy.

"Well, it's after two now and I plan to be here at sunrise, so . . . I can deal with spending a few hours apart." He sounded smug. "But first I want to check your place though. Do a sweep."

"Sunrise?" she asked as he got out of the vehicle, shutting the door behind him. Gah, that pretty much negated what she wanted to do, but she'd just sleep alone tomorrow. She wouldn't tell him until then.

When he didn't answer she realized he had no intention of doing so. Frustrating male. She followed after him to the front door of her townhome. Once they were inside he shut and locked the door behind them with practiced efficiency, shut off the alarm, reset it, then did his normal sweep.

While he was upstairs she kicked off her boots by the door and headed to the kitchen. After tonight she was exhausted and wanted a glass of wine. A big one. When she was working she didn't drink and the shifters tonight had been in full-on party mode. Which meant she'd been running around nonstop.

At least Bo had closed his club after the party, something he rarely did. But with everything going on, he'd decided to start closing around two or three in the morning for the foreseeable future. His place might be considered neutral but the people who'd bombed Howlers couldn't be trusted to follow that rule. Obviously.

"We're going to have to talk about that whole sunrise thing," she said without turning around when she heard Rory step into the room. If he wanted to, he could be ghost quiet, but she knew he was making enough noise for her sake. "Because I plan to sleep in. Oh, you want anything to drink?" She let out a sound of victory when she found her wine bottle opener buried in a drawer. She needed to hang it on a hook or something.

"Oh, I plan to get my fill of something before I leave," he murmured in a positively wicked voice that had her abandoning her wine bottle and glass.

She turned to face him and a shiver rolled down her spine at the heated look in his eyes. "What's that?" She knew the answer but she wanted to hear him say it. After last night she wanted more of him. While she wasn't sure how much more she'd be comfortable with, she was glad he didn't plan to leave right away.

He stalked across the kitchen to her until they were standing inches apart. His hands were shoved in his jeans pockets, as if he was restraining himself from touching her. The tattoos on his arms were pulled taut along with his muscles. She wanted to reach out and trace her fingers over each tendon and striation.

"I need a taste of *you*." His Scottish accent kicked up just the slightest bit, sending her heart rate into overdrive.

There was something about his accent that made her crazy. Okay, everything about the male made her crazy.

His hands went to her hips and before she realized his intent, he lifted her onto the nearest countertop. Leaning down, he brushed his lips against hers. "Tell me to stop and I will," he whispered, his warm breath skittering over her face.

She inhaled the spicy, masculine scent of him. Her breath hitched as she nodded. She trusted Rory. It was herself she wasn't so sure about. But if she could stay grounded in the present, she thought she'd be okay for whatever he planned. And if she wasn't, she knew he'd stop as soon as she said the word.

The anticipation of the unknown built inside her as he kissed his way along her jawline, little nips more than anything. Her nipples beaded tight against her bra when he pressed his teeth against her earlobe.

He made a growling sound she felt all the way to her core. That deep rumble came from his chest and she loved the possessiveness to it.

When his big hands slid up the outside of her thighs, moving her dress higher, she didn't even think to stop him. On instinct she lifted her hips so that he could shove the hem up and out of his way. She wanted to feel his mouth on her.

She dug her fingers into his shoulders. "When you said taste..." She trailed off, unable to finish the thought. What if he had something else in mind?

He leaned back a fraction to look down at her. "I'm going to bury my face between your legs and I'm not stopping until I taste your come."

The bold, raw words made her inner walls tighten with a need she hadn't felt in a very long time. She had absolutely no response because finding her voice right now? Impossible.

He kept his gaze pinned to hers as he tugged her black thong down her legs and tossed it to the ground.

She could barely hear anything above the rushing of blood in her ears as he pressed his huge hands against her inner thighs, spread them wider. It had been a long time since she'd done this and the fact that it was Rory about to pleasure her? Yes, please. When he knelt down, she couldn't tear her gaze from his dark head as he moved between her legs. It was one of the most erotic things she'd ever seen.

His chest rose and fell erratically as he stared at her pussy. He inhaled deeply, the action making a hint of embarrassment swell inside her. It was so intimate, so raw. Before her life had been ripped away from her, she'd had lovers, but no one like Rory.

Because there was no one like this man.

He was thoughtful, giving, and even if he didn't think he was a good male, she knew the truth of it. He was the most honorable male she'd ever met. She wanted to feel him kissing her more than she wanted anything.

And when his tongue flicked up the length of her slick folds, she forgot everything else. The only thing that mattered now was Rory and his teasing, talented tongue.

She slid her fingers through his hair as he began a sweet, slow rhythm of strokes against her. She rolled her hips into his kisses, urging him to move faster, to do something more. God, she'd forgotten what this was like. To let go like this, to just be free and enjoy herself.

His beard tickled her inner thighs, the sensation adding to her pleasure. She laughed lightly at the feel of it.

He groaned against her. "You taste like heaven," he growled, the rumbling sensation hitting all her nerve endings.

Feeling completely uninhibited, she rolled her hips again, meeting his strokes with her own movements. His tongue was pure wicked talent, sending pleasure out to all her nerve endings as he teased her. Needing release, she started to squeeze her legs around his head, but he placed two big palms against her inner thighs, held tight.

For just a fraction of a moment, the loss of control, the feeling of being held in place made her freeze, until Rory groaned again.

Everything inside her relaxed, then almost immediately all her muscles pulled tight when he focused on her clit. His tongue lashed her sensitive bundle of nerves, making her feel out of control. Her fingers dug into his scalp but he didn't seem to mind.

Reaching between their bodies, he slowly teased her wet entrance, his thick finger barely pushing past her folds.

It wasn't enough. She was so close but needed an extra push.

Holding him tight, she rasped out, "More."

Without pause he slid his thick finger inside her and held it there. He stopped to look up at her, his expression dark, dangerous. Just like the man. "Good?" he rasped out.

Breathing erratically, she nodded.

He pulled his finger out of her slowly, then pushed back in. Slowly. Her inner walls tightened around him and as he continued stroking she closed her eyes and let her head fall back.

It was too much and not enough. As if he sensed what she needed, he sucked on her clit, pushing her over the edge.

Her climax punched through her, sweeping out to all her nerve endings as he continued working her with his finger and mouth. This orgasm was better than last night's because it was Rory touching her, Rory giving her this pleasure.

He tore his mouth from her clit, but kept his finger buried inside her, his hand cupping her mound as he stood between her legs. She looked down at their bodies, the way her legs were spread for him, the way he held her most intimate area as if he owned her.

In a way, he did. He'd completely stolen her heart, even if she wasn't ready to admit it yet. Not to him anyway.

He brushed his mouth over hers, her taste fresh on his lips. The action was primal and erotic. He growled against her lips before pulling back, his jaw tight as he watched her.

She wasn't sure what he planned next so she reached for the button of his jeans. His erection was very clear and she wanted to feel it, to touch more of him. She wanted to see him find pleasure, wanted to see the way he looked when he came.

But he withdrew his hand from her mound and clasped her wrist in place. "Not tonight." His breathing was more erratic than hers and she was the one who'd just come.

She frowned, even as pleasure still lingered in her body, her limbs feeling loose. She didn't feel like she owed him, she just wanted to give him what he'd given her. "But what about you?"

He shook his head, the tendons in his neck pulled tight. "Not yet." He spoke as if he was barely in control of himself.

So she didn't push, even though she really wanted to. And she almost melted at his next words.

"I'm going to go next door and think about you coming against my mouth as I stroke myself off." He pressed a hand against his very clear erection.

"Let me do it," she murmured.

She started to take over again, but he shook his head. "Not yet." His voice was strained, the muscles in his neck corded tight. He looked barely in control so she didn't push.

She wanted to. At least part of her did. But the last thing she wanted to do was start something then have a breakdown in the middle of it if things got too intense. Not because she thought Rory would judge her but because she simply didn't want him to see her like that. She'd made a lot of progress over the last eight months and she was going to listen to her instinct. She wasn't quite ready yet.

But she hoped she soon would be.

He kissed her again, this time a little more savagely. The way he ate at her mouth, like a man starving, took her off guard, but she leaned into it, into him. She clutched onto his shoulders and held tight as his tongue flicked against hers. His hunger was a potent thing, live and wild.

When he pulled back she was breathing hard again.

He stepped back, taking all his warmth with him. “Lock the door behind me and set the alarm.”

She nodded because she couldn’t find her voice. When she slid off the counter she felt exposed, but not vulnerable. Just a little bit wicked, with her dress hiked up to her waist and her pussy bare for him to see.

“You’re gonna kill me.” He groaned, palmed the front of his jeans once, then turned and stalked from the room.

On shaking legs she tugged her dress down then trailed after him. He’d already shut the door and no surprise, he must have used his key to lock it. She set the alarm before collapsing against the door for a moment. Right about now she was starting to regret her idea of sleeping alone. Not because she was afraid of the nightmares. She just wanted to be with Rory.

* * *

Rory looked at the clock on his nightstand. Three o’clock. He hadn’t been gone from Liberty’s very long and he knew she was still up. Or she had been a few minutes ago. Even with the insulation between their places he’d heard her moving around thanks to his extrasensory abilities.

He wished he was with her, had contemplated pushing her a little because he was pretty certain she’d have let him stay. But she needed this space and he had to respect it.

Even if he didn’t like it.

He lifted his hand to his nose, inhaled her sweet scent. Yeah, he never wanted to wash his hand or his mouth again. He could still taste her. If he hadn't already been addicted to her, tonight would have done it for him. He was an absolute goner. Even a few hours apart from her were too much. He'd forgone a shower because he hadn't wanted to wash her scent off—but he had taken care of himself. He'd been too damn hard not to. Calling her again would just get him worked up when he heard her voice, but he had no control where she was concerned.

He snatched his cell phone from his nightstand and called her.

"Hey," she said, picking up on the first ring. "Everything okay?"

"Yeah, I just miss your voice."

"We just saw each other." He swore he could hear her smile.

"We did more than just see each other, sweetheart."

She sucked in a little breath. "Next time you have to let me return the favor," she said in a rush. "That wasn't fair, holding out on me."

The thought of her hand stroking him, or her sucking him—yep, he was hard again. He'd had way too many fantasies about what it would be like to have her mouth on him. Had jerked off like a freaking teenager for months to the thought of her in any state of undress, much less of her actually touching him.

"Are you still there?" she asked quietly.

He cleared his throat. "Yeah, sorry. And yes to what you said. You already in bed?"

"Yes. How about you?"

He could hear the rustling of her sheets, knew exactly how she looked all curled up in her bed. He wished he was there right now. "Yeah, can't sleep though." He tucked a hand behind his head, stretched out on his bed and stared at the ceiling.

"Me neither. It's weird without you here."

No kidding. She wanted the space and he was giving as much as he could. Didn't mean he couldn't talk to her. "Earlier you said you were on your own from the time you were seventeen." Not really a question, but he wanted to know more about her. She'd told him enough about herself over the last eight months so that he knew she was from Alabama, had put herself through college, didn't have any living family and didn't like wearing the color orange. Hell, he'd gone with her to retrieve all the stuff her former landlord had put in storage when she'd been listed as a missing person.

But there were some things he still wanted to know about her. Specifically how she'd ended up in a Hell realm. She'd been very vague on that and he hadn't pushed.

"I don't hear a question in there, but yeah. My mom was an alcoholic and had terrible taste in men. Well, terrible taste in everything really." She laughed, the sound sad more than anything. "To make a long story short, she brought home yet another boyfriend to live with us. Normally she dated—and I use the term dated loosely—morons who were lazy, but harmless. This guy, however, thought he had a right to everything in our trailer, including me. So I packed up what little I had and stayed with various friends during my senior year of high school. I just wanted to finish my degree and get the hell out of that town. I'd already filled out like a hundred applications for scholarships for college and I wasn't going to let her hold me back."

"Hell, Liberty." He'd known she'd put herself through college, but he hadn't imagined all that. The woman amazed him more and more every day.

"That better not be pity I hear in your voice." He could practically see her frowning.

Rory snorted. "Definitely not pity. More like respect."

"Oh..." She cleared her throat almost nervously. "Well, what about you? If I'm sharing, you get to share too, Mr. I-have-more-secrets-than Oak Island."

An unexpected laugh rumbled up from his chest. She had an obsession with the History Channel that he found adorable. "You've got to stop watching that show. It's ridiculous."

"You love that show." She sounded almost affronted.

No, he loved her. "What is it you want to know?"

"Well . . . Ian said something earlier tonight. Before you two started rolling around like lunatics."

He growled low in his throat, imagining any number of things Ian might have said to her. His brother meant well, but Ian was worried about Liberty hurting Rory. Fuck it. If she did, he'd deal with it. Because he wasn't going to be a coward and not fight for his female.

"Don't growl like that. He didn't say anything bad, just, I don't know. That you and he had been . . . rejected by everyone. What did he mean by that? You've always said your mom was amazing."

He sighed, shifted against the sheets. "She was. She was a beta and..." He'd never told Liberty that his mother had been raped by his father, that he hadn't been wanted.

Not really. Not that his mother had ever made him feel that way. But hell, how could she have wanted him? "Look, it's late and—"

"No way, you don't get off that easy. Come on, tell me what your brother meant."

Rory scrubbed a hand over his face. Ian and his big mouth. He made a mental note to kick his brother's ass again. "Okay. You probably don't even remember but you once asked how Ian and I only recently found out about our other siblings."

"I remember. Ian said your father got around."

His jaw tightened. "Yeah, he did. It was the truth, but . . . not all of it. Our father is a monster. And that's a tame description. He raped my mother as well as Ian, Bo and Cynara's. Probably did the same to more females. He doesn't care about the species, he just wanted to procreate as much as he could." Rory had met him once, didn't know where the disgusting male was now. He hoped the monster was back in Hell. He never should have escaped in the first place. One day Rory planned to destroy the male, but it wasn't today so he shoved that thought aside.

"Rory, I'm so sorry."

"No pity, okay?" he asked, mirroring her earlier sentiment.

"That's not pity. I'm just sorry." Her voice was soft, quiet.

He cleared his throat, needing to get all this out now. She deserved to know everything about him anyway. If they were going to be mates—and they damn well were going to be mated one day—he owed it to her to tell her where he came from. "Things are a little different now, but over a hundred years ago a being of mixed blood, *me*, wasn't exactly accepted. My mother's pack didn't know what to do with me. I was considered defective because of my heritage."

"That's bullshit," Liberty snapped, the fire in her voice soothing all his edges.

He half-smiled. "Yeah well, it's the way it was. I was never fully accepted and there was this . . . female I thought I was in love with, and who I thought loved me too. But she only wanted to be with me in secret. She told me it was because of her family, that she needed to break it to them slowly." As if he'd been such a horrible match that they needed time to adjust to the concept.

A familiar wave of self-loathing swept through him as he remembered how he'd been grateful for that female's scraps of affection. How he'd ignored the fact that she showered after every time they had sex, as if she couldn't wait to rid herself of his scent. It had been to hide their relationship from everyone, something he hadn't wanted to admit.

"But she never wanted anything from me other than sex. At a pack meeting her mate-to-be announced their impending mating. That was how I found out. She came to me later that night, wanted to keep screwing me until she got mated. Said that no one had to know, as if I should be happy she still wanted me." He let out a harsh, bitter laugh.

"Rory—"

"No, you don't have to say anything." He didn't want to hear pity or anything else in her voice. He couldn't stand it. "So now you know my pathetic story. Once my mom died I left the pack and haven't looked back."

"Rory, I'm so sorry."

He shut his eyes and tried to shut out the sound of the sympathy in her voice. This is why he didn't share about his past. "It was a long time ago. Listen, I need sleep. I'll see you in the morning." He cut her off, knew he was being a dick, but couldn't stop himself as he ended the call. Talking about all this just brought up all those feelings of insecurity, reminded him how it had been before he'd met his brother Ian. He'd been so alone, so—

Bang, bang, bang!

Sitting up in his bed, he frowned until he realized that was coming from his front door. He was downstairs in seconds. After disarming his security system, he yanked open the door. He scented her before he'd even pulled the door fully open.

Liberty stood there wearing slippers, loose plaid pajama pants and a red T-shirt that stretched across her full breasts. Her hard nipples were perfectly outlined and yep, just like that he was hard again. He was pretty sure he had a problem around her.

"What the hell was that?" she snapped. "You just hang up on me?" Without warning, she lunged at him, pulling him into a tight embrace as she buried her face against his chest.

God, he loved everything about her. His arms went around her as he pulled her close, inhaling her sweet scent. He hadn't thought he needed anyone, but how wrong he'd been. Her comfort soothed the darkest part of him. "I didn't want to talk anymore," he growled.

"You don't get to pick and choose how you open up to me. I want to know *all* of you," she said into his chest, her voice muffled. "And fair warning, if I ever meet that bitch I'm going to punch her in the face."

A startled laugh escaped him as he tugged her inside and shut the door. Liberty was one of the least violent people he'd ever met. Seeing her so fiercely protective of him filled him with warmth.

"I'm not joking," she murmured, pulling back to look up at him. "And I'm going to stay here tonight."

He wanted her to, but he also knew how important it was for her to spend a night on her own. He didn't want to take that from her just because she felt sorry for him. Before he could protest she continued.

"It's already after three and if you plan on showing up at sunrise you'll be waking me up in a few hours. I need my sleep so it's selfish on my part really." She smiled at him, something she didn't do often, and he felt it like a punch to his solar plexus.

"You're a terrible liar, but okay." That was pretty much all he could get out as he lifted her into his arms.

She let out a short yelp of surprise, but wrapped her arms around his neck as he headed for the stairs.

What he'd thought was love before was nothing. To say it paled in comparison wasn't even an apt description. This thing he felt for Liberty was all-consuming. If he lost her, it would be like losing his soul.

CHAPTER SIXTEEN

"We should take the collar off her, force her to change back," Roland growled, staring at the she-wolf in the cage.

The female wolf bared her canines but couldn't do much more than that before she whined in pain. With the silver spikes digging into her neck she couldn't do a damn thing. And even if she escaped the cage she'd never get past the two of them to the only exit of the small room they'd turned into a prison.

Ezra shook his head and lifted a Polaroid camera. "It's almost impossible to make someone shift back." Unless stopped from shifting via drugs, a shifter's wolf side would automatically take over when they were threatened. To try and make her shift back to human would be a waste of everyone's time. Right now they didn't have time—and Ezra didn't like explaining himself. Not to mention Roland already knew this shit. He was a shifter, this wasn't a secret among their kind. Moron.

Roland just grunted, crossed his arms over his massive chest. The male was stupid and strong, the main reasons Ezra had recruited him. Roland thought he was smarter than Ezra was, which meant he was easy to manipulate, and since the fool was very strong, Ezra had extra muscle on his side.

This was the type of male he needed for a takeover of another's territory. Someone easy to control. He had to remind himself of that when he wanted to snarl at the other male.

He snapped a dozen pictures, figured that was enough for what he intended. He smiled when he looked down at the exposed photographs he'd set on the fold-out card table. It was clear the female was in pain in the pictures, which was exactly what he wanted.

He turned one of them over, scrawled a quick message. *Soon this will be you, Rhea.*

The bitch would pay for what she'd done, for killing his brother and for getting the rest of his pack killed. He was going to make her suffer too, make sure she knew he was coming for her. He wanted her to be afraid long before he made his move. Nothing would stop him from getting his revenge.

"Is May ready?" he asked as he collected the photos into a pile.

Roland opened the door to their little prison and dragged the cowering female in. God, she was so annoying. But she'd proven useful.

"You're going to deliver a message to the Stavros mansion," Ezra told her.

Her dark eyes widened as she glanced at the cage. He saw pity in her eyes when she looked at the female. "What kind of message?"

He held out the stack of photographs. "These. You'll drop them off and then leave."

She stilled for a moment before taking the pictures. For just a second he saw hope flare in her eyes. He knew what she was thinking. That she would drop them off and beg the other pack to take her in, to save her. Likely in exchange for information on him.

He took great pleasure in smothering that hope. "And if you try to escape or tell them where we are, you'll regret it." Ezra nodded at Roland once. The male grabbed a vest they'd rigged with explosives from a dark corner of the room. There was also a camera and a listening device on the vest.

She looked at the vest, paled, but didn't fight him or Roland as they slipped it over her head. She'd been such a fighter in the beginning, it was almost a disappointment that she wasn't fighting now. Maybe she'd finally learned her place. He respected her even less for that.

He secured the vest into place with silver locks. "If you try to mess with it, I'll set it off. If you try to tell them anything at all, I'll set it off. If you even look like you're thinking of running, I'll set it off. Got it?"

Trembling with fear, she nodded.

He inhaled deeply, breathing in her terror, reveling in it. "We'll have eyes and ears on you the whole time."

Swallowing hard, she nodded again. "Got it."

"Good. Let's go." They didn't have time to spare. He wanted to deliver the message before sunrise, before anyone realized the little bitch was missing. He'd let the Stavros pack know how powerful he was, how he'd taken one of their own right from under their noses.

Soon that huge mansion and all this territory would be his. So would Rhea, before he killed her. That bitch would beg him to kill her by the time he was done with her.

CHAPTER SEVENTEEN

3 months ago

Rhea grinned down at her screen, smiling at Conall's latest message.

"I thought you hated those things," Taylor said as she strode into the training room.

"What things?" Rhea stood next to a table of blades, looked down at them. "Are you crazy?" She had a freaking collection. What was Taylor talking about?

Taylor rolled her eyes. "Phones."

"Oh. I don't hate them."

"Yeah but you hate texting."

Rhea's phone pinged again and her heart rate increased just the tiniest bit. Up until a few months ago she'd hated texting. She didn't anymore. Not when it was a connection to a certain dragon shifter who'd been consuming her thoughts. "What are you doing here?"

"Chloe said she left one of my hoodies—that she borrowed without asking, I might add—down here. And don't deflect. What's up with you and that phone lately? You've had it attached to you."

She smiled sweetly. "None of your business, Ms. Nosy."

Taylor just lifted an eyebrow, grabbed said hoodie from the table, and headed out, but not before saying, "I'll find out what you're up to."

Rhea just rolled her eyes. Nosy freaking packmates. There was never any privacy around here. As soon as her packmate was gone, she glanced down at her phone again and read his latest text. *It's official, I'm putting in my resignation today.*

She smiled and tapped out a response. *Pretty sure you can't resign as Alpha.*

Pretty sure I can. I make the rules.

She had a brief flash, wondering what he would be like in bed, if he'd be Alpha twenty-four-seven or if he'd be relaxed, fun. She swallowed hard, fought the heat rising in her cheeks even though no one could see her. Everyone was either out on patrol or eating dinner right now. It was why she'd come down to the training room; she'd known she'd have privacy. *What would you do if you weren't Alpha?*

Not deal with whiny children all day, every day. She could actually envision his annoyed expression and the image made her smile.

Delegate. Or hide.

They just find me.

She typed, *then come down to Biloxi, hide out with me,* but didn't send it. Her fingers froze on her phone. She hadn't meant to type it. Even if she did mean it. Too many emotions warred inside her. She was playing a dangerous game. She quickly deleted the message then typed, *sorry you're having such a rough week.*

Thanks. How's pack life?

Same old, same old. I've gotta run, pack thing. Call you later? She felt bad lying, but right now she needed space, even from texting with Conall. She needed time to get her head on straight.

Rhea didn't want a mate. Didn't want a relationship. She should put a stop to all her communications with Conall. Or at least limit them.

But even the thought of that made her wolf claw at her insides, telling her to shut the hell up, that that was never happening. She rolled her shoulders but it did nothing to ease the mounting tension inside her.

Space. That was all she needed. A good, long run then maybe a sparring session with someone would help get her head straightened out. It would have to. Because she was never, ever going to have a relationship with Conall. She just needed to remind herself of that.

* * *

Present day

Rhea knocked on Conall's door with more force than necessary. After they'd visited that bar in Pass Christian—and come up with nothing—he'd flown off without her. He'd told her he'd check in with Finn and would see her later. The way he'd said later had sounded a lot like *never.* Which freaked her out way too much.

After she'd checked in with Finn—and they'd confirmed the sketches from Gray matched two of the missing female wolves from their file—her Alpha had told her to get some downtime in case he needed her soon. So she'd skipped the party at Bo's club, which wasn't a disappointment since she wasn't in a freaking party mood anyway. Right now, she wanted to punch stuff.

Unfortunately sleep or even just rest had been elusive the last few hours. She and Conall had never hashed anything out and he hadn't even wanted to talk to her. He'd just completely shut down on her and she absolutely couldn't handle it. Now he wasn't even returning her texts.

She should let it go, let *him* go. That was what she kept telling herself, but her wolf was having none of it. The bitch was clawing her up, telling her to make this shit right.

Only, she didn't know how to make it right. Coming here would probably make things worse but . . . she *had* to see him.

A clawing, growing, obsessive hunger was making her beyond irrational right now. She was even contemplating kicking his damn door in when he yanked it open.

"I didn't return your texts for a reason," he snapped, crossing his arms over his chest. He had on loose pants—and nothing else. His gray eyes had shifted to a bright silver and every muscle in his body was pulled taut. And damn it, she wanted to trace her fingers over every inch of the male.

"I know, I thought maybe we could talk." And just maybe she could explain to him why they couldn't mate. She just . . . hell, looking at him now she was having a really hard time forcing the words out for a second time.

"Talk about what? You don't want me as a mate, fine. We're done." He started to shut the door, but she shoved at it with her boot and stomped into the foyer.

"You're being a dick!"

He lifted a shoulder, his eyes cold.

"So because I won't mate you, we can't even be friends? You won't even let me explain myself!" She shouted the last part, seriously wanting to pummel him.

"I don't want to be your fucking friend, Rhea," he growled, stepping closer. "I thought that was perfectly clear." A bright orange and gold fire flickered all around them, taking her off guard for a moment.

She didn't feel any heat and it wasn't burning anything, but it was very real.

"I never wanted to hurt you," she whispered. Even thinking of him injured shredded her. "I just . . . the thought of getting you killed destroys me."

Something flickered in his gaze before the coldness returned. "I've lived a long damn time. If I die, I die. You think I don't have the same fear for *you*? That I'm not terrified I could get you killed too?"

"But you're a dragon! And an *Alpha*." She'd seen him fight and the male was a terrifyingly beautiful warrior when in action. He made everything look so easy where she fought tooth and nail in every scrap she'd ever been part of. "I'm the weak link! If someone wants to hurt you, they'll target me. You have to know that."

He glared right back at her. "You're one of the strongest warriors I've ever met! You're not weak. Not even close. The first time I saw you go into battle, you killed a dragon. So take your bullshit argument and get the hell out of my house."

No! She didn't want to leave, didn't want to be apart from him. Right now she felt as if she was being ripped apart inside. Her head was telling her one thing, but her heart agreed with him. The worst of her anger faded, leaving a sickening fear that she'd ruined everything with him. That he wouldn't forgive her. She had to explain, no matter how insecure it made her feel. "I wasn't strong enough before. I . . . It was my fault Damien was murdered. If I'd been strong enough I could have been his partner, fought back harder with him."

Conall's expression softened a fraction, but not by much. "It wasn't your fault. It was never your fault. A psycho killed him and hurt you. That's not on you. Never was. Even if you'd been trained back then, there's no guarantee you'd have been able to save him. There are no damn guarantees in this life, something you know more than most, and it's why you shouldn't fight this thing between us. The life we live is hard and full of risks. I'm not a coward and I never thought you were, until now."

His words made her planned arguments freeze on her tongue. He turned away from her, headed for the stairs, his fire flaring even brighter around the entrance. Now she felt the warmth, but it wasn't hot, creating a circle around her.

When she took a step after him the fire parted for her, flickering around her. "Conall—"

"Shut the door on your way out," he said without looking at her.

She balled her hands into fists at her sides, her claws pricking at her palms. His dismissive tone was beyond pissing her off, even if she'd brought it on herself. She started to respond when an unfamiliar scent tickled her nose. "What is that sweet . . . caramel and cotton candy smell?" It was a cheap perfume, that much her wolf senses told her. A punch of jealousy like she'd never experienced swept through her. "Have you had a female here?" She didn't care if she was acting totally nuts. Her wolf was not in control right now—and Rhea was happy to let her leash completely slip.

He turned on the stairs, his wicked mouth curving up into an almost smug expression. "So what if I have? You don't want me."

Without thinking she reached for the nearest thing she could find on the foyer table, a small bowl filled with seashell and starfish-shaped potpourri that smelled like coconut and the ocean. Feeling crazy and not caring, she threw it at him.

He ducked, moving with the speed and grace of a fifteen-hundred-year old predator as it smashed against the wall near the stairs behind him. Potpourri rained down the carpeted steps. "You asshole." She growled it, her wolf snapping at her.

His whole body tensed and his gaze bored into hers. "You don't like the thought of me with someone else?" His words were harsh, demanding as he stalked down the stairs toward her.

She was fuming. "You still haven't answered my question." And damn it, she needed an answer. Her chest constricted at the thought of him touching someone else, of someone touching what was *hers.* She could barely see straight for the rage that created inside her.

He paused, his eyes glowing bright as he moved even closer. Only a few feet separated them now. Power rolled off him in potent waves, his dragon's fire covering every surface. She knew that wasn't his mating manifestation so she didn't know why he was doing it. "There was a female in my house earlier."

Pure reflex had Rhea striking out at him with her fist but he grabbed her wrist in a tight, unforgiving grip. She let out an angry cry, trying to strike out again with her other hand, but he grabbed that wrist too. Before she realized it he had her pinned back against the front door, her wrists above her head. His strength was incredible, yet he wasn't hurting her.

If she really fought she knew she could escape, but . . . she didn't want to. She wanted to wrap her legs around him, for him to sink himself deep inside her. Damn it, she just wanted to give into what her heart wanted, to be *selfish,* to take the male she needed more than her next breath.

"Why do you care if someone was in my house?" he snarled, getting right up in her face.

"Because you're mine!" The words shocked her but she knew they were true. Her wolf was in her voice and she knew her beast was definitely in her eyes. Right now she wanted to crawl out of her skin, to hunt down any female who'd dared to—

A smug, wicked smile spread across his face, as if he'd just won something. He rolled his hips against her, his hard erection pressing into her lower abdomen. She moaned at the feel, rolled her hips against his, even as she wanted to claw his eyes out for letting someone else touch him.

"You're smelling the human cleaning lady," he murmured, his gaze dark, hungry. "She was here today while I was out with *you*. I've never even seen her and I've never touched another female since I met you."

The relief that spread through her was so potent she would have lost her footing if he hadn't been holding her in place. She'd never imagined she could be so jealous, so territorial, so freaking crazy. This was not her MO. Even with her former betrothed she'd never felt like this. She'd been more than satisfied to take a passive role back then, to stay home while he took on that warrior role. Not now. She could never be anything other than Conall's partner in every sense, and would never share him.

"You make me insane," she breathed out, her gaze falling to his beautiful, full mouth. She should be pissed that he'd manipulated her into saying what he wanted, but she was just relieved that the truth was out there. She wanted to nip at his bottom lip, claim what was hers.

"Welcome to my world. I've been fucking nuts since the day we met." The fire surrounding them barely flickered now as the bright glow of his mating manifestation took over, illuminating everything star bright. The glow was so different from his fire, seeming to emanate from his every pore.

She wanted to bathe in that light. Naked. "Conall..." Rhea didn't know what else to say. She couldn't give him up. No matter how great a risk it was to him, she couldn't walk away. It would destroy her. "I'm too selfish to let you go," she whispered, barely able to get the words out.

He stared down at her, his chest rising and falling erratically, his dragon peering back at her with a clarity she'd never seen before. She'd seen him in animal form before and seen the dragon in his eyes when he was human, but this was different. It was as if he could see straight through to her soul. "Good," he growled, more animal than man. "I was never going to let you walk out that door tonight. And I will *never* let you go. You're mine, Rhea."

Swallowing hard, she nodded. "I am. And you're mine." Because she was apparently way more territorial and possessive than she'd ever imagined. The mating heat was no joke. It was a thousand times more powerful than her will. She felt like a fool for trying to fight it, for trying to fight what she had with this male. He was right. Their lives were dangerous and often cut short. Denying them this incredible link in a misguided effort to keep him safe was unrealistic.

His eyes flared bright. "I'm claiming you now." Not a question.

She nodded, breathing hard. Her nipples pebbled tight against her tank bra and—her clothes burned away as that brilliant fire swept over her, but didn't actually touch her skin. The material simply disintegrated, there wasn't even ash left behind. Surprise ricocheted through her, but she had no time to dwell on it as a rush of heat built deep inside her.

"Mine." He crushed his mouth to hers, still keeping her wrists pinned up against the door.

She arched into him, needing to feel more of him as he devoured her mouth with his. His body was an inferno against hers. The feel of his bare chest against hers sent a shiver of hunger spiraling through her. She'd never thought she'd like the feeling of being dominated but the way he held her was insanely hot.

With his free hand he reached between their bodies, cupped her bare mound. When he slid a finger inside her, he growled against her mouth, pulled back a fraction. "You're soaked."

She nodded, barely able to catch her breath. Her body was primed, she was desperate for him. It had been so damn long since she'd been with anyone, but this was the mate of her heart. She wasn't settling for Conall, not like so many years before with her betrothed. This male wanted her for who she was, all of her. And she wanted all of him, to hell with the consequences.

"Did arguing with me get you hot?" His words were a low, seductive murmur.

"*You* get me hot." She rolled her hips insistently, needing more than a finger. "And yeah ,the arguing got me turned on. Come on, more," she demanded.

His grin was pure wicked, his bright silver eyes similar to the mating glow he was throwing off. "I should make you suffer a little longer." He slid another finger inside her slickness. "But I can't wait." He withdrew his fingers but instead of stripping off his pants he fell to his knees.

"I don't need—" Pleasure punched through her as he sucked on her clit.

The male didn't even work up to it, just went straight for the sweet spot. She slid her fingers through his hair, groaned out his name as he flicked his tongue against her sensitive bundle of nerves with enough pressure to have her ready to come in seconds.

He slid two fingers back inside her, his movements surprisingly gentle for the hunger she felt pouring off him.

He moaned against her, the reverberation setting her off with a jolt. Her inner walls clenched around his fingers with the shock of her orgasm, milking him as her climax surged through her.

Afraid she'd claw his head, she slammed her hands back against the door as she rode through the wave of her first orgasm. And she knew this was just her first of the night. When shifters mated, it was wild and fierce, for days—weeks.

Before she'd finished coming down from her high he had her pinned against the door, his expression raw and a little feral. "I need you." His voice was raspy, harsh.

She'd known he was an Alpha but he'd been pretty laid back with her until now. She hadn't realized how much she craved this kind of take-charge bed partner until now. Nodding, she wrapped her legs around him, wanting more of him.

He encircled her with his arms, held her close as he brushed his lips over hers. She was aware of them moving but didn't care where he was taking them as long as he didn't let her go.

When he stopped in what looked like a living room, he seemed to take great effort to tear his mouth from hers. He set her up against the back of a couch, her butt resting on the edge with her legs still tight around him.

She wondered why he hadn't moved to the front of the couch, but maybe he wanted to bend her over the back of it. The image that brought up sent another rush of heat between her legs.

"My dragon recognized you as my mate long before I wanted to admit it. But I need you to know I love everything about you. You make me crazy but you're more than worth the wait. I know I said it, but for the record, I haven't looked at or touched another female since that day I saw you at Bo's club—staring me down like I was an enemy combatant."

Pleasure rolled over her at his words. She remembered that day very well. He and his sister had shown up out of the blue, claiming to be related to Drake. "You barely looked at me that day," she murmured.

His eyes were like liquid fire as he watched her. "I looked, all right."

"I might have noticed you too," she whispered, a smile pulling at her mouth. Had she ever. Her attraction to him had been unwelcome so she'd locked it down, hadn't even admitted to herself how much she loved the male until—tonight. Now there was no going back. He'd said he was claiming her and she knew what that meant. There wouldn't be any more barriers between them. "I love you, Conall. And I—"

Her words were lost as his control apparently snapped, his mouth fusing to hers again. For a brief moment she felt a flicker of his fire shimmer around them and then it was all skin to skin.

She felt his hard erection against her lower abdomen, automatically reached between their bodies and grasped him tight. She'd been fantasizing about this for way too long. Though she didn't want to lose any contact with him, she had to pull back just a bit so she could see all of him.

With her legs still wrapped around his hips, she looked down at his thick cock, jutting up between them. She stroked him once, twice—

His hand covered hers, stopping her strokes. "We do this my way." Back was the feral male from seconds before.

She wanted to swat his hand away, to take over, but the need in his gaze stopped her. She could be difficult and stubborn, she knew that. They wouldn't always see eye to eye, but this male completely owned her. Right now, during their mating, she would gladly give him whatever he wanted.

His hands tightened on her hips and he turned her around, bending her over the back of the buttery-smooth couch. "Look at us." A soft command.

That was when she saw the long, gold-gilded mirror propped up in one corner. She was just glad the thick cream-colored drapes were shut. No one needed a show of what they were doing and the light rolling off him would highlight them for anyone on the beach or ocean to see.

The thought of watching them do this, however, was erotic. She was average height for a woman and he completely dwarfed her, his broad shoulders seeming even wider as he stood behind her. Everything about him was huge.

She kept her gaze pinned to his as his hand slid down her spine, cupped her ass for just a moment before he teased her slick folds from behind. No surprise she was still wet for him. That wasn't changing anytime soon.

Not when he was in the same room, completely naked, pinning her against the couch. Now that she'd let go of her guilt, she fully embraced everything about this male, about what they had together. What they *would* have. She'd been fighting it for too long.

His eyes closed briefly as he moved two fingers in and out of her. She tightened around him, her body aching. What was he waiting for? She hummed with energy and felt the same thing emanating from him. She was on a blade's edge right now, needing release again in the worst way possible. Her first orgasm had barely taken the edge off.

When his eyes snapped open, his gaze colliding with hers in the mirror, another jolt went through her. This was her male. *Hers.* She was never letting him go.

He grabbed her hips and positioned himself between her legs, his thick cock teasing her entrance. Her inner walls convulsed, desperate to be filled.

When he thrust hard, groaning, "Mine," she felt that word all the way to her core. More than the word, but the intent—the absolute claiming. She'd always belonged to a pack but this was different on every level.

She was his.

He cupped her breasts, the sight of his tanned hands against her light brown skin making her shiver as much as the way he teased her already hard nipples. As he thrust into her, he tweaked the sensitive buds, sending shock-waves of pleasure to her already sensitized nerves.

She was close to climaxing again, just the feel of him inside her, taking her, was pushing her to that edge faster than she'd imagined.

But something was missing, something—

With a savage growl his canines descended and he struck, biting down where her neck and shoulder met. She expected pain, but only pleasure shot through her. All the muscles in her body pulled taut as the first wave of her climax exploded through her, rippling out to all her nerve endings like a tsunami. His claiming ignited a fire inside her.

He growled against her neck as he came inside her, thrusting into her with no control.

"Conall," she cried out as her inner walls convulsed around him. She reached up and back and wrapped her hand around the back of his head as he nuzzled her neck, still moving inside her.

Her orgasm finally started to ebb and when he lifted his head, she met his bright gaze in the mirror again. The glowing was gone since they were mated and she realized she was going to miss it.

Wordlessly he pulled out of her and turned her to face him. Immediately she missed the feel of him inside her.

"I feel like my life started the moment I met you," he murmured, brushing his lips over hers in such a sweet, tender gesture that her toes curled. "Which is insane considering how old I am. But you make everything better, brighter."

She slid her hands up his chest and linked her fingers behind his neck. A sense of peace slid through her, invading every inch of her soul. "I feel exactly the same way. You're mine now and I'm not letting you go."

He scooped her up in his arms and a thrill shot through her at the effortless show of strength—then she froze when a loud banging came from the front of the house.

Bang, bang, bang. On it continued, the knocking incessant and aggravating.

Conall growled, baring his canines as if ready to attack. She felt the feral dragon rippling under the surface, felt the exact same way right now.

"Someone better be dead," she muttered.

"I can arrange that." By his dark expression, she didn't think he was kidding.

CHAPTER EIGHTEEN

Conall scented the male before he jerked open the door, wanted to slam his fist right through the guy's face, but restrained himself. For Rhea.

Who was standing half-behind him with a blanket wrapped around her lithe body. Yeah, probably shouldn't have burned all her clothes off. But getting her naked had been his only priority before. Now *keeping* her naked was a very big priority.

And Solon was standing in his way simply by being here. "What the hell do you want?" he growled at the male.

Solon bared his canines, then froze, scented the air as he looked between Conall and Rhea. "Whoa. Congrats guys," he said, thankfully keeping his distance from Rhea.

Right now Conall couldn't deal with another male touching his female. Not even as a friendly, congratulatory hug. Hell, he could barely deal with the guy looking at Rhea. Once his mating craze wore off he wouldn't be so possessive. Supposedly. That was what he'd been told anyway. He wasn't so sure about that for how he felt at the moment.

"Thanks," Rhea murmured, sliding closer to Conall, wrapping an arm tight around him.

He loved the feel of her touching him, holding him. "You're interrupting my mate and me. Now tell us what you want or get the fuck out of here." Conall knew he was being a dick, but he didn't care. He and Rhea had just mated, he wanted her all to himself for a very, very long time. His dragon was old and possessive and nothing else was a concern.

Solon seemed to understand though. "This is the worst time possible, clearly, but . . . Taylor's missing."

"What?" Rhea straightened next to him, but didn't move away. A thin thread of panic rolled off her. "Are you sure? She wouldn't take any chances with her safety."

"We're sure. She left Bo's last night—after being escorted to her vehicle—but never made it back to the compound. We found her vehicle on a side street near our home. The remains of her shredded clothes were there. Keys were in the ignition and the scent of other wolves were around her car. Faint, but I picked them up." His expression was grim.

"How long—"

"A couple hours ago is the best we can guess from the time she left." He cursed, his expression dark. "This shouldn't have happened. It was a ten minute drive in the heart of *our* territory."

"What's Finn doing?" Conall asked.

"He's already started a grid search and all the trackers are out except you. He sent me here to get you when you didn't answer your phone."

"I . . . crap, I didn't even bring it inside with me." Self-recrimination was in Rhea's voice and on her face.

"You couldn't have stopped this," Conall snapped out. She didn't need to carry guilt for anything else.

"I know." She looked up at him, her expression worried. "Will you track with me?"

He nodded once. She didn't even have to ask, but he was glad she had. They were a team now. "We'll be out in a minute," Conall said, slamming the door in Solon's face.

Rhea stared at him wide-eyed. "That was rude."

He shrugged. "You don't have enough clothes on right now. I don't want anyone seeing you."

"I don't have any clothes at all," she said. "You burned them off me."

"I've got some stuff upstairs. All new. For you." He'd bought a bunch of stuff on the chance this very thing happened.

She blinked in surprise, already heading for the stairs. "Thanks."

"Last door on the left," he said. He hurried up with her, knowing they needed to get to her Alpha's home. Though now that they were mated… "Are you going to move back to Montana with me?" he blurted as they stepped through his bedroom door. "Never mind, we'll talk about it later." He stepped to the walk-in closet, opened the door. He shouldn't have asked now.

When she didn't respond, he turned to find her staring at him with something that looked a lot like awe. "What?"

In response, she turned around and dropped her sheet. She lifted the wild mass of tight, corkscrew curls at the base of neck. That was when he saw the small, tattoo-like symbol in between her shoulder blades. A bright silver flame was etched on her skin. Or more like *in* her skin, if what he was seeing was what he thought it was. "My brother has one of these," he murmured, stepping closer, running his finger over it in awe himself. He knew they needed to leave, but this was damn important. "It's rare, right?"

As far as he knew when wolf shifters got mated, in the case of true mates, a bonding symbol appeared on their bodies. With dragons they were linked for life but there was no outward physical manifestation—unless their true mate was a wolf shifter. He liked that his symbol marked her as much as his scent now did.

"Yes." Her voice was raspy, unsteady, when she turned around to face him. Tears glittered in her amber eyes. "Yours is a wolf that looks like me. What's mine?"

He tugged her into his arms. "A silver flame."

She squeezed him tight. "I have so much I want to say to you but we need to go. But know that I'll go wherever you are. We'll move to Montana as soon as this mess is figured out. I go where you go no matter what."

He kissed her hard and fast. Her answer soothed his jagged edges. He'd go anywhere she was too, and if that meant leaving his position as Alpha, he'd do it. But they'd talk about the future later.

For now, one of her packmates was missing and they needed to find her.

* * *

Finn was tense as he neared the compound.

"They're keeping the woman at a distance," Gabriel said quietly, even though Finn already knew it.

He'd just received a call from his mate, Lyra, that a female who claimed to know where Taylor was being held, was at the front gate of the compound—and said female was wearing a vest of explosives.

It didn't matter that his mate and packmates were all strong enough to withstand almost anything, he wasn't close enough to his mate. Or to his daughter—who was securely locked inside the mansion, well past the actual grounds. But he needed to be close to both Lyra and Vega right now, to see with his own eyes they were okay. As an Alpha he had a responsibility to his pack, but his mate and daughter were his number one priority.

Always.

The fact that they were both ridiculously strong didn't matter to his over protective wolf.

"Rhea's on her way with Conall," Gabriel said after glancing at an incoming text. "Solon said they're on the way."

"Conall doesn't need to come." Finn might have made a pact with the male's clan, but this was a wolf problem and another Alpha in the mix right now wasn't what he wanted. He needed to take care of this without outside interference. His pack had already started scouring the city for any trace of Taylor and then Finn was going to destroy whoever had dared to take one of his own. Hopefully the female at the mansion had something he could use.

"They're mated according to Solon so you know as well as I do Conall will be glued to Rhea . . . forever."

Surprise jolted through Finn. He'd known that this was a possibility between them. Hell, a probability, but he hadn't thought it would happen so quickly. Not with the pushback Rhea had been giving the male. Now Rhea's loyalty would always be to her mate and if he was a betting wolf, she'd be leaving for Montana soon. "Fucking dragons stealing our wolves," he muttered. First Victoria and now Rhea. His wolf side was agitated, but he was happy for his packmates.

"I see her." Gabriel straightened as Finn turned onto their street. Over the last couple years he'd bought up homes in the historic area so that his pack owned everything for miles, spanning out over multiple streets in the sprawling neighborhood.

In case a situation like this ever presented itself. The last thing he needed was nosy human neighbors calling human law enforcement because they saw or heard something strange. Like a freaking explosion before their morning coffee.

He threw the SUV into park and jumped out, Gabriel not far behind. A woman a little over five feet stood in the middle of the street about twenty feet back from the gated entrance of his pack's compound. The mansion was on a couple acres so even with the explosive vest he could see, she wouldn't do much damage to the structure of his place. On the other side of the street, a stately home with an immaculate lawn was quiet, though he scented at least a dozen of his packmates nearby, hiding in the shadows. Everyone should be far back enough to be out of range, though if the vest was rigged with silver it would burn like a bitch if anyone was hit with shrapnel.

The abject terror rolling off the female was so potent he could taste it in the air. She stood there, trembling, a bundle of something in her hands.

Photographs, he realized, as he jogged toward her. "Stay twenty feet behind me," he murmured to Gabriel.

Even though Finn sensed his Guardian's annoyance at the order, Gabriel did as commanded without question and fell behind him.

Finn stopped about thirty feet from the woman. Daylight would be breaking soon. He wished he knew that Lyra was safely inside, especially with the sun rising soon but he had to lock down all thoughts of his mate as he stared at this stranger. If he got careless or distracted, his people could get hurt.

"Who are you?" He kept his voice low. It was clear she was already terrified. Adding to that wouldn't help the situation.

"My name is . . . May." Her voice was hoarse, her words stilted. She spoke softly but he could still hear her with his supernatural senses. "He . . . he, wanted me to drop this off to you. He's watching and listening." She tapped her vest and though he couldn't see, Finn figured there was some sort of video capability.

"He? Would that be Ezra Meyer?" He kept his gaze tight on her face as he asked. The fear she exuded would make it difficult to scent anything else, even a lie.

But her expression gave her away. Even from thirty feet he saw the way her eyes dilated. She swallowed hard. "I don't know that name."

Yeah, she was definitely lying. "Okay. Leave what he brought for me and you can go."

She shook her head. "I... I..." She cleared her throat, trying to push past her stuttering. "I can't. He said you had to take it from me personally."

Finn could have analyzed the situation to death. Ezra likely wanted him to get close to the female so he could injure Finn. But what the male didn't know, or likely didn't, was that Finn was incredibly fast.

Instead of debating his options, he went with his gut and using a burst of supernatural speed and the natural gift he had as an Alpha, he was at her side in milliseconds, grabbing the bundle and back where he stood before she'd blinked.

She stared at him with huge brown eyes when she realized she no longer held the pictures. Yeah, he was *that* fast.

He looked down at the handful of Polaroids, his wolf clawing and snarling as he saw the images of Taylor in wolf form. She was in a cage and a spiked collar, most definitely silver, was secured around her neck, the spikes inward, digging into her.

That sick bastard.

Finn shoved his wolf back as he flipped through the pictures. When he saw a flash of writing on the back of one, he flipped them all over. The first message made him see red. *Soon this will be you, Rhea.*

So this was definitely personal.

Another message made him pause. The handwriting was different, smaller, more feminine if he had to guess. *Thirty minutes north, rural cabins, old campsite, occupied by almost one hundred wolves, deep in the woods. Females aren't there willingly. Please help us.* A crude map was drawn as well as a few roads listed. He'd need to look at a map but he could guess the area. No way could he narrow down the location exactly. Not until he looked at Google Earth and let Elana do her magic.

Still . . . He looked up at the female. Her eyes were still wide as she watched him. "Anything else?" he asked.

"He said I had to leave and that if anyone tries to follow me, he'll kill me." She whispered the last few words, and even though all he scented was her fear, he believed her.

He was also pretty sure she'd given him the message with the map. It could be a trap by Ezra, but if so it was stupid because it gave him a layout. Finn could send an aerial scout to see if this map lined up with Ezra's location—once he found it. And find it, he would. If this was from the female, she'd taken a great risk by giving it to him.

He kept his expression neutral. "You're free to go, then." Complete and total bullshit as someone would be following her. "And Ezra, if you're listening, I'm going to enjoy ripping your heart out."

The female took a step backward as an explosion of heat ripped through the air. Finn turned, shifting midair as he dove back toward Gabriel—who'd also shifted.

As his paws hit the concrete, he turned to see what had once been the scared female. A hand lay on the sidewalk. Body parts as well as shrapnel arched out in a giant circle around where she'd once stood.

The rage he'd been holding at bay released in an angry howl. Moments later a chorus of howls joined in from all directions.

CHAPTER NINETEEN

"Why did you kill her?" Roland demanded, looking at the screen on Ezra's hand-held monitor.

They were walking across the expanse of the property he'd secured—not in his name, but one of his holdings. Fallen leaves crunched under his boots. "I always planned to kill her." Which was technically the truth, though he hadn't planned to kill her today. Ezra had intended to keep her around for a while, feed off her fear, but the way Finn Stavros had disrespected him had pissed him off. Now May's death was on the Alpha's head.

He'd needed to show that Alpha he was in charge. Though he'd never seen a wolf move quite so fast as when he'd taken those photos from May.

Ezra disregarded that, however. He would take care of Finn soon enough. Pumping that male full of enough silver would do the job. For now his focus was on the breakdown of the Stavros pack, of decimating the pack's morale.

This war was a psychological one as much as a physical one. He needed the pack to be afraid before his own pack attacked. Breaking them down like this would weaken them. And the note he'd left for Rhea was icing on the cake. Her pack would blame her for this. Maybe not at first, but after a while they'd start to grumble that they were being targeted because of her.

Because with each Stavros wolf he took, he planned to leave a similar message directed at Rhea.

That bitch was going to suffer in more ways than one, and adding to her guilt by hurting her packmates was brilliant. He'd break her down mentally then kill her.

He was a very patient male and he'd waited a long time for his revenge. He intended to savor it.

"But May was easy to keep in line," Roland snarled.

Without thinking he struck out, wrapping his hand around the male's throat. "Too bad. We have a mission to worry about. Keep focused." Or else, was the silent threat. He didn't need to say it.

Roland nodded and when Ezra let go, he sucked in a deep breath, his wolf flashing in his eyes.

Ezra snarled and the male bared his neck in an act of submission. Good. "Go check the perimeter, make sure everyone's staying vigilant." Because now wasn't the time to let their guard down.

Roland nodded, his expression dark as he turned on his heel. Ezra watched him leave, wondering if he'd allowed the male too much leeway. Looking around the land, he saw that everything and everyone appeared to be in place.

He'd purchased a spread of property that had once been a campsite. Older cabins spread out over a couple acres, half of them in disrepair, but they were on a well system and they didn't need electricity. They had it, of course, but if necessary he and his pack could live without it.

Even though it was late fall the trees thick with leaves in the forest provided enough decent aerial cover. And he'd added mesh, camouflage netting throughout the canopy of trees for miles, giving them extra cover from prying satellites. Not that he thought Finn had that kind of capability but just in case it was a good idea. Besides, the human government could be spying on him too for all he knew. He liked to cover all his bases.

He spotted various shifters on patrol, all armed and ready for an attack. Good. If the Stavros pack figured out where he was—and he doubted that would ever happen—they were prepared.

He headed for his private cabin and only once he was alone inside did he pull his cell phone out. His phone was encrypted, no one would be able to trace the call. Even so when he was done he'd take the battery out and smash the thing to pieces. He'd learned to be careful during his days running drugs and women. All his paranoia had kept him alive for a long damn time.

He had to make this call. Ezra had been holding off, trying to restrain himself from calling her, but he needed to hear her voice, to hear her fear. He'd tried finding out more about the male he'd seen her with but so far his facial recognition software programs had come up with nothing. Soon enough he'd figure out who the male was and maybe even hurt her through him.

It filled him with dark satisfaction knowing she would be afraid of him. She'd brought this on herself and after what he'd heard Finn say to the camera on May's explosive device, it was clear Finn knew Ezra was behind this.

"What?" Rhea's voice snapped into the phone mid-ring.

A malicious smile curved his mouth. "It's been a long time, Rhea."

* * *

Rory didn't want to leave Liberty, but he had to go. At least he knew she'd be more than protected at Bo's place.

"I'll be fine, I promise." She smoothed her hands down his chest while Ian waited in the entryway of Bo's kitchen.

After receiving a call from Finn that he was calling Rory in as part of the team to do a grid search for missing shifter Taylor, he'd brought Liberty straight over to Bo's place since it was a fortress with supernatural protection. They'd barely gotten a couple hours of sleep, but he was wired and wanted to help. All wedding parties had been cancelled for the foreseeable future and everyone was out looking for Taylor.

Bo and Nyx were out searching too, but they wouldn't be part of any attack on this rogue pack. That much Rory knew. As Alpha, Finn wouldn't allow them to take part in an attack for a multitude of reasons. Though he'd probably let Nyx use her transportation gift to sneak in and get Taylor out of wherever she was being held.

"Come on," Ian said, his voice tight.

"Shut it," Rory said without turning around. He hated leaving Liberty. It was as if he was leaving a part of himself behind.

"I love you, Rory." Liberty's softly spoken words sucked all the air out of the room.

He stared down at her, not sure he'd heard right. "What?"

Her brown eyes were wide. "I'm not telling you because I think you won't come back to me. I'm telling you because it's true. I've been worried that I'm too broken for you and honestly, I'm pretty sure that some days I'm still going to think that. Dealing with life and probably even sex, is going to be a process for me."

He didn't care about that, about how long it took until she was ready. Not after she'd just told him she loved him. "I'm not ever leaving you," he growled out.

She gave him a soft smile. "I know that. And part of me thinks I should let you go, but I won't. I can't. I love you."

"I love you too." The words were foreign on his tongue, but they were right. More right than anything. This female owned every part of him and if it took years for her to be ready for sex, he didn't care. He loved her. And he didn't care who knew.

"And . . . Arya did something to me last night in the cooler. I still don't know what it is, but I'm pretty much immortal. I won't turn into a dragon or anything but I've got the same lifespan as you now. I'll explain all the details later. What I know, anyway. But I don't ever want you to think that I want to get mated because you'll make me stronger. If and when we do, it's because of who you are. Because you are the most worthy male I could ever hope for." She cupped his face with one hand, gently stroking his cheek with her thumb.

He blinked. If she'd told him that she ate kittens for breakfast, she couldn't have surprised him more. It had to be why her scent was different now. Why had Arya done it?

"I know it's a lot to take in," she murmured, smoothing her hands over his chest, her fingers slightly trembling with what he guessed was nerves.

He covered her smaller ones with his. Damn it, he needed to go, but... "We're going to talk about all this Arya stuff later." Because holy shit that was insane. Now wasn't the time to discuss it though. "You're really open to mating?" he asked, because that was the only thing that mattered anyway. Just because she loved him didn't mean she was ready to get mated, but . . . it had sure sounded like she wanted to. Hopefully sooner than later.

She nodded. "Not like tomorrow, but yeah. I'm not letting you go. No one will ever love you as much as I do." There was a fierceness in her voice he felt all the way to his core.

Relief slid through him. "Good." He cleared his throat, forcing himself to ignore the way she felt pressed up against him and the fact that her words ignited a fire in him. His wolf and demon pretty much only heard she wanted to get mated. They didn't hear the 'not tomorrow' part. But damn it, he had to go. "I'll have my phone if you need me."

"I've got mine too," Ian said, coming to stand next to them. To Rory's surprise, he kissed the top of Liberty's head. "Welcome to the family."

She smiled, blushing. "Thanks."

Rory didn't even care that his brother had kissed her. The truth lacing Ian's words assuaged any lingering feelings of violence that another male had touched Rory's female. He'd needed his brother to accept her, even if he hadn't wanted to admit it to himself.

Liberty brushed her lips over Rory's one last time. "Come back to me." A soft order he would obey.

Nothing could keep him from her. Not now, not ever.

Once he and Ian were outside in the expansive back yard, Ian started stripping.

"Thank you." Rory figured he didn't need to explain further.

Ian lifted a shoulder as he tucked his cell phone into his shoes, then wrapped his clothing around them. "For the record, I've always liked Liberty. She's a sweet woman. I was just worried she'd break your heart. You're my brother, I get to worry about you. But she loves you, I could sense the truth."

"You're a good brother," he said quietly. Finding Ian fifty years ago was one of the best things that had ever happened to him.

"No shit. I'm an *awesome* brother. Don't get all emotional on me." He stood back, preparing to shift.

Yeah, that was Ian. He always had a wall up. "Wait, did you know that Arya could grant people immortality?" Or whatever the hell she'd done to Liberty.

Ian shook his head. "No. But she's ancient, so..." He shrugged again, seemingly unconcerned, before letting his dragon take over.

Rory stared at Ian's huge form as he always did when his brother shifted. Just like his brother, Rory had two forms in addition to his human one. A wolf and a demon. But this . . . the beauty of Ian's dragon always stunned him speechless.

The size of a not-so-small-house, Ian's wings glittered brilliantly under the rising sunlight. They were a waterfall of colors, one hue fading into the other starting with gold, then a shocking violet before sliding into a pale lavender. His body was a mix of all three colors, constantly shifting as the beast moved, making Ian appear to be made of moving smoke, or liquid. Long ago Rory had thought it was a trick of Ian's camouflage, but his brother had explained to him that his body was constantly shifting between the three colors, creating the illusion.

Before he'd blinked, Ian's full camouflage fell into place and all Rory saw was a smudged outline moving around. Without warning, his brother picked him up in his giant claws and deposited him on his back.

"I hate when you do that," Rory muttered. Which was precisely why his brother did it.

Underneath him, a rumbling was the only answer he received. Yep, his brother was laughing. The roll of clothes came up to him next. Holding onto the smooth scales along his spine, Rory hunkered down and tucked the clothes under him as his brother took flight.

Though he hated to leave Liberty, he'd made the decision to officially join the Stavros pack. Part of it was purely selfish reasoning. He needed to be part of something big enough to protect his female if it ever became necessary. The other part was his wolf, who craved belonging to a pack. It was part of his DNA.

Tonight was the first step in showing Finn Stavros that he was serious about being part of the pack, that he could be depended upon. Because if Rory had his way, he and Liberty would never leave this territory.

CHAPTER TWENTY

Rhea glanced at her phone as Solon turned down another street. She and Conall were in the backseat on the way to her pack's mansion. No way could she be separated from her mate right now.

Mate.

That word reverberated through her. She linked her fingers through Conall's as she answered her phone. She didn't recognize the number, but it was local. Could be a packmate with a new cell. "What?" she answered.

"It's been a long time, Rhea." The voice was male, taunting.

While she didn't recognize the actual voice since the last time she'd heard it, because he'd been a cub, she knew who it was. "Ezra." The hair at her nape rose.

"You remember me." He sounded pleased.

"No, but my pack figured out that you're the dumbass who thinks he can move into our territory. So I put it together. You're just as stupid as your brother." Next to her, Conall straightened, his hand gripping hers tighter. She was also aware of Solon looking at her in the rearview mirror.

"I'm so stupid I have one of your packmates," he snarled. "I set a bomb off right in the heart of your pack's territory." The cockiness in his tone was hard to miss.

"You had humans set the bomb off and we both know it's because you're too much of a coward to set foot in Stavros territory." She wanted to keep him talking as long as she could and insulting his ego seemed the best way to do it. She didn't know what Elana would need to track this number but knew he'd have to still be on the phone in order for her to do it. Before Rhea could tell Conall to contact Finn, he already had his phone out and was making a call.

She held out the phone so he could see the phone number. Nodding, he started talking quietly into the phone. She cupped a hand over her mouth and the phone as Ezra continued.

"I'm going to tattoo that bitch packmate of yours and do to her what my brother did to you. Then I'm going to share her." He hung up before she could respond, but his words were a punch to her gut.

She swallowed hard, looked down at her phone to see the call was definitely ended. When she looked at Conall he shook his head. "Finn couldn't get to Elana before the call ended."

"Maybe she can still figure out where he's calling from. Or where he got the phone from." Rhea doubted it even as she said the words. If Ezra had been ballsy enough to call her, he'd have made sure his phone was untraceable. By now he'd probably smashed it to bits.

Conall wrapped his arm around her shoulders. "We're going to get Taylor back."

She leaned into his embrace and simply let him hold her because she didn't trust her voice. It had taken a long time to become the woman she was and a fool's words wouldn't undo all that hard work. Still, she could admit he'd rattled her because now all she could focus on was getting to Taylor. The thought of another female suffering like she had made her wolf want to lash out, claw up everyone who got in her way.

She straightened as they turned onto the main road where the mansion was. "What's happened?" A cluster of packmates were crouched down in the middle of the street.

"Ah..." Conall cleared his throat. "Finn told me there was a situation when I called. Female from Ezra's pack showed up to deliver photographs of Taylor in a cage. An explosives vest was rigged around her and someone, he's assuming Ezra, set it off. Your pack is cleaning . . . her up."

Her stomach twisted. That sick bastard needed to die. "We should help."

"No." He looked forward at Solon, who was starting to slow the vehicle. "Finn wanted us to head straight into the compound. He needs to talk to you," he said, turning to her again.

There was something in his expression that made her go still. She wanted to get out and help, but nodded instead. "Okay."

It seemed to take forever to drive through the gates and make their way up to Finn's office and Rhea was growing tenser by the second. One of her packmates was out there, alone, hurt and held captive by a monster.

When they finally reached the door of Finn's office, she was grateful to have Conall by her side for a multitude of reasons. Having her mate beside her completed her in a way she hadn't realized she'd even needed. He was a rock, a steady presence she knew would always, *always* have her back. She felt that vow rolling off him, the knowledge settling deep in her bones.

She scented everyone before they stepped inside. Finn, Lyra and Gabriel were all standing behind Finn's desk looking down at Elana, whose fingers were flying across her keyboard.

Lyra and Gabriel remained in place but Finn strode around the desk to meet all three of them. He nodded once at Solon. "Go gear up now. Be in the training room in thirty."

Solon was out the door like a ghost.

Finn pinned her with those piercing blue eyes, his expression dark. "We're going to kill this fucker."

"I know." She wanted to do it herself.

"Elana hasn't been able to find much on the phone number he called you from, but that's not what she's focusing on now anyways." He turned back to his desk, raised his eyebrows at Elana.

She swiveled her laptop around. "I think I've found it."

Rhea looked at the screen, frowned, even as she felt the burst of hope roll off the others in the room at Elana's words. On screen there was an image from Google Earth showing a raised 3D image of . . . somewhere with a lot of trees. "What is this?"

"The shifter who died brought pictures of Taylor," Finn said. "There was a message from Ezra and one that I think was from her." He handed her a photograph of Taylor in a cage. "Turn it over."

Rhea's stomach soured even more as she saw the image, but she did as he said. *Thirty minutes north, rural cabins, old campsite, occupied by almost one hundred wolves, deep in the woods. Females aren't there willingly. Please help us.*

"You think this is real?" She handed the picture back to him.

"I do."

"What did the other message say?"

He cleared his throat. "Doesn't matter."

Something about his reaction made her stomach tighten. She couldn't scent a lie because he didn't exactly answer, but she knew he was hiding something from her.

"There's a campsite roughly thirty minutes north of us, by vehicle," Elana interjected. "I did some digging and found out that it was bought by a corporation. And without getting into all the details, that corporation doesn't technically exist. It's buried in layers of bullshit paperwork. And it's the only place I can find bought in the last year that I can't figure out who the owner is. That alone makes whoever owns this property suspicious. It's worth checking out at least."

"We need to do more than check it out," Rhea snapped, her wolf slipping its leash. They needed to send out a hunting party, like ten minutes ago.

"We're heading out in less than an hour. Everyone's gearing up now and I want you to head up a team," Finn said.

She nodded. "Conall and I can leave now. He can fly us in and we can do recon ahead of time." No way could she wait an hour. Not after seeing those pictures of Taylor, seeing her packmates cleaning up what was left of that poor female.

And not after that taunting call from Ezra.

Finn shook his head. "We move in together as a team in case it's a trap."

Rhea had never defied her Alpha. Even when she hadn't always agreed with his orders she'd never gone against him. Until now. "Finn, they have Taylor. We can't waste any more time." And Rhea simply couldn't stay here another minute longer. Because the trip was more like an hour and a half including the drive time. That felt like a lifetime to someone being tortured. She knew from experience.

"An hour to prep isn't wasting time. And I don't have time to argue." His eyes went pure wolf and next to her Conall growled low in his throat.

Shit. Of course he'd feel protective of her even if Finn wasn't threatening her. And this was exactly why two Alphas could never, ever occupy the same territory. It was impossible.

Clearly sensing the growing tension, Lyra moved around the desk incredibly fast. She laid a hand on Finn's forearm as he faced off with Conall. "He's not challenging you. He's protecting his mate." Her voice was soothing.

Rhea did the same thing to Conall, touching him gently. "And he's not threatening me." Good Lord, they both looked ready to rip the other's head off. "He's just being my Alpha."

Aaaand, that was apparently the wrong thing to say. Conall swiveled to her. "He's not your Alpha anymore," he snarled, his dragon glaring at her with heat and possessiveness. He didn't even sound human.

Before she could respond, Nyx and Bo appeared in the office in a whirl of wind and noise. Thank God for the interruption.

Papers flew everywhere and a few books fell off the shelves, but for the most part the office and everyone were unharmed. Nyx had gotten a better grasp on her transporting powers since the last time Rhea had seen her do it. It was still pretty freaky.

Nyx looked at Finn, her blue eyes anxious. Her jet black hair was pulled back in a tightly plated braid. "I got Gabriel's text. You guys have a location for Taylor?"

Of course. Rhea immediately cursed herself. Nyx could save Taylor by flashing in to a location and then flashing out. But Rhea thought the demigod had to have physically been to the location before transporting to it. She wasn't really sure of the specifics of the female's powers, but she knew there were parameters to it.

"Can you get to Taylor using this picture?" Finn held out a photograph.

Nyx looked at it for a long moment, shook her head. "There's nothing identifying the location. No window or anything. I don't have a sense of the space. It's just a cage. This could be anywhere in the world."

"I think we have a physical location." Finn nodded at the computer screen. "Can you use a 3D map of the terrain?"

"Ah, maybe. I've never tried before."

Next to his mate, Bo frowned, clearly not liking it.

"Maybe?" Rhea asked.

Nyx nodded. "I can try, but how big is that place?" she asked, motioning to the image.

"About fifty acres, give or take," Finn said.

"It would be a big risk trying to get there, especially without a current photograph of the land. And I'm not talking some 3D image. I mean a real photo."

Elana swiveled her laptop back around, started working on her computer, likely looking for a current image of the old campsite.

But there was no guarantee she could find one and no guarantee Nyx and Bo and whoever else would even be able to find Taylor once they transported to the property. Not to mention there was no guarantee Taylor was even there. Still, Rhea was done waiting.

She nudged Conall and tilted her head to the door. "Gonna go gear up," she murmured, hoping Finn didn't question her further.

Because she *was* going to gear up, but she wasn't going to be leading any team. She'd seen the coordinates on the screen and was going there herself. Well Conall and her were. Instead of heading downstairs, she motioned to a hallway. "My room is this way." She had plenty of weapons stocked in there. She didn't need to get anything from the training room. And her room was a lot closer to the roof.

"Are we doing what I think we are?" Conall's voice was so low she barely heard him.

She nodded once, glad he'd said "we". "Unless you don't think we should." She would respect her mate's opinion. Right now she knew she wasn't thinking clearly.

She needed to get to Taylor, to save her from the same fate she'd suffered through.

His jaw clenched tight. "Let's talk in your room."

Her room, which was more like a small apartment, was on the next floor up. Once they were alone inside she shut the door and leaned against it.

The words burst out in a rush. "When Anson raped me he let his packmates watch. He wanted to humiliate me. Ezra was young, but he was there. He saw it. It's what Ezra meant when he called. I can't let that happen to Taylor." Rhea could hear the desperation in her voice, questioned herself again whether this was the right decision. She loved and respected her Alpha but she didn't agree with him right now. Conall was a powerful Alpha and could camouflage himself. They could go in as a team and recon easily.

Fire licked out all around Conall in a burst of energy before it quickly disappeared. He cursed low and she could sense he was holding back rage. Rage because of what had been done to her so long ago. "Whatever you want to do, I'm in."

Relief punched through her but there was no time to savor it. She nodded at an antique armoire near one of the big windows. "There are a ton of weapons in there. Can you grab the two Glocks, the small crossbow and backup ammo for all three?" She was already moving to her walk-in closet as he crossed to the armoire, opened it.

The clothes he'd given her were fine, but she needed tactical gear. She had pants specifically designed to hold extra weapons. It took her less than a minute to dress and slide on her double shoulder holster. She knew she'd probably end up shifting and fighting but she wanted to be prepared for every situation. Especially since they had no idea what they were headed into.

"This goes without saying," she said, sliding her weapons into their holsters before picking up her favorite crossbow. The carbon body weighed barely seven pounds and was powerful—and she was very accurate. She tucked the extra silver arrows into a pocket specifically made for them. Twenty should be good. "But you can take anything you want from my stash."

The look he gave her was pure predator and when he smiled all she saw was his dragon peering back at her. He looked almost amused. "Thanks, but I'm good."

"I figured, but I wanted to offer." The male could fly and breathe fire. Of course he didn't need any other weapon. He was a powerful machine of death and destruction over fifteen hundred years old. She'd seen him in action, knew how very deadly he was. But she hesitated. "You don't have to do this, you know. We can wait and go with my packmates."

He shook his head once, his expression set. "I can launch from the roof."

Yeah, they really were on the same page. Still . . . a bit of unease slid through her. "I've never defied my Alpha before."

"Good thing he's not your Alpha anymore." The statement was so savage, so final, she knew that it was true.

Even if she would always love and respect Finn, she couldn't be mated to an Alpha and still follow another one. She reached out, cupped Conall's cheek. His stubble was rough against her palm. She wondered how she'd gotten so lucky to have a mate like him. "Thank you for doing this."

He grabbed her hip, tugged her close in a completely proprietary hold. "You don't ever have to thank me."

Leaning up, she gave him a quick, hard kiss. "Let's go."

* * *

"I wish I could go with you," Lyra muttered. Her agitation was clear, raked over Finn's senses as they waited for everyone else to arrive in the training room.

"I know." His petite mate could be a vicious warrior when she wanted, but he was secretly glad she wasn't going with him, even if he hated that she couldn't walk in sunlight. When she was out of harm's way he could focus and fight better. "I'm glad you'll be here with Vega." And that was the truth. His daughter, a half-vampire, half-wolf shifter, was powerful, but she was only eighteen and they'd both do anything to protect her. He felt a lot better knowing Lyra would be here to watch out for her.

When Chloe jogged in, strapping a blade to her hip, he frowned. The only person they were waiting on now was Rhea—and she was usually earlier than anyone. He scanned the faces before him, counted twenty-five. Not including Ian and Rory, who'd surprised him by coming to help. Everyone else would be staying close to home, protecting their compound in case this whole thing was a trap.

"What is it?" Lyra asked quietly.

"Rhea should be here." She'd left his office well before he had. Nyx and Bo were still up there while Elana tried to find a photograph of the property, though at this point it didn't matter. They'd be there soon enough.

Vega glanced over from where she'd been talking quietly to another packmate. "I saw her headed to the roof with that dragon a while ago. Did they mate? Because I could scent—"

Finn's heart rate kicked up. "To the roof, you're sure?"

"Yeah. She had a really cool crossbow strapped across her back. I asked her if I could practice with it later and she said yes."

"What else did she say?"

A casual shrug. "Nothing."

Finn scanned the group, lasered in on Drake, who was leaning against a wall, arms over his chest. Even if he wasn't part of Finn's pack anymore, the male had volunteered to help. "Drake."

The huge male straightened and strode over, winding his way through the quietly murmuring wolves. "What's up?"

"Do you know where your brother is?"

"Wherever Rhea is, I imagine." There wasn't a trace of sarcasm rolling off the male, but his answer annoyed Finn.

Finn held his temper in check. "Did he and Rhea leave already?"

"I have no idea." There was pure truth in the statement.

"She did," Lyra said a second later, holding out her phone.

His mate had texted Rhea, asking where she was, and had received a response. *I couldn't wait. Tell Finn I'm sorry. We're about to reach the property line. Going dark.*

He reined in a curse and started barking out orders. "Chloe, Solon, grab your teams…" He continued on, making sure everyone was geared up and ready for the infil.

They'd all been sent 3D images of the area and knew the plan. "Everyone will keep earpieces in when we're set to breach the target." They were going to surround it and move in at the same time while Drake and Ian flew overhead with riders to feed them more intel if necessary.

Once everyone started to file out, heading for their vehicles, he motioned to Rory, Ian, and Gabriel.

He looked at Ian, a male with amber eyes identical to Bo's. "Can you take more than one rider?" This male was only here for his brother Rory's sake, that much was clear. He had no allegiance to Finn or his pack.

"I physically can, but I won't." His voice had a slight Irish accent and there was just a hint of apology. "My dragon won't let anyone but Rory or Bo on him. Or Nyx," he added as an afterthought. "Trust." The one word was enough of an answer.

"Okay. Thank you for doing this." Finn looked at Drake. "Can you take me and Gabriel?" He knew the male could, but needed to ask out of respect. Drake was here because he wanted to be and Finn would never forget that.

"Of course."

"Let's head out then." He pulled both Lyra and Vega in for a tight hug. He was pissed at Rhea, but now wasn't the time to focus on his errant packmate.

He had a job to do: bringing Taylor home alive and eliminating the threat to his people once and for all today.

CHAPTER TWENTY-ONE

Rhea held on to Conall's scales as he flew over the canopy of trees. The wind ruffled her curls and rolled over her skin, but she barely felt the chilly air. She was too amped up on adrenaline.

The flight had been quick and silent and now that they'd reached the coordinates according to the map on her phone, she knew they were in the right place. At least no one could see her. His dragon form had a natural camouflage and since she was on top of him they wouldn't be able to see her from the ground.

And she scented plenty of wolves everywhere down below. Could hear snippets of conversation, but with the wind rushing over her and the distance to the ground it was hard to hear much more. There was a sort of mesh netting strung up between all the oak, pine and magnolia trees, the manmade material blocking all views of the ground.

"Freaking camouflage," she muttered even though he couldn't respond and it was pretty damn obvious what it was. The covering was telling in itself. No one put up that sort of military-style camo unless they wanted to hide something. Probably from satellites and drones—or nosy dragons. Not to mention there were a bunch of shifters down below. Shifters who didn't belong in Stavros territory.

This was all the validation she needed. They were at the right location. "Can you burn away all the camouflage without damaging the trees?" Because from what she'd seen, the male had some serious control over his fire. "Fly downward if you can."

Though she could feel him beneath her, she couldn't see much other than a smudge of color here and there. But she certainly felt the freefall when he dipped down. She held on tighter until he straightened out, moving in a big circle around the tops of the trees. The flapping of his wings was whisper quiet.

"Okay, I'm going to call Finn, let him know this is probably the place." With what Elana had found online combined with what she could see, it had to be. And even if it wasn't, there shouldn't be any damn wolves in Stavros territory. They'd broken shifter law plain and simple, whoever they were. She'd started to call him when a terrified female scream ripped through the air, the sound echoing all around.

Panic slammed through Rhea. There was no way to tell if it was Taylor, but it didn't matter who it was. Someone was in trouble.

She slid her crossbow off her back, held it securely in front of her. "Go in hot and head straight for the screaming. Burn all the camo as you do."

Conall dipped low, a burst of fire blasting over the tops of the trees in a horrifying yet beautiful wave of orange, spanning out in all directions.

She pushed up to her knees, her crossbow at the ready as he breached a cluster of trees, heading straight down into enemy territory. She tightened her legs to keep her balance.

The drop was rapid and she probably should have been scared, but she knew Conall would never hurt her. Knew in her bones he simply wouldn't let her fall. If she tumbled off him, he'd catch her.

Rhea was aware of shouts of alarm as they descended. The screaming woman hadn't stopped and as they dove into the camp Rhea quickly catalogued her surroundings.

Decrepit-looking cabins spanned out over a couple acres. Wolves in human form were all running around, some armed, some not. A naked female with dark hair was running barefoot toward a line of trees. Two males were in pursuit. Even at this distance, Rhea could see the blood running down the woman's throat, from where spikes had been.

She must have gotten the collar off.

Good for her. Rhea was going to make sure this woman survived and kill everyone involved in the kidnapping. "Go in lower," she said quietly, knowing Conall would hear her no matter what.

Not that it mattered who heard them at this point because everyone had for sure seen her. They might not be able to see Conall, but they could see her and the fire was a pretty big giveaway what she was riding on. She was aware of snatches of conversation, some males worried about the fire, some racing after her and Conall with guns. *Bullets aren't going to do much against a dragon, but have fun trying,* she thought. They wouldn't even hurt him.

He swooped down even lower, his camouflage gone now. His wings spanned out wide, glittering like emeralds as they dove toward the two males.

One of them looked over his shoulder, his eyes widening. Dumbass had just realized he was being chased by a dragon. She pulled the bolt back, let it fly. It nailed the male right in the head. He started to fall but Conall was moving at warp speed so she never saw the guy hit the ground. He'd be dead though. Especially with a head shot from a silver arrow.

Her heart rate kicked up as they neared the other male who had given up chasing the woman and was now running for his life. She could see his terror in every line of his body. He started to shift to his wolf, hit the ground with all fours. She drew the crossbow back again, let the next bolt sing through the air.

It hit him right in the head while he was mid-shift. "Can you grab the female?"

Conall dipped even lower so that they were mere feet off the ground. Faster, faster, he flew, heading straight for the woman who hadn't turned around once—and a line of thick trees.

Rhea's heart jumped in her throat. She wasn't sure how they were going to stop in time without crashing into the trees. He was moving like a rocket with no sign of slowing. Bracing for the impact, she held onto his scales tight.

Suddenly he banked sharply to the right. She heard a frightened female yelp right as they turned, then shot upward.

Rhea held on tight, crouching low against his body as he burst through the treetops. The male really was a creature of beauty. His scales gleamed like diamonds before his camouflage suddenly fell back into place.

Just as quickly he banked again.

Rhea's stomach pitched and she tightened her legs around him. She really didn't want to get sick but all this twisting was taking a toll.

They flew back down toward the treetops, breaking through them once again. Just like before Conall let his camouflage drop, let everyone below see what he was. He obviously wasn't worried about being targeted.

Rhea scented everyone's terror and was surprised when Conall reached back with one claw and deposited the naked female in front of Rhea. She hadn't even realized he'd managed to grab her.

The dark-haired woman stared at Rhea, her eyes wide with stark terror.

Too bad there was no time to comfort her. "We're here to save you. Your captor, Ezra, has one of my packmates. Do you know where he's keeping her?"

The woman shook her head and hunkered down against Conall's back.

Rhea wasn't going to grill her. Instead, she said, "Hold onto his scales. Neither he nor I will let you fall. I promise." Without waiting for a response, she scanned the spread out cabins. Males were running in every direction. Four raced to the west.

"Head west," she ordered.

Conall swooped in that direction. As they turned, a staccato popping sounded below. She hunkered down as a barrage of bullets flew past her, some striking Conall's right wing.

She growled, fought the urge to shift right then and there. She knew from Drake that in dragon form, he'd just push the bullets out, but still. She didn't want her mate getting shot up.

She popped back up, ready to fight back when Conall let loose a stream of burning blue fire, incinerating the cabin the shooter had been trying to hide behind and whoever had shot at them.

She'd seen that blue fire only once before; knew what it meant. It burned hotter than anything imaginable and a dragon was only able to release it when they feared their mate was in imminent danger. In that moment she realized how truly powerful Conall was. He could destroy everyone here without help from *anyone.*

He turned again, making a slight right as he headed after their original targets. She knew he could just incinerate them, but was glad he was letting her fight too. She drew back the crossbow and fired, hit one, then another—

"That's Ezra." The voice of the female before her was so low, so trembling with fear, it took Rhea a moment to realize what she'd said. "He's the monster that took all of us." Her voice cracked on the last word.

Rhea's gaze narrowed on the back of one of the running males. Of the two left, one was blond—Ezra for sure—and the other had black hair. She aimed, killed the black-haired male. Ezra wasn't getting the easy way out. She could kill him with a bolt to the head, but nope. He was going to know who killed him, see her face before he died.

"I need to do this hand-to-hand," Rhea said to Conall, hoping he understood why. The burning, growing need to destroy this male who'd dared to attack her pack was too much. She could do it too, had faith in her abilities.

Screw this male and all that he stood for. Anson's entire line should have been wiped out a hundred years ago. Today she'd make sure they were. She needed to do this. For herself, for her pack, for freaking closure on the darkest part of her life. She thought she'd put everything behind her, but evidently not.

Conall shot out a stream of regular fire, making the hope for vengeance in Rhea wilt—for only a second.

His fire arched past Ezra, creating a huge wall in front of the blond male. Conall dropped the last few feet, slowed his flight as they neared the ground. She did a mental fist pump in the air. He wasn't going to try to stop her from fighting.

Going on instinct, Rhea jumped from his body, her boots slamming to the ground. She trusted that Conall would take care of the female while she fought.

She didn't break pace as she raced for Ezra. Only fifty feet to go now.

He swiveled, recoiling from the wall of fire. There was nowhere for him to go.

Except to meet his fate.

Forty feet.

She could simply shoot him with a bolt—or one of her guns. But neither she nor her wolf liked that idea at all. It had to be hand-to-hand. With blades.

Or claws.

Something up close and personal.

Her legs ate up the distance. She was aware of almost nothing but getting to her enemy.

Thirty feet.

She slid her bow off her back, set the quiver on the ground. "You wolf enough to fight me?" she demanded as she pulled a three-foot blade out of a sheath strapped to her back, stalked closer.

She wanted to slice him up, make him suffer. Apparently she wasn't as evolved as she'd always thought. But this male had done a lot of harm, had blown a defenseless shifter up right in front of Rhea's compound, and he'd kidnapped and likely raped and tortured others.

He would pay.

He was big—much bigger than her. Wearing cargo pants and a ripped T-shirt, he faced off with her, rage—and fear—glittering in his dark eyes. He looked so much like Anson she wanted to claw his eyes out.

The male looked past her, no doubt at Conall who'd shifted back to human form, but Rhea had to tune out her mate and the female who'd shifted to her wolf form.

"This is between you and me," she growled at Ezra, wanting to make him pay for every crime he'd ever committed. He'd never seen her fight before. She'd been a different female all those years ago. Untrained. She hadn't even realized she was a warrior, a tracker, until later. Now he'd get to see who she'd become—and die by her hand.

Conall was next to her in an instant, his own anger pulsing off him in fiery, orange flames. She risked a glance at her mate. He was naked and covered in fire, flames licking over his entire body. "Please find Taylor. She needs help. So do the other women. And I need to do this alone."

She could see the war raging in his supernova eyes. It almost hurt to look at him. She turned away, kept her focus on Ezra. Oh yeah, he was going to die.

"Don't ask me to do this." The words were ripped from Conall, his voice pure dragon. His fire shot as high as the tree tops, surrounding them in a brilliant inferno. She didn't feel the heat though.

And she understood what he was saying. He was an Alpha and a dragon. She was asking him to let her do this alone.

"Don't ask me to be someone I'm not." Because she wouldn't do that to him. She'd fight to the death to protect him, but she wouldn't try to change his nature.

"Just this once." His voice was more animal than human. She knew what he was doing, that he was putting aside his Alpha self and letting her fight this battle. This, more than anything, told her how much he loved her. Respected her. And she needed respect as much as she needed his love.

It made her love him even more. "I swear it."

His knuckles skimmed down her cheek but she kept her gaze pinned to the threat twenty feet away. Otherwise she might back down and let Conall just incinerate the guy. "No one will be able to penetrate the fire. You and the she-wolf are safe from an outside attack. When you've killed him, find me. The fire won't ever harm you."

His words warmed her from the inside out, but she locked down all emotion, simply nodded once. She needed to end this now.

"I love you," she murmured as he raced into a wall of flames.

She heard him echo the same, his voice still ragged, all animal as he disappeared.

Heavy beads of sweat rolled down Ezra's face and his clothing was soaked all the way through. The fire must be blistering.

Or he realized he was about to die by her hand.

She swiveled the short blade once. "You haven't answered me."

He whipped out a gun in response, his movements fast, but not fast enough.

Blade in hand, she jumped to the right as a bullet whizzed past her head. Using her inborn supernatural speed, she sprinted straight for him, jumped high into the air when he aimed again.

He fired but she was well out of range now.

Talk about weak. He could have gone for blades, claws or even wolf form, but no, he pulled out his gun as a mortal would have.

Two more bullets zinged past her. Still in human form she extended her claws, raced up a tree. Using the trunk as a platform she shoved off it, aiming for a low-hanging branch above him.

"Die, you stupid bitch!" He continued firing, but she was too fast.

She leaped down behind him, sliced out with the blade before he'd fully turned to her. She slammed it down, slicing off his hand. It and the gun fell to the ground.

He screamed in agony, blood spraying everywhere as he completely swiveled in her direction. His eyes were wild with pain and—surprise.

He was surprised she'd taken him on, gotten the first strike. And would definitely kill him.

She thrust her blade into his chest whiplash fast, before he could even release his claws.

He stared at her in horror. "This wasn't . . . supposed to..." He trailed off, gurgling on blood as pain fired out to all his nerves.

"What?" She twisted the blade once. "This wasn't supposed to happen? I wasn't supposed to beat you? Or Finn wasn't supposed to? You're a weak minded fool if you thought you could come into our territory," she growled.

His mouth opened and closed soundlessly as he looked down at his chest. Blood gushed out. His claws had released now, but it was clear he couldn't move his arms, couldn't do much of anything.

She slid the blade deeper, leaned down so that her mouth was next to his ear. "You're not even an Alpha." She pulled it out then, lifted her blade high as he fell to his knees, struggling to draw in breath. "And I've killed a fucking dragon. You're no contest."

In a swift, sharp arc she sliced his head from his body. A fountain of blood sprayed out as his head flew through the air.

For the briefest moment she saw a flash of movement in the flames, thought Conall was still there, but as Ezra's severed head rolled into a tree with a thunk, it took all her attention.

She stared down at it, his dead eyes staring up at her in shock. As if the fool couldn't believe she'd killed him. The kill felt anticlimactic, but the male wasn't as strong as he thought. Not even close.

How he'd ever thought he was strong enough to take over Stavros territory, she'd never know. Delusions of grandeur likely.

Wasn't her problem now. He was dead and gone.

She turned, saw the rescued she-wolf standing on all fours, watching her. "You'll be safe if you stay within the flames. I'll come back for you, I promise."

The she-wolf yipped in understanding.

Good enough for Rhea. She raced for the flames at full speed, feeling Conall's embrace stroking over her skin as she sprinted through them, as if the fire was alive. For all she knew it was connected to him on an intrinsic level. Everything about her mate was beautiful, even his fire. Especially his fire.

As she burst through the other side of the flames Finn, Gabriel and Rory dropped down from the trees looking every bit the warrior wolves they were.

She couldn't see Drake, but knew he had to be nearby. Possibly Ian too. Didn't matter. "Ezra's dead," she said, sprinting toward Finn. "Conall went to find Taylor." Bright orange flames licked everywhere, not burning, but covering the trees and cabins. She'd never really understood the extent of Conall's power until that moment. All the wolves from earlier were nowhere to be seen. Must have fled, or attempted to flee into the woods. Or some were probably dead from Conall's fire.

Finn nodded once, his expression dark as he turned to Gabriel and Rory. "Kill any male on sight." He turned back to her as the two males raced off in opposite directions. "The team will be here in less than ten. Let's find your mate and get him to extinguish that fire. Last thing we need is humans sniffing around here."

Shit, yeah. She hadn't even thought about that. The fire might not be burning through the forest but the flames weren't invisible. Some of them were licking across treetops. Not exactly stealth mode. Nodding, she fell into step with him as she followed the scent of her mate.

She could feel her Alpha's anger toward her as they walked.

"I won't lie and say I'm sorry." Because she wasn't. At all. If she and Conall hadn't arrived, who knew what would have happened to that female being hunted down. Or any number of the females being held prisoner. Not to mention Taylor. For all she knew Ezra had given a standing order to kill captives if their camp was attacked. She refused to believe that though.

Finn snorted, clapped her on the shoulder once. "I wouldn't expect you to."

Good. She was glad her mate hadn't interfered, tried to protect her. The way he'd let her fight, let her be herself, told her all she ever needed to know about her mate. She'd definitely picked the best male.

CHAPTER TWENTY-TWO

Conall ripped open the cage Taylor was being held in, tossing the door behind him onto one of the two males he'd just killed. She stood on all fours in wolf form, wobbling on her paws, and he could scent her blood. That damned silver spiked collar was still around her neck.

He'd hated leaving Rhea, hadn't been able to actually go. He'd gone back, to make sure he could protect her if necessary, watched as she'd sliced off that male's head. Once he'd seen her decapitate Ezra he'd disappeared back into his flames and gone hunting for Taylor. Rhea would probably be pissed when she found out but screw it, he was new to this whole mated thing. He simply hadn't been able to just leave her.

"I'm going to pull the collar off, okay?" he asked Taylor.

She just made a whining sound.

Crouching down next to her, he slid his fingers under the spiked collar and yanked once. It snapped easily under his grip. Unlike wolves, silver didn't bother him.

Growling, she shifted almost instantaneously. Naked, but way more pissed than afraid, she panted heavily as she rubbed at her throat. It was already healing but her skin had red welts and marks. "Thank you."

He shook his head, not wanting her thanks as he turned back to the dead males. He pulled a T-shirt off one of them. "I know this isn't the best option, but here." He tossed it to her over his shoulder before taking the males' weapons. "You want to go wolf or you want to use these pistols?"

She moved up beside him, the shirt almost reaching her knees. "I'll take the guns for now. I was wolf for too long."

He nodded, headed for the door of the small cabin. "You ready?" He wouldn't insult her by asking if she wanted to stay and hide inside. It was clear from her expression she was ready to fight and he fully understood that need.

Her red hair was tangled around her face. She nodded. "Let's go."

He opened the door slightly, peered outside and saw Rhea running his way. He'd known she wouldn't be far behind. Her wild hair bounced everywhere as she raced for the cabin.

He was so damn proud of her strength. The female was everything he ever could have wanted in a mate.

He flung open the door fully and was off the porch in seconds. Leaving her alone to fight that monster was the hardest thing he'd ever done in his fifteen hundred years. Leaving her period made his dragon want to burn this whole forest down. To take away any and all potential threats.

But he'd had to let her do it. Sort of. At least he hadn't interfered with the actual fight. That was a big concession as far as he was concerned.

He trusted her skill, had seen her in action to know how deadly she was. Still, leaving his mate like that had been too much. He'd just found her. He couldn't lose her.

Conall pulled her into his arms, held her tight. "I went back," he murmured. "I had to know you were safe."

"I thought I saw you." Her voice was quiet, with no recrimination.

"Never again," he growled into her hair, crushing her to him. "I can't leave you like that again."

"I know. And I wouldn't want you to." Her fingers dug into his back as she gripped him, the strength of her embrace easing him inside.

"Stop the fire," Finn ordered him, jerking to a halt as he reached them. "If any humans see that, we're screwed."

Conall didn't take orders from anyone, but he controlled his flames, pulled them back because he knew he was close to losing control of it. With his mate in danger, it had exacerbated his restraint. He could scent and hear wolves fighting in the distance, knew the Stavros pack had arrived. The rogue wolves had clearly tried to flee into the forest, but they wouldn't get far.

"Taylor, you good?" Finn asked his packmate.

She nodded. "Fine. They didn't hurt me—other than that messed up collar they put on me. Freaks. All the females here are unwilling, from what I've picked up from different conversations."

"I know." He tapped his earpiece. "Got a team that's already freed them. Their captors tried to flee." Finn looked at Conall and Rhea. "The males have run into the woods. We need to round them up."

Conall's dragon rankled at the order in the other male's voice, but he nodded. Yeah he knew what to do. "Where's Drake?"

"In the air with Ian. Can you do aerial recon, catch any stragglers?"

Conall didn't want to leave Rhea again, but he nodded because she wasn't under a direct threat anymore. Now they needed to find and destroy anyone belonging to the rogue pack.

"I'm going with him. I can use my crossbow." Rhea's tone was final. She was flat out telling her Alpha what she was doing—her *former* Alpha.

That soothed all the jagged edges inside Conall. He just needed her with him.

Finn paused a moment, the surprise clear in his eyes, but he nodded. "We'll meet back here when we're done." He pointed at the closest cabin. It had a rusted rooster weathervane on top of it.

Wordlessly Rhea grabbed Conall's hand and they raced toward open space so he could shift.

* * *

Rhea stalked toward the pile of bodies they'd stacked in between the main cabins and felt nothing but anger for the dead shifters. They thought they could just take she-wolves they wanted then try to move into Stavros territory? They all deserved their fate. "Hold off on burning them," she said to Drake and Conall.

Both males nodded, but Finn frowned. "What's up?"

"The females we rescued want to see them." It had taken an hour, but they'd rounded up every single male from this rogue pack and killed them all.

Packs looked out for each other, protected the weak. Always. But Ezra had clearly recruited the worst of the worst and destroyed the definition of what a pack should be. And the females he'd taken had all been packless, unprotected. They were currently waiting in the extra SUVs Finn and the others had brought. Rhea wasn't sure what they were going to do with the females but she knew Finn would be getting them help. Probably find them packs if he didn't take them in himself.

"I don't know if that's such a good idea." Finn scrubbed a hand over his face, glanced at the maimed bodies.

"It might help give them closure and they asked me to ask you. They haven't had any control in their lives for a long time. I think we should give them what they want, let them see that these monsters are dead." Rhea thought letting them see the dead males who had hurt some of them was a great idea. It might help with their healing process. God knows killing the male who'd hurt her had given her a lot of closure all those years ago. It was one of the reasons she thought she'd been able to move on.

Jaw tight, Finn nodded once. "Okay. Then we burn the bodies and head out of here. We've been here too long as it is."

Yeah, and just because they were out in the country didn't mean that someone hadn't seen Conall's light show of fire earlier.

"You want us to burn the cabins too?" Drake asked.

"Burn it all. Once everything's incinerated, extinguish it. Won't matter if humans find the aftermath as long as we're not here when they get here. They can make whatever conclusion they want about this mess then." Finn's voice was hard and she knew he was holding all his anger in check. It wasn't directed at anyone here, just the situation in general. When he headed in the direction of the vehicles, where most of Rhea's other packmates waited, she stayed.

"I'm going to ride back with the females," she said to Conall. "I think it'll be good to have as many females as—"

He nodded. "I understand and agree."

She wrapped her arms around him. Of course he understood. They might be in the first stages of their mating but this male was an Alpha to his bones. He understood what it meant to look out for those who needed it most. "I love you," she murmured, laying her head against his chest.

Someone had found him pants, but he was still shirtless. His skin against hers was warm. She turned her face away from the bodies, not wanting to look at them while she was holding him.

"I love you too. I'm ready to go home so we can start our life together," he said quietly against the top of her head.

She knew he meant Montana and the truth was, she was ready too. She was ready for the next step in her life. At her age, she knew things couldn't stay the same forever, and she'd always embraced change. Now more than ever. She'd miss her packmates, but she was ready to start a new life with her mate. "Me too."

* * *

On bare feet, Rhea stalked across the lawn when she saw Finn try to duck behind some trees. "You can't hide from me forever, Finn Stavros." They'd gotten all the females back to the mansion and they were now being looked at by Ophelia and even Victoria, since she was still in town. Some of the women hadn't been raped at all, but many of them weren't so lucky. And those psychological wounds wouldn't be going away anytime soon.

"I'm not hiding," he growled, stepping into the sunlight. He was still covered in blood and dirt, but didn't look as if he'd been injured.

"Oh really? Then what are you doing out here?" She shoved her hands in her pockets. She didn't want to have this conversation, but she needed to do it sooner than later.

He mirrored her, shoving his hands into the pockets of his cargo pants. "Checking in with the warriors on patrol."

She snorted. The perimeter of their place was secure and as far as everyone knew, they'd eliminated the threat. "I thought Alphas were supposed to be able to lie convincingly."

"Dragons keep stealing my people," he grumbled, no heat in his voice, an expression almost like a pout on his face. "I thought I could pretend a little longer that you really aren't leaving. I'm gonna miss you, Rhea." He rubbed a hand over the back of his neck, clearly uncomfortable. "You've been with me almost the longest of anyone."

Her throat tightened at his words. Finn wasn't overly emotional or affectionate with anyone. Sure touch and affection were important with any shifter pack, but Finn had always had an edge to him, always kept a certain distance from his packmates. Being the Alpha, he had to. In case he ever had to make the decision to eliminate a packmate for a crime. It was like no matter what, he always had to have a barrier in place because no one—except his mate and daughter—were immune from any potential future judgment. They'd always had a close relationship though, because he was right. She had been with him a very long time.

"I'm going to miss you too. But it's not like I'm leaving forever. I'll still be back." Her pack, her *family,* lived here.

He lifted a shoulder. "I know. Still gonna miss you and your sass."

She laughed. "You'll have Chloe. She's got way more sass than me."

His mouth curved up a fraction, but she saw the sadness in his eyes. That was what pushed her over the edge. Blinking away tears, she lunged at him, pulling him into a tight hug.

He gripped her back, his hold just as tight. "That dragon better treat you right," he growled.

A watery laugh escaped as she sniffled against his chest. "I wouldn't worry about that." She knew he actually didn't or he'd have never allowed Conall into his territory in the first place. "And hey," she said, stepping back and swiping at a few errant tears. "I'll be with Victoria now too. And you see her more now than when she lived here. We'll still see each other."

Finn nodded once, his jaw tight. "Yeah."

It wouldn't be remotely the same and they both knew it. While she was sad, she couldn't deny she was excited to start her new life with Conall. Her mate was her world now.

"No one will ever replace you," he continued, his voice rough. "You're one of the best damn trackers I've ever seen."

Her throat was too tight to answer so she just nodded.

He cleared his throat. "So when do you leave?"

"Probably after Bo and Nyx's wedding." With the last few parties cancelled, Rhea thought they were only doing one more—the actual wedding.

"Damn."

"I know." It was only a few days away. "I guess I could stay a few weeks and—"

He shook his head once. "No. I'll change out the rotation and figure all that shit out. But it's not for you to worry about. You're mated now. That bond is your priority."

At that she smiled, glad he understood. "Yes." And it was the best feeling in the world, knowing she was mated to such an amazing male.

Finn slung an arm around her shoulders, kissed the top of her head. "Come on. Let's head inside."

She wrapped her arm around his waist, a sense of sadness and joy mixing through her, making her feel a little bittersweet. Things were changing so dang fast. Leaving behind the life she'd had for so long was a little scary. Still, she'd never been so excited about anything in her life and with Conall as her mate she knew she could take on anything.

CHAPTER TWENTY-THREE

"Thanks for talking with me," Rory said to Finn, his new Alpha. That thought was odd, a little disconcerting to his wolf who hadn't followed a leader in a very long time. Even when he'd been part of his mother's pack, he'd known he was stronger than his old Alpha. That male hadn't been a threat and Rory hadn't cared about him.

Finn nodded once, leaned against the front of his desk. His body language was clear: make this quick. "Thank you for your help today."

Rory nodded. "Those bastards deserved what they got." By the state of some of the females brought in, the males deserved more than the quick deaths they'd been given. But torture wasn't any shifters' style. That was more a vampire thing.

"So what's up?"

He scrubbed a hand over the back of his neck. Liberty was downstairs, helping Ophelia and Victoria get the new females situated. Nyx had brought her over earlier because Liberty had asked Nyx to. Because she wanted to help out with females who might have been through the same type of situation she had. She truly was one of the kindest females he'd ever known. He wanted to make sure she was looked after, no matter what. "If something happens to me before Liberty and I mate, I need to know that she'll have the pack's protection."

"*Your* pack."

Rory frowned. "What?"

"You said 'the pack'. It's your pack now, Rory." Finn's gaze was hard, assessing.

"I know. It's weird to say, I guess." He'd told Finn about most of his history with his old pack because joining with a new one meant he had to lay himself bare to an extent. He had to be honest with the wolves he hoped to become packmates with.

Finn simply nodded again, his ice blue gaze hard to read.

"I know she'll have my brothers and Nyx, but I just . . . need to know she'll be protected."

"And if she doesn't mate with you?"

He didn't have to think about it. "I want her protected no matter what." Even if she ended up with someone else—and that would likely destroy him—he still wanted her taken care of, looked after.

Always.

If she chose someone else over him, that was her choice. It wouldn't diminish his love for her. At this point he didn't think she would, but he always felt the need to prepare for the worst.

Finn's shoulders relaxed a fraction. "Good answer. You have my word she'll be protected. Even if things don't work out and you leave the pack, she'll be under my protection."

Rory blinked at the Alpha's words. "Seriously?"

"Yes."

He didn't want to push his luck, but... "Can I ask why?"

"Why not? She's a good female, she lives in my territory and she knows about the supernatural world. She's one of mine now. The strong protect the weak. Always." The Alpha said it with such a matter-of-fact attitude, Rory understood right then why this male was the leader of one of the strongest packs in the world. He inspired loyalty not through fear, but respect and love.

Yeah, Rory wasn't going to leave this pack anytime soon. There'd have to be a damn good reason to drag him away. While he didn't agree that Liberty was weak, he also didn't think that was what Finn meant so he didn't comment. "Thank you."

Finn nodded, pushing up from the desk. "Her scent is different now, which I'm sure you know."

"It is. And I know why, but I think it's something she needs to tell you about personally." Unless Finn directly asked, then Rory would tell him.

"Fair enough. We've got a lot of stuff going on this week and Rhea's leaving in a few days so I'll want to move you into a security rotation. Unless you'd prefer to do something else? I know you and your brothers have your own businesses and holdings. I could use help at Howlers for security and your resume fits that bill. Or I'm looking into expanding with a few more restaurants. I know you've got experience there too."

God, he hadn't even thought that far ahead. Rory and his brother, well both brothers, had a shitload of money. But he and Ian had gotten wealthy mainly from investments and businesses that were run by very capable, smart people. They only checked in once in a while to make sure they were still making money. The people who worked for them were too afraid to screw with their finances.

Most of their time had been spent in a Hell realm the last fifty years. And the last eight months he'd been pretty much focused only on Liberty. But he'd been getting antsy with the need to do more since returning to the human realm. "Let me talk to Liberty first. She's still . . . healing." Emotionally anyway. He wasn't sure how long it would take, but he knew he didn't want to be working insane hours, spending too much time away from her.

"We can work any job out so that your schedule works with hers. I do it for all the mated couples. The only thing I require as a member of the pack is that everyone contributes their fair share. Sometimes it'll be more, sometimes less. And if you hate a job you've been given, we'll switch it up."

"Thanks." He held out a hand, relief filling him. Being part of this pack would be a good thing, even if it would take some getting used to.

Finn pumped his hand once, nodded. "I know you'll always have a loyalty to your brothers. If one of my orders ever divides your loyalty . . . we'll cross that bridge if we ever get to it."

"Thank you. What do you need me to do?" he asked, moving toward the door. It was clear Finn had a ton of stuff to take care of around the mansion and he didn't want to get in the way of that. He'd just needed to know that no matter what his female was taken care of.

"Nothing for now. Check on Liberty and if she's ready, you two can head out."

"Will do," he said, opening the office door. While he wouldn't have minded staying and helping, it was clear the pack—his pack—had enough people to deal with everything. And he was ready to go home with Liberty, to be alone with her. Their time together last night had been interrupted and any time he had with her, was heaven.

* * *

Liberty stretched out on Rory's bare chest, savored the feel of his skin against her palm. She was still dressed, but he'd opted to wear boxer shorts. Having all that sexy skin on display was making her a little crazy, but she was more than happy right where she was. He made her feel safe just by being close.

"I talked to Finn today, about pack stuff," he murmured. Moonlight streamed in from the partially open curtains, illuminating her room.

She had on a nightlight though, which helped her to see better. "Is everything okay?"

"Yeah, he uh, gave me some options for different jobs with the pack."

She turned so that her chin was propped on her hand and looked up at him. "You don't need to work with them though, do you? I thought you had other businesses."

"I do, but to be part of the pack I have to be a contributor. I want to."

"I wondered how all that worked," she murmured. "Do they care if you mate with a human?" She felt her cheeks heat up at the question. Liberty knew how Rory felt about her and didn't doubt his love, but she was still confused about the whole mating thing. It seemed to carry more weight than a marriage and now that he'd joined a pack she worried that maybe he wouldn't be able to mate her.

"No. And Finn said he would protect you no matter what. Even if we don't . . . mate." He said the last part in clear distaste. "His pack will always have your back."

She blinked in surprise. There was so much she still had to learn about the supernatural world and the way packs, vampire covens and dragon clans worked, but to have the protection of the Stavros pack even if she wasn't with Rory was pretty incredible. Even if she didn't like the idea of *not* being with him. "Wow, thank you."

"Don't thank me. It's Finn."

Liberty had a feeling that Rory had requested, or maybe, knowing the sexy man, demanded, that she be protected, but she didn't push. "Rhea told me she's leaving in a few days, but that she talked to Chloe and she's agreed to train me with weapons and will teach me how to defend myself."

"I can do that." His tone was definitely offended.

She splayed her fingers over his muscular chest, rubbed in a small circle. "I know. I just think it'll be easier for me to concentrate if I have someone else training me. No way would I be able to concentrate with all your naked skin on display." Her cheeks heated as his gaze darkened.

His eyes dropped to her mouth, giving her that hungry look she found she liked a whole lot. But just as quickly he looked away and smoothly slid out from under her grasp.

"I'm gonna grab a quick shower." He was fast, moving out of the bed before she could say anything, but not fast enough that she didn't see his very prominent erection.

She fell back against her pillow, the air pushing out in a whoosh as he disappeared into her bathroom. She could guess what he would be doing. Probably masturbating.

That thought annoyed her because she wanted to be the one bringing him pleasure. He'd already done so much for her and while she knew he wasn't keeping score, she still wanted to give him what he'd given her. Wanted to see ecstasy play over his face as he came for her. She loved him, plain and simple.

Months ago she wasn't sure she'd ever be at that point again to be with someone physically but she'd come a long way from being that girl Rory and the others had rescued from that Hell realm. She'd gone into the darkness and come into the light stronger for it. Because she wasn't just surviving anymore, which was all she'd been able to think about back in that hell. She was actually living.

And she wanted to live the rest of her life, however long that may be, with Rory. She knew that with a bone deep certainty that was a little scary.

She wanted her mate. It was time she made that clear.

Shoving up, she got out of bed and stripped as she made her way to the bathroom. She might not be sure about a lot of things, but she was sure of her and Rory. He was the only solid thing in a world that felt crazy most days.

CHAPTER TWENTY-FOUR

The bathroom door opened without a sound as Liberty pushed it open. She figured Rory had to hear her, especially with his super sensitive hearing, but he didn't say anything. The mirror was already starting to fog over from the steam billowing out of the glass and stone enclosure. She couldn't see him clearly behind the thick glass stones, but could see his big shadow standing under the shower jet.

Even though he'd gone down on her and seen her mostly naked, this felt different. Because she didn't plan on stopping at oral sex tonight. She'd helped out at the mansion for most of the day, knowing she'd get to come home with Rory.

That thought had filled her with so much joy; that he was hers and wasn't going anywhere. She knew there wasn't a rush to mate, but she still wanted to move forward in their relationship and show him what he meant to her.

Her feet were chilled against the tile as she walked to the shower opening. When she stepped into the shower enclave, Rory was standing under the water, all the muscles in his huge body pulled tight as he watched her with a mix of surprise and lust.

His erection was thick, curving up against his lower abdomen.

On instinct, she stepped forward. Even though he blocked most of the water, some splashed over her. She barely felt it, she was so focused on him.

His green eyes seemed even brighter tonight as he tracked her movements. He hadn't shaved in a couple days so his facial hair was even scruffier, all that stubble ridiculously sexy. There was pretty much nothing about him that didn't turn her on.

With her eyes on his, she reached for his erection, wrapped her fingers around his thick length. Stroked once. Twice.

He shuddered, his eyes rolling back once as she stroked again. He groaned, slammed one hand against the tiled wall and the other against the glass. There wasn't much space so his arms were bent, his muscles flexing under the tension.

"I meant what I said earlier." She stroked again, this time with more pressure. Tendrils of heat licked through her as she watched his eyes dilate. She loved that she could bring this big male to his knees.

His breathing was erratic as he watched her, his eyes definitely brighter now and she realized his wolf was looking back at her. She could see that he was fighting for control, but wasn't worried about him losing it with her.

Rory would never do anything she didn't want.

His cock pulsed in her hand, the feel of that thickness sending a rush of heat between her legs. She wanted to know what it would feel like to have him inside her. "I'm never letting you go," she murmured.

He let out a soft growl at her words and made a move as if he wanted to touch her, but kept his hands pinned in place.

She caressed him again and he groaned, his jaw so tight he looked as if he was in pain.

Moving faster now, she began stroking him in a hard, steady rhythm. It was clear he was holding back and she wasn't sure why. "Come for me," she demanded. He'd given her not only pleasure, but the ability to actually feel again. She didn't want him to ever hold back from her.

Her words seemed to set off something inside him. He came on a growl. He threw his head back, letting out a roaring, growling sound that sent shivers of delight skittering across her skin. She loved that she could make this man lose it. She loved everything about him.

He came all over her hands and stomach and she reveled in it in a way she never had with anyone before. She almost felt as if he was marking her. A year ago, she never would have had that thought. Now . . . she loved the idea of Rory claiming her.

"Liberty," he gasped out as he continued coming. His orgasm seemed to go on forever.

She couldn't stop watching him, stop touching him. Until he tore his hand from the glass wall and stilled her, his bigger hand steady over hers. Breathing harshly, he stared down at her, at his come on her. To her surprise, he rubbed it into her stomach, made a growl of satisfaction as he did.

The action was so raw, so earthy, her cheeks heated up.

"It's a wolf thing." His words were raspy. "I'm gonna want to mark you with my scent all the time."

"I like it." And she did. Way more than she could have imagined, especially the 'before' Liberty. Sex in her previous life had been fine, but it had just been sex. She'd never been in love before Rory and everything about being with him was different. And not just because he was a half-demon, half-wolf.

He shifted to the side so that more water cascaded down over her as he bent to kiss her. His tongue invaded her mouth as he tugged her body to his.

She slid her arms around him, clutched his back. When he bit her bottom lip, she moaned into his mouth—then pulled back, stared up at him with wide eyes. "How are you hard again?" His full erection lay heavy between their bodies.

"You're naked. That's how."

Grinning, she lifted up on her toes to kiss him again. His mouth devoured hers in what was most definitely a claiming.

She breathed in everything about him, that cold wintery scent of his driving her crazy with need. She wasn't sure if it was because of whatever Arya had done to change her, but she'd noticed that her ability to smell was heightened. Before she'd known that Rory had a distinctive scent, but now she felt like she could get high on it. On him.

Her breasts rubbed against his bare chest, the stimulation turning her on even more. Right now under the bright light of the bathroom, in his arms, she felt whole and safe. The feeling was freeing and while she knew it wouldn't always be like this, that she'd still have bad days, she was going to embrace the good ones.

She leaned back to look up at him. Water rushed down over both of them, steam rising everywhere. It was like they were the only two people in the world at the moment. Something she was more than okay with.

His green eyes were bright and his expression so caring, so full of love, it melted her. Yep, she was never letting him go.

"I want you inside me," she whispered, the only words she could get out when he looked at her with such adoration.

A shudder went through him as one of his big hands slid between their bodies. His palm was a little roughened with calluses as he glided lower, lower, until he cupped gently between her legs. "You're sure?" he asked, even as he began slowly teasing her slick folds with a finger.

Her inner walls tightened, needing to be filled by him. She nodded.

"Say it." A soft demand.

She realized he needed her to be audible, struggled to find her voice when her senses were going into overload. "Yes."

He slid a finger inside her, let out a guttural sound as he closed his eyes. "You're so wet."

She clutched onto his shoulders as he slid another finger inside her. She loved the feel of him teasing her. Her inner walls tightened around him.

Pressing her against the wall, he bent down to cover her mouth with his as he began moving, oh-so-slowly inside her. His fingers were thick and long, the sensation of them filling her almost perfect. She needed more though.

Too many sensations bombarded her. The tile behind her cooled her back, but she felt a fire raging through her. Building and expanding out of control, she desperately needed a release.

Rory barely grazed her clit with his thumb as he continued thrusting his fingers inside her.

She pressed down on his bottom lip with her teeth harder than she'd meant to.

He jerked back, his hand stilling with his palm cupping her and his two fingers buried deep inside her. "We'll stop," he said, already starting to pull out of her.

"No." She dug her fingers into his shoulders. "I need more." Did she ever.

She was glad when he didn't question her. She didn't think she could stand it if he questioned everything she said, if he was so worried he'd break her that this wouldn't be enjoyable. She knew her mind and appreciated that he accepted that. That he trusted her. It meant more than he'd ever know.

With his bright gaze pinned to hers, he grasped her hips, lifted her up against the wall. On instinct, she wrapped her legs around his waist as he settled her against the wall. She'd thought he'd thrust right into her, but apparently he'd decided to take his time.

She couldn't decide if that was a good or bad thing. Her nipples were tight buds, aching for his touch.

As if he read her mind, he dipped his head to one of her breasts, sucking on one nipple with a sharpness that punched out to all her nerve endings.

Her inner walls clenched even harder now, aching. She let her head fall back against the tile as she dug her nails into his shoulders. "Feels good," she rasped out.

He made a growling sound against her breast, the vibration ricocheting through her, making even more of her nerves spark to life.

He shifted his body slightly as he continued teasing her nipple with his wicked, talented tongue. She'd experienced last night just how gifted he was with his mouth.

She rolled her hips against him, trying to urge him to do more.

His chest rising and falling erratically, he lifted his head, his eyes sparking with too many emotions to filter through. "I never imagined someone like you. Ever." His voice was hoarse, guttural.

"You're more amazing than anyone I could have imagined," she whispered. It was true. She'd never thought someone like Rory could exist. He'd been by her side for the last eight months and if she needed to wait another eight months to be ready for sex, she knew he'd be right here by her side, waiting. It was one of the reasons she loved him so much.

He looked as if he wanted to say more, but his jaw tightened when she lifted up against him, rubbing her slick folds against his cock.

She was done waiting. She was taking what she wanted. What had happened to her in the Hell realm wasn't going to define her life. Yes, it had changed the direction of it and shaped who she was now, but she wouldn't let a monster take away her future.

Not when her future was this male and he was the most beautiful thing she'd ever seen. "Mate me," she blurted, the words tumbling out before she could analyze them. She wasn't even sure if they were the right words. She just knew she wanted to be mated to Rory for the rest of her life.

"I should give you more time." The muscles in his neck corded tight as he held her up against the wall.

"I don't need more time." When you know, you know. She'd had enough bad shit happen to her and now she was damn well going to grab the best thing that had ever happened to her and not let him go. "You're what I want. Forever."

He made a savage sound of approval, as if he couldn't voice anything more. He cupped her mound again, shuddered as he slid two, then three fingers inside her. She arched her back off the wall, crying out his name as he moved his fingers inside her. It wouldn't take her long to come, but she wanted all of him.

Thankfully he wasn't going to make either of them wait. He withdrew his fingers and positioned his cock at her entrance. She ached for him to fill her. His fingers clutched onto her ass as she held onto him.

He hovered where he was, intent to take his time. No way. She impaled herself on him with one stroke, taking him by surprise.

"Fuck," he growled, gripping her ass and holding her in place.

She sucked in a breath at the feel of him filling her completely. Her inner walls convulsed around him, her climax within reach. She tried to move, but he held her tight, his fingers digging into her as he tried to catch his breath.

She didn't want that. She wanted to feel him thrusting into her over and over. Going on instinct, as she seemed to do with his male more often than not, she nipped at his chest with her teeth.

Which was apparently the right thing to do.

He pushed her against the wall and began thrusting, his gaze intent on her the entire time.

She couldn't look away if she'd wanted to. She felt pinned in place in more ways than one as he thrust into her, over and over.

Her nerves felt as if they were on fire, dancing with pleasure as he filled her. The way he held her up against the wall, as if she weighed nothing, made her even wetter.

She started to reach between their bodies, but he shoved her hand away and tweaked her clit with his thumb.

The pressure was perfect, unexpected, and it sent her over the edge. All her stomach muscles tightened as pleasure rocked into her in a sharp burst of sensation.

Her climax surged through her, taking over any sense of reason or coherency as he pushed into her over and over. She buried her face against his neck, raking her teeth over him in a wild, instinctual gesture. Her clit pulsed under the onslaught of his teasing, the sensation starting to border on painful as he continued stroking her.

When he began nuzzling her neck, she arched into him, her breasts rubbing against his chest as another, slightly milder orgasm started to crest.

"Too much," she rasped out, just before she felt the sharp sting of his canines.

The prick of his bite lasted for only a moment before it blurred into exquisite pleasure. All her nerves felt alive as he groaned against her neck.

He gripped her impossibly tight as he emptied himself inside her, the warmth of his orgasm filling her. All she could do was hold on as he continued thrusting inside her, his orgasm as long as hers, until she collapsed against him, wrapping her arms around his neck.

She was glad he was strong because she was barely holding herself up against him.

She wasn't sure how much time passed, but eventually he pulled his head back from her neck. Water pounded down around them, the sound seemingly over-pronounced as they stared at each other.

When his gaze strayed to her shoulder, he frowned slightly, then shifted so he looked down over her shoulder.

"What?" she murmured, concern filling her.

He ran his finger over the back of her shoulder. "I wasn't sure it would happen, but . . . you have a small, circular tattoo on your shoulder."

Blinking, she tried to look but couldn't see anything from the odd angle. "You mean like Nyx does?" She'd seen one on the demigod and it was a mirror of the one Bo, Ian and Rory had on their chest when they were in demon form. She'd wondered if Nyx had gotten it when she'd mated Bo.

He nodded, looking unsure of himself. "Yeah. It's a symbol of my heritage."

She smiled, insanely happy to have that tattoo on her. It made her feel even more accepted. "I can't wait to see it."

Her words clearly eased whatever worry he'd been feeling. "You're mine now." He rolled his hips against her once, his cock half-hard and starting to lengthen again inside her.

"Always." And he was hers. Forever.

* * *

Rory idly stroked his hand down Liberty's spine, loved being able to touch her anywhere he wanted. Anytime he wanted. As long as she let him.

He wasn't sure what time it was, but it was late. Maybe even early Monday morning now. The past few days had rushed by in a blur of activity and insanity. The only thing that mattered to him was that he and Liberty were mated.

He still felt like maybe he'd dreamed it all, and soon he'd wake up and reality would crash over him. With her lean, naked body stretched out over him he knew everything between them was real. And he was never letting her go. When she'd told him to mate with her, he'd almost said no. Almost.

Nothing could have stopped him from fully claiming her. Not when she was telling him to do it. Part of him felt selfish, wondered if he should have waited a little longer, but that hadn't been much of an option.

Not when she'd been naked, wrapped around him, *wet* for him, and ordering him to claim her. Nope. He only had so much self-control.

He drew in a ragged breath, forced his erection back down. Sort of. It was damn hard with her draped across him, her breasts pressed against his chest.

Well too damn bad for him. She was exhausted and he wasn't going to wake her up simply because he was horny again. But the female was an addiction. One he never wanted to recover from.

He rolled his shoulders once, shifting against the sheet. He turned toward the window as a shadow passed over it. The tension fled him as he realized it was just a cloud moving in over the full moon.

The bright moon soothed his wolf side. It didn't matter that shifters didn't need a full moon to shift—what a weird human myth—his animal side still loved to run around under the moon. Soon he wanted to take Liberty out with him. She was more than comfortable with him in his wolf form, but he wanted to take her out to the woods, to go running. Or hell, maybe even just along the beach. He couldn't actually pass for a large dog, he was way too big, and he'd have to go slow so she could keep pace with him, but—

"Do you remember the first time I opened up to you about . . . what happened to me?" Liberty's quiet voice cut through his rambling thoughts.

He stilled at her words. Her breathing had been so steady he'd thought she was finally asleep. "I remember everything you've ever told me about your time there."

It was the truth. The first time she'd truly opened up to him had been not long after her rescue. Only a couple days. She'd been living in his brother Bo's house, as had he, and they'd been watching something on TV. Whatever it had been, he couldn't remember. Because all his focus had been on her.

Some of her first words on the subject still stuck with him, were embedded in his brain. He knew he'd never forget them and his only wish was that he could bring the monster who'd hurt her back to life just so he could torture and kill him again.

Her previous words played in his head, even as he tried to shove them back. *I didn't get to eat whenever I wanted. Back in that place. When I'm around you, I feel caught between the girl I was before and who I am now. And I'm not really sure why I'm so comfortable with you. It's scary all by itself. For so long I was afraid every second of every day. I was even afraid to go to sleep because I never knew when he'd be back. I just knew that he would return. It didn't matter how many times I escaped. He always brought me back.*

"I never really told you about how I ended up there," she said now.

No, she hadn't. And he'd never pushed. Because the details she'd told him about her time there had been enough. "You don't have to tell me if you don't want to."

"I know." She idly traced her fingers over his chest. "I want to."

She cleared her throat so he tightened his hold on her, wanting her to feel supported.

"The two females you buried, they were the reason I ended up in that place."

Once, months ago, he'd told her that he was sorry about her friends. After they'd found Liberty, helped her escape that hellish camp, he'd gone back that same night and buried the other human females who'd died there. Liberty had told him in no uncertain terms that the females weren't her friends.

"They hired me to plan a party, some beach-themed bachelorette party for a friend. One of them had an interest in the occult, thought she might have some inborn powers. Like a witch, I guess. I'd never heard of anything supernatural before and I didn't even know any of this until we were stuck in that realm." She took another breath and he could feel her heart racing out of control.

He smoothed a hand down her spine, continued rubbing up and down. Almost immediately her heart rate slowed. Not completely back to normal, but she wasn't as stressed and he was glad that his touch comforted her.

"I got to know both of them a little when planning their friend's bachelorette party, so a week after, when one of them called me about planning a party for the two of them, I didn't think anything of it. Work by word of mouth was pretty much how I operated. When I got to the address, a pretty nice cabin out in the country, it was a freaking horror show inside." Her voice was tight as she shifted against him so she could look at him. Her eyes were sad as she gave him a half-smile.

"They'd killed two men. Homeless, I found out later. They used them as a sacrifice to open a door to a Hell realm. They thought they could release *something* from it and control it to do their bidding. They'd planned to use me as a sacrifice too, but things went haywire, a portal opened and sucked all of us in to that hell."

Not the real Hell but he knew what she meant. "That's insane."

Sighing, she nodded before shifting back down and tucking her head against his chest. "I know. It was like I'd walked into a horror movie and things kept getting worse and worse. But they had it a lot worse than me there." She shuddered and his grip automatically tightened again.

"I'm sorry." His words felt weak, inadequate. He remembered what his brother had told him about finding the women in cages. One had already been dead and the other took her own life when Ian had freed her, stabbing herself with one of Ian's blades. He also knew they'd been shared among the males of that half-demon camp run by Koighans. Unlike Liberty, who'd belonged to the leader.

He felt his demon half rise to the surface, had to shove his rage back down. Now wasn't about him or his anger. It was about listening to her.

"I wasn't glad for what happened to them, but I was glad that I didn't get thrown into one of those cages. I still feel guilty about that. About being glad that I just had one monster to deal with and not all of them." Her voice was soft.

Fuck that. "They were murderers who got you sucked into a Hell realm against your will. And they'd planned to kill you." She had nothing to feel guilty about. He didn't say that though. When dealing with guilt or other emotions, he understood that the mind wasn't always rational.

"I know, I just . . . I remember their screams at night sometimes when I try to sleep. It's hard to deal with sometimes."

Ah, hell. He buried his face against her hair. "I'm so sorry, sweetheart." He'd give up anything, even his own life, to take away all her pain, to go back in time and reverse everything that had happened for her to end up in that place.

She didn't say anything, just curled up against him and threw her leg over him. He felt the wetness of her tears against his chest and wanted to slay all the monsters in the world for her.

But for now, he pulled the covers up over them and held her close. "I'll always be here for you," he said quietly against the top of her head. "No one will ever hurt you again. Not if I have breath in my lungs."

CHAPTER TWENTY-FIVE

Finn pulled Lyra into his lap, more than exhausted after the last week or so. It seemed like it was always one thing or another he had to deal with. Insane demigods or Akkadian demons trying to escape into this realm. At least this recent threat had been easier to handle.

Some fool who'd thought he could take on Finn's territory, his pack, *him*. He was glad Rhea had killed the wolf, though part of him wished he'd had that pleasure himself.

"What is going on in that sexy head of yours?" Lyra nuzzled his neck, raking her teeth over his pulse point.

The music from the live jazz band in Bo's club was going full steam. With everything back to normal—for now—Bo and Nyx had finally gotten married. And tonight's reception had no apparent end in sight. He'd snagged one of the private booths at the back and finally had a moment alone with Lyra. Those moments were too few as far as he was concerned.

"How sexy my mate is," he murmured, sliding one hand up her unfortunately covered hip.

Lyra had worn a purple dress—though she'd informed him the correct term was eggplant—and the thing was designed to make him crazy, wrapping around his delicious mate's body like a second skin. He couldn't wait to slowly peel it from her, to reveal every inch of her. "I was thinking soon we might grab one of those rooms behind the red door." Her teeth sank into his neck and he let his head fall back as a wave of ecstasy swept through him.

He loved it when she bit him. He didn't bother fighting a moan as she tugged, drawing just a bit of blood from him. Damn it, they did need some alone time and those rooms were right there. Before she'd come back into his life he'd have never considered getting one of the private rooms. Had never really come to this club except for work. But he'd already gotten a key—

"Dude, you guys. Not in front of the kid." Vega's voice snapped them both back to the present.

Lyra didn't move, but she did snicker as she shifted slightly on his lap. Over his extremely uncomfortable erection.

He fought back a groan of frustration.

"Just a couple hours ago you were telling me you were an adult now," Lyra said to their daughter.

"I am, but I'm still your kid and I don't need to see all this." She motioned with a hand between them, her blue eyes filled with a sort of horror. "Much less hear you two talking about going behind that door." She whispered the last part.

Lyra laughed while Finn scrubbed a hand over his face. He'd just learned about his daughter a little over a year ago and he had absolutely no problem *never* talking about anything related to sex in her presence. "What's going on? Are you ready to go home?"

"No way, it's early. I just . . . well, I wanted to know if maybe I could go to an after party."

Finn frowned, looked at Lyra. It was already two in the morning. What kind of after party was she thinking?

Lyra just lifted her eyebrows, letting him make the decision. Damn it, not what he wanted to do. He'd made his daughter cry twice in the last year and he still felt guilty about it. Though to be fair he'd just been trying to forbid her from going on a date with a human. Of course now he realized that using the word forbid to his daughter had been his first mistake. There should be a guidebook for parenting. "Who's going to be there?"

"Ah, well, I think Keelin and Ophelia are going."

He nodded, not scenting a lie from her. Keelin and Bran had made it into town for the wedding because Keelin was actually part of the wedding party. So if she was going then Bran would be too. "And?"

"Some of the staff from here. Cynara," she said quickly.

Yeah, Finn had met Bo's half-demon, half-vampire sister. She was a good female and if Keelin and Ophelia would be there, he could deal with it. "Where?"

"Cynara's place."

Finn knew the female had a place on the beach not too far from here. "Just keep your phone on you."

She blinked in clear surprise. "Seriously, I can go?"

He lifted a shoulder. "We trust you." She was eighteen and a powerful hybrid. He knew she could take care of herself, she was just untrained. So if a more powerful being attacked her—nope, he wouldn't be thinking of that. The pack would be there to look after her and he couldn't keep her wrapped in cotton for the rest of her life. Even if he wanted to.

"Thank you guys!" She half dove into the booth and tackle-hugged them.

His heart swelled even more as she wrapped an arm around his neck and smacked a kiss against his cheek. "You're the best!"

She was gone in a blur of motion, her blue-black hair the same color as his own flying out behind her as she hurried back to the dance floor.

"You're sending Gabriel to shadow her, right?" Lyra murmured low enough for only his ears.

He snorted, already pulling his cell phone out of his pocket. "Not even a question." But he didn't even have to text his Guardian. Gabriel was on the edge of the dance floor, nodded once at Finn in total understanding and moved closer to where Vega was dancing.

"I seriously don't know how I'm going to deal with her going to college." Lyra wrapped an arm around his neck, cuddled closer to him as she set her head against his shoulder.

He'd never been more content in his life than he was now. His mate in his lap, his daughter safe and secure with friends and packmates surrounding her. "Me neither," he murmured. He didn't even want to think about it, but he knew the time was coming soon enough. He had maybe seven months to get ready for it because Vega wanted to start with summer school instead of the fall semester next year.

"Who are you gonna send with her?" Lyra asked.

"I thought maybe Chloe would be a good fit." He hadn't figured out who else to send with her just yet. She wouldn't be living on campus and she'd have to deal with two guards living in the same building she did. Maybe even more. He knew it sucked, but that was just the way it was going to be. Powerful or not, she was a target because of her bloodline.

"Yeah, I was thinking the same thing. Maybe Gabriel, but he might stunt her ability to make friends too much."

Finn just grunted. It was true. "He'll also keep any males away from her." Which was fine with Finn.

"I like the way you think." Lyra's voice was surprisingly approving.

He laughed, turning to look at her. "I thought you'd tell me how wrong that was."

"Screw that. I don't want any male near my baby girl."

They both looked out at the dance floor where their "baby girl" was talking to a very adult vampire male who had definite interest in his gaze. Finn hadn't even realized he'd started growling until Lyra placed a calming hand against his chest.

"We trust her," she murmured, shifting so that her face was all he could see. "We have to act like it or she'll resent us forever. She's gotta be free to live her life."

"I know." Didn't mean he had to like it. But Vega was growing up and they couldn't stand in her way. Not if they wanted to have any sort of relationship with her. Besides, he trusted Gabriel to watch out for her. She could direct all her annoyance to him. Which yeah, was shitty, but Finn didn't care. Powerful Alpha or not, he'd rather his daughter be angry at someone else than at him.

He reached into his pants pocket, pulled out a single gold key. "Room two."

Lyra's grayish-violet eyes brightened supernaturally with hunger and need. "I can't believe you've had this the whole time." With supernatural speed she was off his lap and standing by the edge of the booth.

He moved just as fast and scooped her up in his arms before she could take another step. Vega was well protected. For the next few hours he wasn't going to worry about anything other than pleasuring his mate.

The outside world could wait. Lyra completed his life in a way he'd never fully imagined. The last year had only shown him how incomplete his life had been without her in it. He loved to show her exactly how important she was to him every chance he got.

* * *

Rhea tugged the hem of her dress down her legs as the cooler door flew open.

Liberty stood there, wide-eyed, looking between Rhea and Conall—who was currently zipping his pants up.

"Yep, it's what it looks like in here," Rhea said, feeling only a little bad. "Sorry." But she wasn't. Conall had decided to get frisky and well, the walk-in fridge had been the closest place they could find for some privacy. The cold temperatures didn't affect them, especially with the kind of heat they generated together.

Even though her cheeks tinged pink, Liberty shook her head and strode toward one of the racks where trays upon trays of food were lined. She picked up what Rhea thought was cucumber cups stuffed with crab. "I've come to learn that shifters have absolutely no shame. I just caught two people going at it under one of the food tables. Seriously," she muttered, avoiding eye contact with them as she picked up the tray. "Y'all are freaks."

Conall held the cooler door open for her, grinning back at Rhea, who just followed behind Liberty, still trying to get her dress situated as she stepped into the kitchen.

"I think her mate is going to be a good addition to the pack," Rhea said as Liberty disappeared through the swinging door that led back to the club. The scent of Rory on Liberty and vice versa was unmistakable. Once shifters mated it was clear to anyone standing close to them that they were officially off-limits.

"He'll never replace you." His words were so sweet, sincere, emotion clogged her throat.

She hadn't even been thinking in those terms, but she was glad that her pack had another warrior to join with her leaving. Not that they even needed it, but more strength was always a good thing. "Thanks," she murmured before clearing her throat.

Empty glasses had been stacked next to one of the industrial-sized sinks and plates had already started piling up in both of them. Rhea knew that Liberty had a whole crew who were supposed to be helping out with the cleanup, but had a feeling that whoever they were, were slacking off because it was such a fun party.

"What?" Conall stilled beside her, his expression worried.

"Nothing. Just thinking that someone needs to be back here cleaning up right now. They can't leave all this until the end of the night. The party's not ending anytime soon and—"

Grinning, Conall leaned in, brushed his mouth over hers. She could taste herself on him from when he'd had his face buried between her legs earlier. She wanted to drag him right back into the cooler.

"Not your problem tonight," he said. "Let's head back out there, enjoy ourselves some more."

She'd definitely been enjoying herself in the cooler with him, but something was bothering her and had been for the last few days. "Does your clan know you're mated to a wolf?" she blurted. They'd be headed back to Montana in a couple days and he hadn't said much about his clan's thoughts on her. Sure, she knew that Arya loved her—the female had made that abundantly clear—but an Alpha dragon mating with a wolf wasn't common.

He nodded, frowning. "Yes. Everyone is pleased." Suddenly, he stilled in a way only supernaturals could do. "Why? Are you not . . . pleased to be an Alpha's mate?"

"No! I mean, yes, I'm happy. But I just wondered if anyone had an issue with me being your mate? I mean, you came down to Biloxi for—"

"You."

"Wait, what?"

"I came down here for you."

"I thought you were here for the wedding stuff."

His mouth curved up in a wry smile as his big hands settled on her hips. His hold was possessive. "No. It has always been about you. I bought that place almost eight months ago because I knew I'd eventually be down here—for *you.* Even when I didn't want to admit what my dragon half knew from the moment we met, everything was leading me to you. The wedding celebration was simply an excuse to see you. And to convince you that you're mine."

A weight she hadn't realized had been on her chest lifted, making it easier to breathe again. She threw her arms around his neck, kissed him hard. Yes, she was still a little nervous about taking up the role of an Alpha's mate, especially to a clan of dragons, but she could do anything with her mate by her side. "And you're mine," she murmured against his mouth. "I'm never letting you go."

CHAPTER TWENTY-SIX

Two days later

Rhea slid her hand into Conall's as they headed for the entrance to Howlers. She'd finally packed everything and was having the majority of her belongings sent to Montana. They planned to leave tomorrow and Solon and Chloe had wanted to meet up for drinks one last time.

Her heart ached a little no matter how freaking happy she was.

This was her pack, her people. She was really going to miss them. She was a little bummed that Finn hadn't been able to get away from pack business but after everything that had gone down recently she understood more than ever that he had to take care of the pack first and always.

Conall's fingers tightened around hers as he held open the door for her. When she stepped into the entrance of Howlers, she stopped dead in her boots.

Her entire pack was there, everyone smiling widely underneath a sign that read "We'll miss you!"

Finn, Solon, Lyra, Chloe, Gabriel, Spiro, Jason . . . She looked around at everyone she'd lived with and worked alongside for decades and burst into tears. She hadn't expected this at all. Everyone had been so dang busy today and yeah, she'd been a little disappointed that only a few packmates could hang out during her last night. But she hadn't expected a party.

"Damn it," she muttered, swiping at her eyes as Solon and Chloe tackle-hugged her. She never cried. But screw it, she wouldn't be embarrassed. She wrapped her arms around them tight, not bothering to fight her tears as they sandwiched her. She was aware of Conall heading over to where Drake and Victoria were standing by a high-top table and was glad he was giving her a little space to say goodbye.

"I'm gonna miss you," Solon said, his voice uncharacteristically thick with emotion.

"Bitch'll be back to visit," Chloe growled, her own voice watery. "Or I'm coming up to Montana. Either way works."

Laughing, Rhea stepped back but still had her hands loosely wrapped around both their shoulders. "Of course I'll be back. And you two have a standing invitation to visit. Always."

"No way," Finn said, coming up to join them. "These dragons keep stealing my people. You can't have anymore."

"Don't be a hater, Finn." Victoria, hurrying over on five inch heels, looped a sash over Rhea's head as she reached them. It read 'Adios Bitches!' Aaaand, she wanted to cry all over again.

"Besides, wolves are taking over the Petronilla clan, bitches!" Victoria continued, raising an unopened champagne bottle in one hand.

Rhea's eyes widened. "Bitches?" It was pretty rare for Victoria to curse, let alone publicly like this.

"She's had way too much to drink," Chloe whispered, but Victoria clearly heard her.

"That may be true, but..." She trailed off, looking around, Rhea assumed for Drake, who was just watching her with a mix of amusement and lust.

"But?" Solon prodded.

But Victoria had lost her train of thought as she hurried back to her mate. Rhea waved at Conall to join her and the others but he shook his head and motioned for her to go talk to everyone who was waiting. Yep, she loved her mate.

Finn wrapped an arm around her shoulders, kissed the top of her head. "Almost everyone's here tonight and they all want to say goodbye. We've got a table full of presents—mostly gag gifts, I'm sorry to tell you. I've worked it so that those on shift are gonna trade out with others here so everyone gets a chance to talk to you before you go."

Rhea didn't respond, her throat too tight with emotion.

"But first, a shot." Ophelia, petite and mischievous, appeared from out of nowhere, thankfully balancing a tray of shot glasses on her hand.

"I think I'm going to have to carry Victoria back to our place," Drake murmured, watching his mate on the dance floor with the other wolf shifters. Victoria had a glass of champagne in her hand and had been dancing for the last straight hour. Neither she nor her packmates appeared to be even close to done for the night.

Conall just laughed into his beer. His brother wasn't wrong. "I might be right there with ya," he said, automatically scanning for his mate. Though probably not. Rhea was making the rounds, talking to all of her packmates, but she hadn't had much to drink. His mate was incredibly loved, something that was clear, and he was so proud of her. He was going to make damn sure his own clan accepted her. If they didn't, he'd resign his position.

Simple as that.

He wasn't too worried though, not after the way the clan had accepted Victoria with open arms. Not to mention his mother adored Rhea and no one in their right mind would ever cross her. But Rhea was so damn easy to love. Everything about her was real. Yes, his clan would love her too. He had no doubt.

"I think it's official that wolves are the craziest of any shifters." Drake stared at where one of the she-wolves was sitting on the shoulders of another she-wolf and was holding up a beer funnel for her.

"They're like college kids," he agreed, shaking his head. As insane as the wolves acted, Conall understood why. One of their own was leaving and they'd almost lost one of their own when Taylor had been kidnapped. They needed to let loose, celebrate being alive.

"I think those two are actually in college." Drake took another sip of his beer, staring in a kind of fascinated horror. "At least they're not setting anything on fire."

Conall wasn't even going to ask what that was about. "Where are the females they found?" He knew that Finn had been working to get all the captured females ready to either go back to their former lives, to stay with the Stavros pack, or to place them with different packs if they chose.

"Back at the mansion. They were invited, according to V, but none of them wanted to come."

He nodded, understanding. He doubted any of them felt like partying right now. None of them had been at Bo and Victoria's wedding either. He was glad Finn's pack was doing the right thing and helping them, not that that was ever a question. He cleared his throat. "What time did you guys want to head out tomorrow?"

He shrugged. "Whenever we wake up. What about you?"

"That was the plan for us too. You want us to pick you up on the way to the airport?" Conall and Drake would be using his clan's private jet. Their pilot was on standby twenty-four-seven.

"Yeah. To be safe let's make it late morning." His gaze was drawn to the dance floor again. "I have a feeling Victoria's gonna want to sleep in."

"I'm so happy you found her," Conall murmured. His brother had been to Hell and back—literally. He deserved all the happiness in the world.

Drake lifted his beer, tilted it for a toast. "And I'm happy you found the mate you deserve."

Conall clinked his glass. "To our better halves."

"I'll drink to that." Very soon he would have his mate all to himself. He had a bunch of crap to deal with once they returned home, but he planned on holing up with her for at least a week after that.

His clan had proven they could live without him for a week. They'd just have to deal for a little while longer. Because his mate meant everything to him.

Everything inside him warmed when he heard her loud, familiar laugh. That sound drew him like a beacon. He turned, saw her standing next to one of the big windows at a table of younger she-wolves. Her head was thrown back, her curls bouncing as she shook with laughter.

Until her he'd never realized what love was. He was never letting her go.

CHAPTER TWENTY-SEVEN

One month later

Conall nearly snarled when another knock sounded on his office door. But he scented who it was so he reined in his annoyance. "Come in," he snapped. Okay, he sorta reined it in.

Greer, the clan healer, poked her head in, a grin on her face, clearly undeterred by his tone. Her copper-colored hair was pulled back in a ponytail and she had on reindeer ears that flashed red and green lights.

"What the hell is that?"

"A gift from Victoria. We're both wearing them." She stepped into the room and he got the full view of her ensemble. She had on red and white striped tights and some sort of green and white top that he thought Christmas elves might wear, and bells on her pointed shoes. At six feet tall she was the typical height for a dragon shifter. And a ginormous Christmas elf.

"You look ridiculous," he muttered, looking back at his tablet, even as his lips twitched. He was being cranky and he knew it. But he couldn't seem to stop himself.

"Sooooo, watcha doing?"

He rubbed a hand over his face. Christmas was two days away, he had a shitload of financials to go over before Rhea got home from training and everyone in the freaking clan had decided they had a problem they needed him to deal with. Not to mention he and Rhea hadn't had sex last night.

Which he knew was a stupid reason to be in a foul mood, but he missed his mate. She'd been passed out from exhaustion by the time he'd gotten in, and then she'd gotten up before he'd woken up. She'd left him a sweet note and they'd talked today, but . . . he missed his mate.

"Did you come here to harass me? Or do you really need something?" He pushed his tablet away from him and leaned back in his chair. It was clear Greer wasn't going anywhere.

"I just came by to let you know a certain skank was here with her mate. They're at Drake and V's place. I heard her tell her mate that she wanted to come by and talk to you in private. Thought I'd give you a head's up in case you wanted to be elsewhere." She winked at him before turning—and jingling—and exiting his office.

"Thanks!" he called out after her. Greer only called one person on the planet a skank; Fia Devlin. His former betrothed. Their conflict had nothing to do with him and he had no idea why Greer didn't like the female.

Not something he was going to worry about right now. Deciding that work was a pointless effort, he shut down his files and financial programs and turned off his tablet—right as there was another knock on his office door.

Scenting who it was, he strode to the door, opened it, and wasn't surprised to see tall and elegant Fia standing on the other side. He nodded once at her but didn't invite her in. Instead, he stepped out and shut the door behind him. "What brings you to my home?"

The Petronilla clan had a huge spread of gated, private property neighboring the ski resort they owned and ran. No one who wasn't invited was allowed on their land so as Alpha, his door was always unlocked. Still it was unusual for Fia to search him out. Without her mate as well.

A wave of nervousness rolled off her. "I just hoped you'd have a few minutes to talk."

He didn't bother glancing at his watch. His mate would be home soon so whatever this was about needed to be over fast. Not that he thought Rhea would care about Fia being here, he just didn't want to deal with this bullshit. But he feigned a polite smile and motioned down the wood corridor. "We can talk in the sitting room. Did you want anything to drink?"

"No."

Once they were settled in impossibly uncomfortable high-back chairs his sister had picked out for a room he was almost never in, he resisted the urge to growl at Fia. She'd left her long, black hair down and was as usual, elegant in clearly tailored, custom-made clothing. Her long, white winter coat was draped over her arm and she kept tapping her heeled boot nervously.

When it was clear she wasn't going to start whatever this conversation was about, he said, "Look, I don't want to be a dick, but can you just say what you need to say? I've got a lot going on right now."

Surprisingly, his words seemed to relax her. "Yes, sorry. I, uh, okay, this is going to sound silly I'm sure but

I just wanted to let you know that I'm really happy you found your mate."

Truth rolled off her, crystal clear.

He'd never felt any animosity for her, at least not for a very long time, but her presence still surprised him. She'd left him to mate with a male from another clan, but that had been well over a millennium ago. "Thank you." He cleared his throat, trying to find some diplomatic words that she clearly needed. Why else would she be here?

"Look, I don't even know why I'm here really. I just . . . your sister is mated to my brother-in-law and my mate is dear friends with your brother. Best friends really. I guess I just wanted to make sure everything between us was water under the bridge. I don't like feeling awkward when we visit, like we're intruding on your land."

Sighing, he leaned back in the uncomfortable chair. "I haven't thought about you in a long time, to be honest. And I never loved you." As soon as the words were out he realized that sounded like a blow, but thankfully she smiled.

A real one. "I know. And I knew we would never be true mates. Especially not after I met Gavin." She blushed before clearing her throat. "I suspected Rhea was your mate when she showed up at your property gates a year ago as part of your security crew. I saw the way you looked at her and I'd hoped..." She lifted a shoulder.

He smiled at that. When members of the Devlin clan had shown up at his clan's gate, Fia with them, demanding to see Drake, her childhood friend, Rhea had insisted on coming with him. She'd been so fierce and determined. "I understand why you left your clan and everything for Gavin now. And I've never held any anger toward you. My pride was hit but that was short lived and very long ago. So yes, water under the bridge. I don't ever want you or your mate to feel unwelcome on our land. I know how much my brother cares for Gavin." Gavin was one of Drake's oldest friends and Conall would never do anything to hurt that relationship.

The relief that punched off her was potent, hitting him with an intensity he hadn't expected. Hell, this was probably a conversation they should have had a long time ago.

Before she could respond, the front door opened and the sound of Rhea and Gavin's voices trailed in a second before the two of them stepped into the foyer.

When he saw Rhea his heart skipped a beat and everything else fell away for a long moment. She wore combat boots and cargo pants—which were ripped. He frowned at the sight as he realized how rumpled she was. Even her leather jacket was . . . He was at her side in a millisecond. "Are you okay?"

He ran his hands up and down the tattered and burned sleeves of her new leather jacket. She had his essence protecting her so no dragon fire should ever be able to harm her.

She snorted and wrapped her arms around his neck. "Yes, but your mom is the devil. She wanted to spar with roman candles today. Like she'll ever need to use one. I seriously don't understand her some days . . . *Most* days."

Rage like he'd never known burst inside him, his dragon rising to the surface with the intensity of the sun. "My mother attacked you with a—"

"No! God, no. I wasn't wearing the jacket when this happened." Rhea laughed, the sound beautiful music. "I told her that no one was sparring with those things because that's just plain insane, and she wanted to 'play with one' anyway, as she put it, and she burned almost everyone's coats. Mine actually escaped unscathed compared to everyone else."

His rage immediately dimmed, his dragon settling back into place now that he knew Rhea was unharmed and safe. Wrapping his arm around her shoulders, he turned to the others and cleared his throat. Damn it, he wanted alone time with Rhea, but he could be polite for a few more minutes. Hopefully. "If you two haven't eaten, please join us for dinner." He didn't even sound sincere, but he was trying.

Gavin seemed to be smothering a smile as he shook his head. "We actually have eaten, over at Drake's. But thank you. We'll be heading out soon. Got a plane to catch, but we'll be back in a couple months. Thank you for your clan's hospitality."

"You're both welcome anytime." After saying goodbyes, he practically slammed the door on them and locked it. No one else would be bothering them tonight.

He'd just turned back to Rhea when she jumped him, wrapping her legs around his waist as her mouth crushed against his. "I'm gonna ask later why she was here," she murmured, nibbling her way along his jaw. "But all I care about right now is getting you naked."

He groaned at her words and the feel of her pressed against him, his cock already rock hard.

Conall wasn't sure how much time had passed but much later, they were both naked, sated and stretched out on the floor of the sitting room. He belatedly realized they'd never shut the curtains as he saw drifts of snow trickle past one of the huge windows from his prone position.

Rhea was tucked next to him, her naked body curled into his. "Can I ask you something?" Her breath was warm against his chest, her voice soft and soothing against all his senses.

"Always," he murmured, stroking a hand down her spine. He loved touching her.

"Back in Biloxi, that day when we saved the women, could you have killed everyone? With your fire?"

Okay, that wasn't what he'd been expecting. He'd thought she would ask about his earlier visitor. "I . . . could have. Maybe not all your packmates. Some of them are strong enough to withstand dragon fire, especially your Alpha."

"Finn is?" Her head popped up as she shifted to look at him.

"Yes." She was strong enough to withstand it now too, something she already knew. Dragon fire would never harm his mate. Technically his essence would eventually break down under enough heat from dragon fire, but it was unlikely to ever happen.

She was silent for a long moment. "I think I get why dragons mate for life in the literal sense now. If you had higher numbers, you guys would definitely take over the planet."

His lips curved up a fraction. "We could *now* if we wanted to. It would be bloody, but we would prevail." There was no arrogance behind his words. Just truth. Dragons could destroy the human world if they wanted, especially with a calculated attack worldwide. But humans would nuke the planet first. No one would win, not really. And who the hell wanted to own a damn planet when it meant inheriting all its problems? His clan was hard enough to manage. "But that's not why. I'm only speaking for myself, but if I lost you . . . I would go insane. I would bathe the world in fire and not care who I took with me. Dragons are not meant to live without their mates. We *cannot.*" His voice was gravelly, harsh.

Her amber eyes glittered and he saw the love he felt for her mirrored back at him. "I couldn't live without you either."

"I have a present for you," he murmured, still stroking along her spine. He loved the way she felt curled against him. Like she'd been made for him.

Laughing lightly, she laid her head back on his chest. "Pretty sure you just gave it to me."

"Ha, ha. Something else." Something sacred to his kind.

"Another Christmas present? Dude, I think you have a problem." There was no censure in her voice, just muted laughter against his chest.

He smiled at her words. Yeah, he'd gone a little overboard with the presents this year. Under their glittering tree shiny, wrapped boxes overflowed. But it was their first holiday together. He was going to spoil her, even if she didn't seem to want anything.

"It's something I've been working on for months. I want to give it to you tonight though."

She made a soft *hmm* sound and he realized she was fading fast. He knew she'd had a long day. Hell, a long week. They both had. But she'd tackled being an Alpha's mate exactly as he'd expected. Full-on, without fear or hesitation.

His entire clan respected her and it was no wonder. He'd never seen anyone work harder than her. Closing his eyes, he just held her tight. He'd give her the gift later, maybe even wait until Christmas morning. He'd created a blade forged in dragon fire, one of the rarest things on the planet. His kind rarely made them because they could be used against them. But it would protect her in various ways, giving her the gift of seeing other dragons even when they were camouflaged. And it was virtually indestructible.

Because nothing was more precious than the strong, smart woman he held in his arms.

She was *his* gift. And one he would treasure for the rest of his life.

EPILOGUE

"Thank you both for coming to see me. I know it's your day off," Finn said to Rory as he and Liberty stepped into his office.

The room looked as if Christmas had thrown up in it—Lyra or Vega's touch, Rory imagined. The holiday was only a couple days away and while Rory didn't really care about it, Liberty did so they'd decorated their home as well, inside and out in epic proportions. Anything to make his mate smile. And okay, he found that having a little holiday spirit wasn't exactly a hardship. "No problem. What's up?" He loosely linked his fingers with Liberty's as they both sat in chairs in front of Finn's desk.

Finn pushed a manila file across the desk. "After Liberty and Chloe," he said, nodding once at Liberty, "found that center that helps women get back on their feet, I had some of my guys check the place out."

Rory knew what he was talking about. Liberty had been working with Chloe over the last month, taking self-defense lessons, and Liberty had mentioned it was a shame there wasn't a place that could give therapy to supernatural women who'd gone through hard times or abuse. Chloe agreed and after some research they'd discovered there actually *was* a place relatively nearby that did just that. They were right on the border between

Stavros territory and the territory of an Alpha named Knox.

"You're not going to shut them down, are you?" Liberty sounded horrified at the thought.

And Rory was right there with her. Not that he was worried the Alpha would do that. Finn was too good of a male.

Finn frowned. "What? Hell no. No, we're actually planning to start one here in the city. It's something I should have done a long time ago, but . . . Anyway, I sent some guys to check out the owner and no one can get a read on *what* she is. The only thing everyone agrees with is that she's very powerful."

"Okay." Rory wondered where Finn was going with this.

Finn rubbed a hand over the back of his neck as he looked back and forth between them and Rory had a feeling he wasn't going to like whatever the male had to say. It was something in his body language. Finn's muscles were pulled taut, his jaw too tight. "I want to send someone in to talk to her. A female—"

"No!" Rory was on his feet before Finn had finished. Alpha or not, Rory wasn't going to listen to this, much less let his mate go into some unknown place without backup. Because it was clear that was where Finn was going with the conversation.

Liberty tugged on his hand, drawing his focus back to her. "Please let him finish," she said quietly.

He returned to his seat, but all his muscles tightened as he prepared to argue. Taking orders from an Alpha was difficult at times and he wondered if it was because he'd been alone for so long.

Finn pinned him with that ice blue gaze, his expression more frustrated than angry. "I want to send someone in to meet the owner, someone who the woman will trust. Liberty has been through a lot." He cast her a quick look, his expression softer.

It was the only thing that eased off some of Rory's anger. Finn seemed to have a soft spot for Liberty and really, who could blame him. She was perfect.

"And if I send in Chloe or anyone else, they'll never get through the front door. She'll sense if they're lying about being abused. All I want is for Liberty to get an appointment, talk to her and set up a meeting between the owner and me. I want a sit down with her and discuss some things. Like who the heck she is. This is a file of information Elana's been able to find on the place and its owner." He tapped his finger against the manila folder.

Rory lifted an eyebrow. "It's pretty thin."

Finn nodded. "No kidding. They've been operating for *decades*. And this is all we've come up with on the owner."

At that, Rory raised both eyebrows. "And you've never heard of her before?"

"She's not in my territory and never been on my radar. Still . . . she's close enough to my territory that I want to know more about her."

Sighing, Rory picked up the file and flipped it open. He froze at the image of the woman in the first photograph. It had been taken recently, or at least he assumed from her style of dress. She had on jeans and a flowy looking top with sandals. Her espresso hair was pulled back into a ponytail and though he couldn't see because her profile was turned toward the camera he knew her eyes were a brilliant blue. He hadn't been sure before, but seeing her standing next to someone else, he guessed she was exceptionally tall for a woman. It made him wonder if she was a dragon.

"What is it?" Liberty asked, her hand settling on his forearm.

He looked at her, then Finn. "Remember how you once said there might come a time when my loyalty might be divided between you and my brothers?"

Finn cursed, nodded. "Yeah."

"I don't think this is *that* extreme, but . . ."

"You know who she is?"

"Not exactly." But he'd seen a photograph of this same woman, almost fifty years ago, in his brother's possession. It had just been of her face, but there was no mistaking it was the same woman. Not with those sharp cheekbones. "I think Ian might know who she is. I need to talk to him before we commit to anything. I owe my brother that."

Sighing, Finn sat back in his chair. "Well, she's been operating for damn near forty or fifty years out of there. I can wait another day or two. Just don't lie to me," he growled softly. "That's all I demand. If you can't tell me something we'll deal with it. But don't ever lie to me."

Rory felt the Alpha's command roll over him and it only rankled him a fraction because he understood. "I won't. I swear it."

Finn stood, motioned to the file. "Take it with you. I've got copies. Get back to me once you've talked to Ian. And enjoy the next couple days off."

Rory wasn't so sure about that now, but he nodded anyway and stood with Liberty. They were both silent as they made their way out of the mansion and down to his truck. Only once they were on the road headed back to their place did he say anything. Though they'd had the option of living at the mansion, he preferred keeping his place with Liberty. He might be half-wolf, but he was also half-demon. He liked his privacy.

"Decades ago, not long after Ian and I met each other, I found a picture of the woman in that file in one of his drawers. By accident." He tilted his head at the file, even if it was clear who he was referring to.

Liberty flipped it open, looked at the image again. "Who is she?"

"No idea. When I asked him about it, he said she was a woman he knew. I pressed and he shut me down. I've never brought her up again and I've never seen the picture again. But the way he looked at it, she was more than a friend." The sadness—no, more like grief—that had punched off his brother had made Rory think the female had died. Apparently not.

"Hmm." Liberty shut the file, her expression thoughtful.

"What?"

"Well, if he's hung up on her it would explain why he acts like a player but never actually sleeps with anyone. Maybe she's the one that got away."

He glanced at her as they pulled up to a red light. "You've noticed that?"

Liberty snorted. "Please. He's not as smooth as he thinks. Besides, one of the females from the pack asked me once if he was gay. Said he flirted like mad but never actually followed through—with anyone."

Rory just nodded in agreement. He knew his brother better than anyone, but there were secrets even Ian kept and he'd never pushed. Now he hated that he had to push. But it was unavoidable. "How do you feel about going to talk to the female?"

Liberty shrugged and he didn't sense any fear. "Just because she's powerful doesn't mean anything. According to Chloe, she's done a lot of good over the years. She's helping women who otherwise don't have anyone to turn to. If it hadn't been for Ophelia I would have literally had no one to talk to after that hell. Obviously other than you, but you know what I mean. I wouldn't have had anyone to talk to in a therapeutic sense. She's doing a lot of good. I'm not afraid to talk to a woman like that. And I doubt Finn would send me in somewhere if he was truly worried about my safety."

It was clear from his mate's tone that she wanted to do this. "We'll talk to Ian, see what he says about her." Whether she could be trusted. If not, Rory wasn't letting Liberty within fifty miles of the place.

Liberty nodded and casually set her hand on his thigh as they drove. The action was so innate, he knew she hadn't even thought about it. "I love you so much," he murmured.

She turned to him, her expression softening. He showed her every damn day, but still, he didn't just blurt the words out at random times. "I love you too."

When they came to another stoplight he leaned over and captured her mouth in a demanding kiss, tasting his sweet, sweet mate.

No matter what the future held for them, he was going to be by her side every step of the way. Fate had given him this wonderfully brave female and he was never letting her go.

Thank you for reading Into the Darkness. If you don't want to miss any future releases, please feel free to join my newsletter. I only send out a newsletter for new releases or sales news. Find the signup link on my website: http://www.katiereus.com

ACKNOWLEDGMENTS

It's time to thank the usual crowd! I work with an amazing group of people and I'm incredibly thankful to each and every one of them for their help in making sure my books get published. In no particular order, Kari Walker, Carolyn Crane and Joan Nichols, thank you all for helping me get this book into shape. You all provide such different insight and I'm so grateful you took the time to read Into the Darkness. I owe thanks to Sarah Romsa for all the behind-the-scenes stuff she does to keep me on track. Because of her, I get more time to write. To my fabulous readers (always!), I hope you enjoy this latest installment as much as I enjoyed writing it. I'm thankful you read my books. I'm also thankful to Jaycee of Sweet 'N Spicy Designs for another great cover. And as always, I'm thankful for my family, who supports me and for God, because of too many blessings to count.

COMPLETE BOOKLIST

Red Stone Security Series

No One to Trust

Danger Next Door

Fatal Deception

Miami, Mistletoe & Murder

His to Protect

Breaking Her Rules

Protecting His Witness

Sinful Seduction

Under His Protection

Deadly Fallout

Sworn to Protect

Secret Obsession

The Serafina: Sin City Series

First Surrender

Sensual Surrender

Sweetest Surrender

Dangerous Surrender

Deadly Ops Series

Targeted

Bound to Danger

Chasing Danger (novella)

Shattered Duty

Edge of Danger

A Covert Affair

Non-series Romantic Suspense

Running From the Past
Dangerous Secrets
Killer Secrets
Deadly Obsession
Danger in Paradise
His Secret Past
Retribution
Merry Christmas, Baby

Paranormal Romance

Destined Mate
Protector's Mate
A Jaguar's Kiss
Tempting the Jaguar
Enemy Mine
Heart of the Jaguar

Moon Shifter Series

Alpha Instinct
Lover's Instinct (novella)
Primal Possession
Mating Instinct
His Untamed Desire (novella)
Avenger's Heat
Hunter Reborn
Protective Instinct (novella)

Darkness Series

Darkness Awakened
Taste of Darkness
Beyond the Darkness
Hunted by Darkness
Into the Darkness

ABOUT THE AUTHOR

Katie Reus is the *New York Times* and *USA Today* bestselling author of the Red Stone Security series, the Moon Shifter series and the Deadly Ops series. She fell in love with romance at a young age thanks to books she pilfered from her mom's stash. Years later she loves reading romance almost as much as she loves writing it.

However, she didn't always know she wanted to be a writer. After changing majors many times, she finally graduated summa cum laude with a degree in psychology. Not long after that she discovered a new love. Writing. She now spends her days writing dark paranormal romance and sexy romantic suspense.

For more information on Katie please visit her website: www.katiereus.com. Also find her on twitter @katiereus or visit her on facebook at: www.facebook.com/katiereusauthor.

Made in the USA
Charleston, SC
29 March 2016